Dandelions for Dinner

A Farm Fresh Romance

Book 4

Valerie Comer

Dedication

For Jessica

There is always hope.

Books by Valerie Comer

Farm Fresh Romance Novels
Raspberries and Vinegar
Wild Mint Tea
Sweetened with Honey
Dandelions for Dinner
Plum Upside Down (summer 2015)

Riverbend Romance Novellas (e-book only)
Secretly Yours
Pinky Promise

Christmas Romance Novella Duo
Snowflake Tiara
(with Angela Breidenbach)

Fantasy Novel
Majai's Fury

Acknowledgements

Many thanks to Melanie Pike, Sally Shupe, and Iverna McAnulty for being awesome beta readers on a quick turn-around. These gals *rock*!

Hugs and blessings to Nicole O'Dell. I'm so thankful for her, every single day.

A huge shout-out to my fellow travelers within the Christian Indie Authors Facebook group and my blogger buddies at www.inspyromance.com. What amazing folks to share the writing journey with.

I appreciate the readers and fans of my Farm Fresh Romance stories! I'm thankful for everyone who has posted reviews, liked my Facebook page, and especially to those who've joined my email list and written to tell me how much my stories mean to them. What an encouragement!

Thanks to my husband, Jim, who embodies romance in my life. I'm grateful... and very much in love! Thanks to my kids, their spouses, and their charming little daughters (my grandgirls), for being my inspiration, my support, and my delight.

I'm deeply thankful to Jesus, who makes all things new and sheds light and hope into dark corners. I write to honor Him.

Chapter 1

*A*llison Hart had perfected the art of staring out the window and checking her watch simultaneously. The contractor said he'd be here by ten, and it was now quarter after. If guys could be on time driving in Portland city traffic, how hard could it be on northern Idaho's rural roads?

Waiting. Who had time for it? She tapped her foot and crossed her arms, not that there was anyone to see her. No one who lived at Green Acres was home today except her, which suited Allison just fine. She'd arrived at the communal farm three days earlier, and she'd already experienced about all the togetherness she could handle.

The rumble of a vehicle grew louder, and a white pickup with the emblem of Timber Framing Plus emblazoned on the side turned into the driveway.

Finally. Allison strode for the door, buttoning her cardigan against the cold March day as she went.

The contractor slammed the truck door and turned toward her, hard hat in hand.

Wait a minute. This wasn't Patrick at all. This guy had a shock of black hair — unlike Patrick's thinning salt-and-pepper — to say nothing of those dark brown eyes, slightly angled. Skin that on anyone else might look tanned but combined with the rest definitely tagged him of Asian descent.

Japanese? Thai? Didn't matter. He could be Martian for all the difference it made. The biggest problem was, he wasn't Patrick.

The guy tucked his hard hat under his arm and stretched out his hand. "Hi, I'm Brent Callahan from Timber Framing Plus."

An Irish name? Unexpected.

"Allison Hart."

He had a strong grip, like he knew what he was doing, even though he didn't have the other man's years of experience.

"Where's Patrick?"

"Back in the office. He sent me out to check the footings."

The wind had built up speed crossing the Galena Valley to get to her. Would it slam straight into the mountain beside the farm and come to an abrupt halt or find some other direction in which to continue? Either way, she should've worn something without the big holes in her bulky cardigan. She wrapped both arms around herself in an attempt to stay warm. "I was under the impression he was coming himself. I have a list of questions for him."

Brent grinned. "Nothing I can't answer, I'm sure. I've worked for him since high school."

Her eyebrows shot up. When was that, last week?

"Ten years, ma'am." He winked, set the hard hat on his head, and turned toward the construction site, where the perimeter of the new farm school lay outlined in concrete.

Ten years? That made the guy something like twenty-eight. He sure didn't look it. Allison hurried after him. "I'm sorry. I didn't mean to doubt your experience. I just expected Patrick. It's his business, after all."

Brent turned to face her, dark eyes unreadable. "Timber Framing Plus is a large company. We work on more than one project at a time. Patrick oversees them all, but that doesn't mean he and his two best friends put into place every piece of wood that makes each structure."

"But he said…" Allison's words trailed away as she tried to recall the exact words in their discussion.

"What did he say, ma'am?"

Her temper flared. "My name is Allison, not ma'am." It was a temptation to make him call her Ms. Hart so he'd remember which of them was the real boss on this site. Ma'am made her think of someone old with an unsavory reputation.

He tipped his head. "Allison. What did Patrick say, exactly?"

"He said he'd oversee the project personally."

Brent laughed and shook his head. "And he will. From his office in Coeur d'Alene, where he can keep an eye on all the structures we're erecting this season. Available to any of his foremen, day or night, with whatever questions or problems we might encounter."

"But—" Allison hated losing, but this was obviously not a battle she was going to win. If Patrick's office were any nearer, she'd march right in and give him a piece of her mind. A two-hour drive might be worth the satisfaction.

She looked at Brent, but he was striding away from her. He made a fine figure in navy work pants and shirt. Not a big guy, but not scrawny either. Good looking.

A disaster. She'd counted on Patrick. Somebody with

experience. Somebody who was safe.

Not that being older made a man safe to be around. She knew that all too well. Her dad had been nothing but trouble to any woman he came within flirting distance of. And Mom had repaid him in kind. Only a shared desire for convenience and prestige had kept the two of them married all those years.

It hadn't provided any security for her and her sister. Thinking of Lori brought all the old aches surging to the surface. Drinking, sex, and drugs had comprised Lori's life since she was fourteen. She somehow managed to keep things together just enough to keep Child Protection Services at bay and retain custody of her little boy.

Finnley. That poor kid. Allison soaked him up every minute she could, but Lori was always quick to move on to another city, another man, another addiction. The little guy deserved so much better. If only she'd been able to make a difference for Finnley by staying in Portland, but her sister had screamed in her face and dragged the boy off to Tucson with a guy named John. Likely an apt name.

Allison blinked the tears away and straightened. The man over there crouching down and poking at the footings wasn't a loser like the guys her sister hooked up with, even though he was Asian like Finnley's father apparently had been. This guy had a real job. She could trust him to build the farm school she'd proposed to the women of Green Acres when they met last fall.

So everyone in this group she'd joined might think marriage was a great thing, but she'd watched her parents. She would escape the curse. She was absolutely, definitely, for sure here to build herself a spinster house and get herself a big dog.

She blinked. Brent Callahan stood in front of her, eyebrows raised as he looked at her.

No room for a man in her life. So totally not interested. Didn't matter if he was ugly and fifty or gorgeous and close to her age.

She met Brent's gaze evenly. "And the verdict is?"

"The verdict is I'll have a crew out here Monday to get started."

"You?"

He narrowed his eyes. "Yes, me. Didn't I just tell you that Patrick assigned me as the foreman in charge of your project?"

No. No, he had not.

oOo

Thanks, Uncle Patrick. Why couldn't Brent's first gig as foreman be for some middle-aged man? Someone who would swing by the worksite a couple of times a week? Someone who would respect Patrick's decision and trust Brent's experience? After all, his uncle had been grooming him for several years to take over the commercial projects.

He didn't need Allison Hart to question his every breath. He didn't need a female client at all, especially not one near his own age. The girl was almost as tall as he was. Her bulky black cardigan came to mid-thigh, topping black leggings and high black boots. Too skinny for his taste. She was probably anorexic. No one could possibly eat normally and look like that.

Too bad, really. She was kind of pretty under the layer of makeup. And while he liked long hair on a girl as much as the next guy, hers swung nearly to her waist.

Not much softness to Allison Hart. It was like she was careful to give off the persona she wanted. Nah. Brent would bet this was whom she really was underneath.

He'd been staring. He tried for a natural smile. "It looks like we'll be seeing a lot of each other for the next few months."

Her jaw twitched. "Great. Just what I needed." She glared at him through narrowed eyes.

Brent's spine straightened on its own. "I have the experience and the credentials."

11

She gathered her hair in both hands and flipped it over her shoulders. "I'd really rather have Patrick."

"I am his fully-qualified representative." He'd nearly said nephew. Bet that wouldn't go over well with skinny Miss Priss. He'd quit calling the man uncle in public years before, when they'd begun working together so closely. It was better on the job site for the crew not to be reminded of their relationship. Most didn't even know, given that Patrick looked totally Irish and Brent... did not.

"I'll be staying at The Landing Pad." Brent thumbed toward the town of Galena Landing. "Along with the guys who will be my permanent crew. Once we get rolling, we'll be here from eight to five Monday through Friday with an hour off for lunch." He quirked an eyebrow at her. "If that meets your expectations?"

Allison's eyes narrowed until he couldn't see the brown orbs any more. "That will be fine, so long as your crew is disciplined, experienced, and gets the job done as soon as possible." She grimaced. "I can't believe he did this to me."

She was seriously starting to get under his skin, and that took some doing.

"I'm sorry Patrick didn't make it clear."

Her eyebrows rose. "*You're* sorry?"

"Indeed. Do you think I enjoy being treated like a second-class citizen?" He leaned closer. "Just because I'm not who you were expecting doesn't mean I am not the right man for the job."

She took a step back.

Good. She was getting the idea. His cell phone rang with his uncle's ring tone, and he reached for it, maintaining eye contact with Allison. "Hi, Patrick. Brent here."

Allison thrust out her hand for his phone, and he turned away.

"How's it going, Brent? Are the footings ready?"

"We can start Monday. Say, it seems you forgot to mention to Ms. Hart that you wouldn't be on the job here every day."

His uncle laughed, but it sounded strained. "She's not too happy, I take it?"

"You got that right."

"Well, it gets worse."

Uh oh. Brent's hand tightened on his cell as he strode toward the truck. Better be out of earshot for this one. "How's that?"

"We ordered all the glass for her job from McGowan Windows."

No secret there. "Yes?"

"The plant burned to the ground yesterday. We have to find another manufacturer." Patrick paused. "And get in line with everyone else."

Brent closed his eyes. So many words he'd quit saying a few years ago vied to explode from his mouth. He tightened his jaw to clamp them back and took a few deep breaths.

"Brent?"

"I'm here." Inhale, exhale. "Please tell me this is your idea of an early April Fool's joke."

Patrick's chuckle had a nervous edge to it. "I wish. It's not just the Hart job affected. We've got three other clients who ordered McGowan windows. And of course we're not the only company. Everyone else is scrambling to get on some other manufacturer's list, too."

"Expected delay?"

"Several months, probably. Those Hart structures have a lot of windows. But I don't have anything confirmed yet. Waiting to hear back."

"This is going to go over like a ton of bricks, you know that?"

"I know." His uncle sighed. "Right this minute I have three other lines lit up with incoming calls. I need to go. I'll let you know as soon as I have some answers."

"Just a sec. I assume we're to go ahead as far as we can while we wait?"

"Yes. We'll try not to lay off any guys. It will take some

juggling, but we'll make it all happen."

"Okay. Thanks, Patrick." But his uncle had already ended the call.

Now Brent had the joy of explaining this to his client. He turned slowly, but she was right there. She'd followed him to the truck and probably overheard every word.

Both hands rested on what would be hips on a woman with curves. Her dark brown eyes stared straight into his from mere inches away. "Well?"

Good thing Brent had become a praying man. He shot a plea heavenward. "We have a problem."

"So I deduced. What is it? How bad?"

"The window manufacturing plant we'd ordered your windows from burned down yesterday. It's totally destroyed."

Her jaw clenched and she shook her head slowly. "Right. That's too bad. Just get them from somewhere else."

Brent opened his mouth and closed it again. Another prayer winged away, this one for patience. He managed to smile, so that was progress. "Not as easy as you might expect. McGowan's plant was one of the largest in the US."

Allison raised her finely plucked eyebrows. "And?"

"And there are dozens of contractors with orders placed, many of them with multiple clients. No other plant has the capacity to simply step in and meet the demand."

"So you're telling me we have no windows coming, and no idea when we can get them."

"Basically. But Patrick's on it. He'll let me know as soon as something is confirmed."

Allison jabbed her finger against his chest. "Do you know that this is supposed to be a school?" Poke. "That we have classes booked and students coming in July?" Poke.

"Hey, wait a minute." He grabbed her hand to stop the jabs, and she jerked away. "It's not like I went to Milwaukee and torched the factory to spite you. This situation is totally out of my hands. It makes no difference if Patrick was going to be onsite or me. This is bigger than Timber Framing Plus. We'll do our best, but we're not miracle workers."

If he were, he knew where he'd start, and his first miracle wouldn't be for Allison Hart.

Valerie Comer

Chapter 2 --

*W*hat had she been thinking?

Allison stared across her open laptop where it rested on the plank table over at the big house. This was like being in some stranger's dining room. Maybe because it was. She barely knew the people who lived and worked here. Green Acres Farm didn't have a separate office, so she was stuck.

She'd hoped her classroom building would be up in less than three months. Everyone had told her it would take longer, but no one had expected the stupid window factory to burn to the ground and double their timeline. Months. It would probably be autumn before she had a place closed in from the weather where she could do her own thing. Being stuck in Sierra Riehl's tiny spare room for that long was not an option. She'd have to insist they clean Sierra's fiancé's junk out of the other half of the duplex.

Allison looked down the length of the farmhouse table, through the great room, and out the expansive windows, listening to the coffee pot gurgle in the kitchen. Caffeine rarely failed to improve her outlook.

Brent Callahan, black hair peeking out from beneath his bright yellow hard hat, pointed his clipboard around the building site while the two guys with him gestured and nodded. The man hadn't done a thing all morning that she could see. If this was progress, she was a monkey's uncle.

She shook her head and tried to focus on her laptop. Already several students had enrolled for classes starting in July. Should she email them and offer a refund? Or could she manage without a finished space?

The men outside the window walked over to the Timber Framing Plus pickup and climbed in.

Allison jumped to her feet and bolted out the door. She stood on the deck as the truck trundled down the lane toward town. Seriously? In what universe had those guys put in a day's work? She glanced at her watch. Okay, so it was noon, but they hadn't been here for any four hours. They hadn't even broken a sweat. They didn't deserve a break yet.

Not that anyone glanced back and saw her on the deck glowering at them, fists planted firmly on her hips. Grr. She gathered her long hair in both hands and flipped it over her shoulder. Shaking her head, she marched back into the house.

"Short day's work." Claire Kenzie, one of the other women who lived at the farm, stood beside the window, looking out.

"Very." Allison flounced back to her chair and tapped the keyboard to revive the laptop.

"Want a coffee?" Claire walked past the table and into the kitchen. The caffeinated aroma filled the place as the pot beeped.

"Sure, thanks."

At the peninsula dividing the kitchen from the dining room, Claire poured some into a mug then frowned. "I don't even know how you like it."

"Just black, thanks."

Claire grinned. "That would help explain how you stay so thin."

Did that require an answer? Allison hoped not. She glared at the screen, feigning preoccupation.

Claire set the mug near Allison's elbow then dropped into another chair, cradling her own cup.

Now they were supposed to visit? This was why Allison needed her own office. She needed to wedge a TV tray or something into that bedroom at Sierra's. Four pink walls hemming her in. She shuddered at the thought.

"They still figuring on having the classrooms ready to move into by summer?"

"No. The factory they ordered the windows from burned down, so they're doing some juggling."

"Oh, no! I hope no one was injured."

Allison grimaced as a pang of guilt stabbed. "I didn't think to ask."

"So what's the revised plan?"

"They don't have a new timeline yet. Obviously, they can't put the windows in until they arrive, or finish the floors or anything as long as rain can drive in. And siding comes afterward, too."

Claire lifted her mug for a long sip.

Allison ignored the fact that the other woman watched her.

"When did you find out?"

"A few days ago."

Claire leaned closer. "When did you plan to tell us? Remember, you're part of a team now. Didn't you think about how this affects everyone on the farm?"

Drat. The woman was right. Allison was so used to sailing solo she kept forgetting that she'd signed on as a team member. What had she been thinking?

She'd been thinking she had enough money now to make her dream come true if she didn't have to buy land as well. She'd been thinking it would be nice to have people around who cared... at least when she wanted them to.

Time to screw her head on at a new angle. A team. This was crazy stuff. She did need them. They did have a right to know.

Allison leaned back in her chair and met Claire's gaze. "Sorry. I keep forgetting. My life hasn't been full of dependable people before. Or anyone with a vested interest."

"I bought a big white board the other day and just need Noel to put it up." Claire grimaced. "It's all a bit more complicated on the straw bale walls than it is on regular old drywall. Anyway, it's for messages the whole team needs to know between official meetings. Your news would be a good candidate for that board."

Allison nodded. "How often are there official meetings?"

"Not often enough." Claire laughed. "Until now, we've been a group who knew each other for years, so we mostly decided things on the fly."

Right. But now they had a newbie in their midst. Someone who was not their best friend. Someone who didn't automatically tell everyone everything. Awkward.

"And the guys, of course." Claire lifted her mug for another sip. "But we didn't count on them from the beginning."

"That's a lot of what appealed to me," Allison admitted. "Sierra's sister told me about you all and your decision to forge ahead with this farm and your dreams regardless of marital status."

Claire chuckled. "Our Mr. Rights didn't bother showing up in college or soon after. A woman can't just put her entire life on hold waiting for him, you know? At some point you have to ask God what He wants of your life and step forward in faith."

Allison tucked her hair behind her ears. "That's been my attitude my whole life. Watching my parents live two separate lives under one roof made me realize marriage wasn't that great." To say nothing of the mess the situation had made for her and her sister. "I'm glad for you girls, honestly, but I hope you've made plans in case you find out your men are cheating on you. You could stand to lose everything you've worked for."

Claire shook her head. "That's God's problem, not mine. I didn't enter into marriage with Noel half-heartedly, expecting it to go foul."

Allison shrugged. In her experience — admittedly from observation, not personal — it was a matter of when, not if. If Claire, Jo, and Sierra had found exceptions, good for them. She wouldn't bank on there being any left for her.

"So, what are you working on today?"

Whew. Nice topic change. "Trying to decide if I should send refunds to the students who've pre-paid or if there's any way to salvage this summer's courses."

Claire's coffee cup clunked to the table. "Excuse me, but how is that your decision to make? Remember what I just said about being part of a team? We didn't give you carte blanche to run the classes any way you like."

Allison surged to her feet. "Sorry. Not used to thinking like this." Did she even want to? "Maybe I should be thankful the contractors are delayed. Maybe I should forget the whole thing and cancel my agreement with them." Yeah, she'd lose her deposit, but what did it matter if her whole dream came crashing down? Besides, then Brent Callahan wouldn't have the power to irritate her so much.

"Don't over-react. Allison, please. Of course we want you here. We all prayed about the decision in the fall after we first met. We're excited about the new possibilities your presence opens up for the entire farm, and for everyone who lives here."

Allison flung her arms out. "It's all so foreign. I don't even know how to work like this. I need an office with walls and a door. I need to make decisions and own them. I need to stand on my own two feet, not constantly wonder what other people think." She parked both hands on the edge of the table and leaned across it toward Claire. "I don't know how to do this teamwork thing."

Was that sympathy oozing out of Claire's eyes?

Great. Just what she didn't need was someone feeling sorry for her about it all. Her life was what it was. No one else could

21

possibly understand how her personality had been shaped. Nor could it be undone because someone said it should.

"Did you pray about coming here, Allison?"

What kind of question was that? "Of course I did."

"And I'm assuming you felt it was the right direction, or you wouldn't be here."

Allison set her jaw. "Yes."

"Then we take the issues one at a time and work through them together." Claire shrugged and drank half her coffee. "We discuss things, we pray about them, and we make decisions together."

"Just like that?"

Claire pulled to her feet. "Yep. Just like that." She grinned, drained her coffee cup, and headed for the kitchen. "I'm thinking soup and biscuits for lunch. You okay with it?"

Allison blinked. Claire had really moved on? Okay then. "Sounds great."

Claire smiled at Allison across the peninsula. "And we'll have a board meeting tonight after Jo and Zach tuck Maddie in bed. We'll get things figured out. Together."

oOo

Brent drove south on Highway 95. Whatever the speed limit was, he didn't care at the moment.

"How did the driver make such a stupid mistake?" he asked into his Bluetooth headset.

"He saw Thomas Road just north of Wynnton and thought he'd misunderstood," answered Patrick.

"And he couldn't just turn the rig around when he figured out he was in the wrong place?"

His uncle sighed. "He's a rookie driver, a young guy who's not from the Panhandle. He didn't figure it out real quick."

"So he got stuck driving a wide load onto a narrow bridge. Good job, dude."

"Brent, take it easy on the kid when you get there. He's already pretty shaken."

"Thomas Road. There it is. East, I take it?"

"Yes."

Brent slammed on the brakes and snapped on his turn signal. Good thing no one was right behind him. As it was, he barely got slowed enough to make the turn in time. "How far from the highway did you say?"

"He's about eighteen miles up, but you'll run out of cell signal long before then. Give the kid a break, Brent. Remember what it's like to be green."

"Yeah, yeah. I'll try. Talk to you when I'm back in range." Brent tapped the button to disconnect the call.

Just the fact that nothing riled Patrick irritated Brent even more. Surely somebody had to get upset over itty-bitty problems like entire window-manufacturing plants burning down and semi trucks carrying the first load of timbers for the Hart job getting stuck on a bridge fifty miles from its destination.

He dragged in a deep breath. It was only a bunch of squared timbers. Inanimate objects. In neither incident had any human been hurt or killed. This was good, and he should dwell on it. Instead, all he could see in his mind's eye was Allison Hart's stiff posture and unyielding face when he told her where her beams were.

Why had he wanted to become a foreman again? Why had his uncle handed over the reins on one of the bigger jobs for the season? Today he'd gladly be one of the crew, just doing what he was told. Being in charge wasn't all it was cracked up to be.

Enough. If he wasn't going to blow up at the poor rookie when he got to the bridge, he needed to calm down. This wasn't the attitude of Christ Jesus he wanted to emulate.

Patrick had told him the true test of greatness was not the heights of the glorious things he accomplished but the depths of the service he provided in humility.

Brent sighed and let the truck's Bluetooth pull worship music from his cell phone out through the speakers. Belting out with Matt Redman settled his heart and mind until he careened around a curve on the mountain road and came face-to-face with the blocked bridge.

Whatever the greenhorn had told Patrick hadn't taken the entire situation into account. It was going to take a crane to get this truck out of here.

Allison Hart was not going to be amused.

Chapter 3 ---

*A*llison shoved the sleeves of her Oregon Ducks sweatshirt up her arms. Finally a day where the sun had a little warmth to it, feeble as it might be. A good day to rake last year's fallen leaves beside Thompson Road.

Nine-fifteen on Wednesday morning. How come she hadn't seen a single sign of Brent Callahan since Friday? He'd quoted her full business hours. With the qualifier this would be "once they got going."

Apparently they weren't going yet.

But they should be. She might not know a lot about putting up timber frame buildings, but it stood to reason the school needed walls and a roof before it needed windows. How come nobody was here erecting them?

Patience. Man, she knew it was a weak point.

Allison pressed the volume button a few more times on the side of her iPhone. Maybe listening to a sustainable living podcast would help her get over her annoyance. She really didn't want to live grumpy all the time, but the cozy togetherness at Green Acres Farm totally encroached on her personal space.

The leaves had partially decomposed, compressed by the snow plowed off the road. A few low banks of tired gray snow lingered beside the gravel. She gave a tentative kick at one. Ouch. Harder than she'd have thought. She might need to get out her steel-toed boots if she kept that up.

She sensed vehicles approaching more than she heard them and looked up. A white pickup — hopefully Brent's — was followed by a semi loaded with squared logs.

Finally. She leaned the rake against the nearest elm and gave the trucks her complete attention.

The Timber Framing Plus pickup careened into the driveway while the larger truck took the turn much slower.

Allison narrowed her gaze. The tarp covering the load was ripped, and some of the visible timbers had long scratches running down the lengths of them. Others had deep gouges in places that didn't look like the carefully hewn ends that would fit together like puzzle pieces.

Had she made a mistake hiring TFP? It sure looked like it.

A third truck, this one with an attached crane, pulled in behind the log load.

She strode across the matted lawn toward Brent, who was just swinging out of his truck. "What happened to those timbers?"

He turned and waved at her before heading to the semi driver, setting his hard hat in place.

Okay, maybe the trucks' engines were too loud for him to have heard her words. He'd hear her soon enough.

The crane truck shifted into reverse, beeping.

Allison stopped to gauge where the driver was going so she could stay out of the way. Surely he was going to park by the gravel pad that'd been flattened in front of the building site. Someday it would be a parking area for the school.

The finished building, bustling with students, teachers, and guests, reared in her mind like the pop-up book she'd given Finnley last time she'd seen him. She had to keep the final goal in mind. Maybe it wasn't a good idea to antagonize the foreman too much. She'd have to keep a close eye. Push him just the right amount, but not so far he balked.

Managing men was not her strong suit.

Allison stood to the side, watching as the crane edged into place then as the semi pulled in beside it. One of the guys scrambled up to unfasten the tarp.

"Impressive."

She lurched. Who'd snuck up on her?

Claire's husband Noel stood beside her. He grinned at her then jerked his chin toward the action. "Good-size beams on that truck. Douglas fir?"

"Um, yeah. But it looks like there's damage to some of them."

He nodded thoughtfully. "I'm sure the company has everything accounted for. Who's the foreman?"

"The guy doing all the pointing. I'll introduce you when he's free." Just before she ripped Brent's head off. Oh, right, she was going to be nice to him if it killed her. It might.

Brent nodded and stepped away as the boom lowered for the first log. Two guys scrambled up the truck to attach the straps while Brent came around toward Allison and Noel.

She held her peace. It was one thing to holler at Brent. He was her employee and would be gone in a few months, though it would take much longer than she'd hoped. But not in front of Noel, a man who would live on the same farm as her for both of their natural lives. Or until Noel got tired of his wife and the farm and amused himself elsewhere like all men did.

Brent stuck out his hand toward Noel. "Mr. Hart?" A big smile crossed his face.

Nice try, buster. "Brent, this is Noel Kenzie, one of the other owners of Green Acres Farm. Noel, meet Brent Callahan from Timber Framing Plus. He's the foreman in charge of the build." Somehow she managed to keep the bitterness out of her voice.

Brent clasped Noel's hand. "Sorry, man. I just assumed."

Lesson number one. Never assume anything.

Noel laughed. "No problem. I've been happily married to Claire for over three years, and we live in the straw bale house over there." He motioned toward the house, hidden behind the trucks. "Zach and Jo Nemesek live on the farm, too, in a log cabin just up the hillside. And there's another couple here who will be married later this summer."

"Ah, I didn't realize it was such a big operation. One big happy family?"

If he only knew.

"No one's actually related." Noel grinned. "Well, Zach's related to his daughter, I guess, and his parents live next door."

"Interesting." Brent turned back to watch the first log being lowered to skids on the ground.

Allison couldn't hold it back any longer. "What happened to those logs, Brent?"

He grimaced and shook his head. "The driver took a wrong turn and got the truck wedged on a curving bridge on a back road out of Wynnton. Took a bit to get him and the load headed the right direction again."

"So the beams are damaged."

Brent met her gaze, his brown eyes unwavering. "Some seem to be. We'll be examining each one as it gets unloaded to see if it's still suitable for the job it was designed to do."

Had he heard her? "But they're gouged."

He tipped his head. "Yes, ma'am. A few are, but in most cases it is superficial. Don't worry about structural integrity. Each will be inspected with that in mind, as well as visibility. We'll order replacements as required."

And they'd take how long to get here?

"Adds a little character," Noel said with a nod.

He must be kidding. Allison looked at Noel, who shrugged. When she turned back to Brent, he was striding back to the lone timber on the ground.

Could she trust Brent Callahan's judgment?

oOo

He was aware of Allison's gaze on his back the entire time it took the crew to unload the truck. While he and Curtis set aside the three beams that had taken the brunt of the damage. While the other guys all jawed.

By then the audience had gotten bigger. Two women, including a very short one with a toddler firmly in her grasp, joined Allison and Noel. The other tucked her hand into Noel's and they shared a kiss.

Okay, so Brent hadn't kept his back turned the whole time, but he'd done his best to ignore the gathering. If he were going to have to work every single day with extra eyes on him, he'd go bananas. And, what, tell his uncle he wasn't up for the job?

Man, he'd worked for this level of trust for years. He wasn't going to let any skinny dictator run him off. That Noel guy seemed nice enough. Hopefully no one else at the farm was as whacko as Allison Hart.

The rookie driver carefully got the semi turned around, out the driveway, and headed toward Coeur d'Alene.

"We're going to go buy some lunch," Curtis said. "Are you coming, or do you want me to grab something for you?"

Brent took a deep breath and let it out slowly. "I'll take a ham on rye, please. The keys are in the ignition."

Allison stared in his direction.

"And don't take too long about it, bud. We've got to get rolling here."

Curtis slapped his back. "You got it." He saluted Allison and headed for the truck, leaving Brent to his fate.

Working this site was going to improve his prayer life abundantly, at least if single sentences tossed heavenward counted. Prayers like, "Please, Lord, help me," and "I could use some patience, God," and "Jesus, give me the right words. Calming words." Definitely prayers.

He walked toward the waiting group, just as Allison crouched down to the toddler's eye level. The little girl dodged in and out of Allison's arms, chortling with glee, then ran a few circles around her.

Maybe if he kept that image in his mind, it would help. See? She liked kids, and this one seemed to like her back. She couldn't be that horrible.

"Hi, I'm Brent Callahan from Timber Framing Plus." He held out his hand to the woman tucked under Noel's arm.

"My wife, Claire," Noel replied. "And Jo Nemesek with her daughter, Maddie-the-Tornado."

Brent shook both women's hands then glanced again at the child. Tornado seemed about right. Giggling, she ran circles around Allison then collapsed in a heap. Allison tickled her, and the child squealed.

Someday maybe he'd have kids. Unlikely, though. What good Christian woman would want to be saddled with the likes of him? The only plan he'd come up with so far was not to get close enough to someone that they'd want to know his past, because lying wasn't a better option than the truth.

Allison stood, dusting her hands together.

Subtle hint to get back to work? Too bad for her.

"That went better than I feared." Brent met Allison's gaze. "I'll notify Patrick which beams he'll need to replace and send with the next load. The good news is that none of them are essential to the first few days' work."

"Excellent." Noel grabbed the tornado and sent her end-over-end to his shoulder, facing backward. "It will be interesting watching this structure go up. I've worked in the bush a lot of years, but never at the harvesting end. Good-looking timbers you've got there."

"Patrick works hard with his sources."

Allison stepped closer. "So how much is this going to slow things down?"

"In the long run? Not at all." Brent met her gaze. "In the short run, a day or two. The new timbers will be rough cut. We'll need to plane them on site and fit the joinery."

"But—" She bit her lip.

"We're doing the best we can, ma'am." He couldn't help grinning as she bristled.

Noel slid the child to the ground. "That's all we can ask. Hey, man, soup's on. Want to come on in and have a bite to eat?"

Allison's face soured.

Brent couldn't decide if he wanted to spite her or see if she were actually capable of smiling. Maybe neither. "The guys are getting me a sandwich from the deli."

"Oh, do come in." Claire put her hand on his arm. "Sit down out of the wind for a few minutes, and get something hot in you."

"Uh…" He glanced at Allison. "I need to give Patrick a call."

She smirked.

"I guess I can do that from inside. Thanks, I'll take you up on your offer."

They trooped up the driveway toward the large house. Pretty soon it wouldn't be the biggest building on the farm. He took a closer look. Wait a minute. "Is this timber frame?"

The toddler's mother, Jo, spoke for the first time. "Sort of, but the wood is hidden between the straw bales. We had to use post-and-beam to carry the load of the roof over that distance."

A low whistle escaped between Brent's teeth. "I haven't seen straw bale up close. Looks good. Who was the contractor?"

Claire grinned. "Jo, Sierra, and I handled the general contractor duties and a lot of the hands-on."

Brent stopped in his tracks. "No way." He glanced at Noel.

The other guy raised both hands, palms out. "It was before my time. These gals really are the bomb."

He noticed Noel hadn't mentioned Allison. Was she a newer addition, too? He glanced her way.

31

She had both arms wrapped around herself, as though that could keep the wind from cutting through her sweatshirt. A little personal insulation would go a long way.

They traipsed up the steps to the wide deck flanking the house, and Noel opened the door with a bow. "After you."

Brent followed Allison in, his gaze going to the lofty beamed ceiling above and the massive rock thermal wall straight ahead. A whistle slipped out.

A rich beefy aroma filled the air, and his stomach grumbled. It'd been a long time since that coffee and Danish he'd called breakfast.

Allison leaned close. "Don't forget to call Patrick." Then she stalked away into the kitchen to wash her hands at the sink.

This was going to be a very long few months.

Chapter 4 --

ickle, fickle March blustered out with slushy snow showers. April strutted in just as emotionally.

Allison paced at the windows in the great room. Over the past two weeks, the skeleton of the school building had gone up. The thing looked massive, even with the forested hillside visible between the posts.

Brent had turned his crew to erecting the frame for her house. She couldn't see it from the great room, and she didn't feel comfortable roaming the bedroom wing of the big house and staring out those windows. Besides, even then, it was barely visible through the naked trees.

She'd appreciate that privacy once she was moved in. Now it drove her crazy. After two weeks of butting heads with Brent Callahan, she'd decided he worked better if she wasn't staring at him, so she couldn't just take up residence in the tree house in the nearby golden willow and watch her house go up.

The guy was obstinate bordering on rude.

Sierra came in the back door, stamping slush off her boots. Her eyes lit up when she saw Allison. "There you are! I've been looking for you."

33

Allison smiled. If she'd done something wrong, Sierra wouldn't look so pleased. "What's up?"

"It's supposed to clear up tomorrow. Want to take a trip to Coeur d'Alene and do some shopping? Or even Wynnton…"

"It's clearing up? Finally. I can get to work—"

"Relax a little, girl! I don't think I've seen you curl up with a good book or even play solitaire on your laptop since you got here. A little shopping therapy will be good for us."

She'd managed to avoid Sunday evening game nights so far. Relaxing hadn't been dealt into her hand of cards when she was born. Her mind scrambled for an excuse Sierra would accept for avoiding this bonding moment. "I thought you guys limited use of your vehicles. All that fuel being sucked into the atmosphere."

Sierra shrugged and glanced toward the kitchen. She lowered her voice. "Sometimes I just need to get off the farm, you know?"

Allison raised her eyebrows. Even Sierra found their lifestyle a little stifling? "I guess I could take a day off. I feel like a caged tiger."

Sierra grinned. "And you look like one half the time, too. Pacing and watching."

"Not trying to make anyone uncomfortable. It's just how I'm wired, to keep moving. I really hate depending on someone else's timeline."

"You're not in the city anymore. We have time to smell the roses. If they ever bloom this year, that is."

Allison managed a laugh. "Once spring arrives, it will come in full force. I'm sure the roses will be blooming by your wedding."

"I hope so. Chelsea is determined I have roses, and I'm determined to have local flowers."

"Your sister is efficient." Allison sobered. "I don't know what I'd have done without her last summer after my parents' plane crash. I didn't even know my father had named me executor, let alone how to plan a funeral or deal with the estate." She'd turned to Chelsea Riehl, an event planner she'd first met in college for help with the funeral. Later, Chelsea had introduced her to Sierra, Jo, and Claire — and changed her life forever.

Sierra rested her hand on Allison's arm. "I'm so sorry. I know I've said that before, but it's still true. I can't imagine doing life without my parents, even though they live so far away."

"Your parents are pretty cool." They might even be one of the few couples that didn't cheat on each other. Allison had been in their Portland home several times with Chelsea and found their apparent dedication to each other enlightening.

"Yeah. Anyway, help me escape for a day? I'm sure I can think of something I need to source for the wedding, if you're up for it."

If she were going to live here for the next fifty years, she needed to make friends with these women. One at a time sounded better than by the threesome. She stepped back to drop contact with Sierra's hand. "Hey, it's my nephew's birthday in a month or so. Maybe I can find a gift for him."

"You have a nephew? I don't think I knew that."

Allison's jaw clenched. "He's going to be four. I hardly ever get to see him."

"Aw. Where do they live?"

"Last I heard, my sister was in Tucson. She must've burned through most of what she inherited from our parents already."

Sympathy poured from Sierra's eyes. "Burned through?"

Allison lifted a shoulder and let it drop, resigned. "She's a drug addict who hops in and out of relationships. I don't know how she's managed to keep custody of Finnley."

"Oh, no. I'm so sorry to hear that. How often do you see them?"

"I ran into her in the mall a few weeks before moving here. That's when she told me she was going to Arizona with her latest boyfriend. I hadn't seen her since the funeral."

"Poor little guy."

Allison blinked. "Yeah. I wish I could do something."

"Well, we'll pray for him and for your sister, too. What's her name?"

"Lori." Allison hesitated. "Do you ever wonder if a person is beyond God's help?"

"Remember Saul of Tarsus? The guy went around imprisoning and killing Christians. God got a hold of his life, and he became the most renowned preacher in all of history."

"Yeah, but that's in the Bible. Ages ago. I mean, I believe God can change people. Don't get me wrong. But there isn't a whole lot of evidence He does it these days."

Sierra regarded her thoughtfully. "It's not usually as dramatic as a light from heaven and a guy getting blinded in the middle of the road, no. But God has His ways of meeting people."

"Do you really think so?" Oh, no. She could feel tears stinging the backs of her eyes. *Show no weakness.*

"I know so. Ask Noel how he met Jesus one of these days. He's certainly a changed man."

"Noel? Really? He seems like such a nice guy." As far as men went.

"He is. He was before, too, but he was doing his best to avoid thinking about God. That didn't stop God from thinking about him, though." Sierra reached for Allison again.

Again she shifted just out of reach. This was such a touchy-feely group. "I guess. I mean, I believe in God. I know what He's done in my life."

"What's that?" Sierra dropped into the nearest deep chair. "Tell me."

"He made me strong." Allison thought back over the affairs her parents flaunted in each other's faces, leaving them little concern for their daughters. And when Dad accused Mom that Lori wasn't even his child, and when she screamed back that he was right, and Lori disappeared... yes, she'd needed to be strong.

Being strong wasn't enough, it turned out. But it was still better than being weak.

"Allison?"

"I'm sorry. The memories are just too painful." Allison paced over to the window and peered out. She still couldn't see her house from here, but she could see a white Timber Framing Plus pickup truck come from the building site, pass the house, and jounce down the driveway. No way was it five o'clock yet.

Sierra strolled up beside her and they watched the truck disappear together.

"Yeah, I'll go to Coeur d'Alene with you. Or, better yet, we can take my car, if you like." Her hybrid Camry had to be better on fuel than the old diesel hatchback Sierra drove. Plus it had the comforts of home. Actually, it had more comforts than home did.

"You sure? That'd be great! I'll help you find a gift for Finnley. What kinds of things does he like?"

Allison stared at Sierra blankly. "I have no idea." Pain sliced through her. Yes, she hurt for Lori, but her sister had made her own decisions, at least at first. But what had Finnley done to deserve being born to a druggie?

That had been one of the times when Lori moved back home for a while and tried to kick the addictions. It was a miracle the kid didn't have fetal alcohol syndrome, or worse.

Maybe there was a God. Maybe He did care about Finnley.

"We're all going to pray for your nephew." This time Sierra got close enough to give Allison a side hug.

They both survived. Who knew that could happen?

"We're going to pray that God gives them a fresh start. He can do it, you know. Just watch."

oOo

It should've made him less twitchy when Allison wasn't watching his every move. For the past week, she'd only shown up two or three times a day instead of constantly raking or weeding or just standing nearby. But he never knew when she'd suddenly be there, practically at his elbow, with a question. More than once he'd nearly dropped a tool in surprise.

He'd handed over a hard hat and told her she wasn't allowed anywhere near the job site without it. She'd looked at it with distaste, but hey, rules were rules, and she was going to abide by this one or he'd toss her over his shoulder and carry her off himself. She couldn't weigh that much. Evidently she'd believed him and wore the protection.

Today he hadn't seen her at all. Not that he was looking, of course. But she hadn't nagged him once.

"Whew." Curtis took off his hard hat and wiped back his hair as he glanced around. "Peaceful in these here parts when *she* ain't here." He said the word as though Allison were poison.

"A little respect. She's our client."

"Oh, come on. I've seen you clench your teeth when she's around. She'd drive a man to drink, she would."

The thought had crossed Brent's mind a time or two, as well. He shrugged. "Don't let her get under your skin. Seriously, no woman should have that kind of power over you."

Curtis looked at him skeptically. "So that's your great wisdom from the lofty age of — what are you, anyway?"

"Twenty-eight." Brent knew he had enough years on Curtis that his age didn't matter. "And yep, that's my wisdom. You're doomed if you let a woman wrap you around her finger."

Curtis clapped his hand on Brent's back. "Is that the voice of experience?"

"It is." What kind of experience wasn't any of his crew's business. "Our job here is to get these two buildings up. This here house, and—" he pointed toward the front of the property "—the school building. Ms. Hart is our client and nothing more. She has a right to see progress."

"Every five minutes?"

Brent lifted a shoulder. "I guess. It's her time she's wasting."

"And yours."

"Sometimes. But Patrick taught me to keep a client in the know, at whatever level he or she needs. Every job is different." He sounded so pious he could almost hate himself, yet it was still true. In the end, Allison Hart was paying his wages. He should be thankful she'd finally started to trust him enough to let him work unsupervised.

Still, it was odd she hadn't come by a single time all day. He doubted it was because she wasn't curious. He glanced down the path toward the straw bale house and saw a glimpse of bright yellow.

Curtis followed his gaze and nudged him. "Get to work, dude," he stage-whispered. "Here she comes."

Brent poked his jaw toward the structure. "*You* get to work. I'm allowed to stand here and supervise."

Shaking his head, Curtis gave another pull on his water bottle and sauntered back into the heart of the place.

"Allison!" Brent feigned surprise as she came to a stop beside him. "I wondered where you'd gotten to today."

Her head swiftly tilted upward, and a surprised look crossed her face. She shifted a step farther from him. "I've been busy."

He pointed a hammer at the structure. "We have, too."

"So I see."

"Come on in closer if you like. I see you've got your safety equipment on."

She rolled her eyes but followed him.

Brent stopped in the very center and tipped his head back. "See? There's your kingpin, holding the entire roof solidly in place."

She stared up for a long moment.

"No response? Come on, you have to admit it looks pretty awesome."

"Yeah. It is cool. Thanks."

Wait. Was that moisture in the corner of her eyes? The hard girl in the hard hat wouldn't be feeling any emotion, would she?

39

"You okay?"

She glanced at him through narrowed eyes. "Yeah, fine, why?"

Brent grinned. "It's all right to be happy, you know. This is going to be your home. I think you chose a great design. You'll love it."

Allison shook her head, ever so slightly. "Okay, I'm excited. I really am. Is that better?" Her pencil-thin eyebrows rose as she challenged him.

"I don't know. I was thinking more of a twirl, or a squeal. Maybe hands clasped in front of you." He feigned a girlish position.

She shook her head again, but this time a laugh escaped. "You're crazy, you know that? I don't do giggles and glee, but I do like this house."

Brent raised both hands in the air and did a two-step. "Well, hallelujah! I do believe my crew and I have been complimented."

"Yeah, you have." The smile slid off her face. "You're doing a good job. Even Patrick couldn't have done better."

"Whoa." He looked over and watched a myriad of emotions play across her face. "Okay, thanks. But what do you want?"

Her features hardened. "Nothing, all right? Nothing but my house and school."

Chapter 5 --

*H*aving a girls' day was more fun than Allison anticipated. She'd been avoiding one-on-one with Sierra after the other woman's mood swings and depression last fall when she'd been convinced she was dying of cancer.

This new, upbeat Sierra was a lot more fun. The other women teased that it was her engagement to Gabriel Rubachuk causing her to glow. Allison hated to burst anyone's bubble. Likely Gabe himself would do that soon enough. Meanwhile, Sierra blissfully shopped for clothing and wedding decorations like there was no tomorrow, and Allison could relax a little.

"You haven't told me what you're looking for in a gift for your nephew." Sierra stuffed another shopping bag into the Camry's trunk. "It's time to shift gears before I run out of money."

Allison doubted that would happen any time soon. She'd been a guest at the Riehls' Portland home on several occasions. It might not be the grand estate her parents had owned — and that she still needed to get rid of — but it was no shack in the slums either.

"I really don't know Finnley all that well. I've only seen him a few times in the last year. What do four-year-old boys play with?"

Sierra shrugged. "You've got me. I don't know any. Does he like to play outside? Build things? Look at picture books?"

Allison's heart clenched. "Lori moves him so often I'm sure they leave stuff behind all the time. If it doesn't fit in her car, it doesn't come. And knowing her, her own things would take precedence over Finnley's." That little guy deserved so much better. He deserved a chance, at the very least — one he wasn't likely to get any time soon.

"So sending him a bike or something like that might not be a good idea." Sierra looked thoughtful, staring across the roof of the car.

"Probably not." Allison sighed.

Sierra dabbed at her eyes.

Oh, man. Now the woman was crying over someone else's nephew she didn't even know. "He'll be okay." Allison hoped.

"It's tough. So many unloved kids, and so many people who want them but can't have any." Sierra looked heavenward. "Are you listening, God? It's not fair."

Her voice stayed flat, but Allison knew Sierra's thoughts were anything but. Allison reached over and touched Sierra's arm. Probably the first time she'd ever done that to anyone. "Thanks for caring. I pray for Finnley every day, asking God to protect him. Asking God to step into Lori's life and give her a good smack so she'll see what she's doing to both of them. She knows better." Allison pondered those words. "At least she once did. I don't know what the alcohol and drugs have done to her brain."

"I'll pray with you. Every day."

"Thanks." Allison met Sierra's gaze, and something passed between them. Was this what it would be like to have a friend? She'd stood on her own all her life, the opposite of Lori. But neither of them had what normal people thought of as friends.

"Let's go grab a coffee and figure out something for Finnley." Sierra pointed down the street. "There's a little coffee shop a few blocks away. We don't even have to drive."

Allison nodded. "You're on."

A few minutes later they sat in a little booth with coffee and pie in front of them.

"Don't tell Jo. I have so missed lemon meringue pie."

Allison grinned. "You need a bigger greenhouse if you want enough lemon trees to supply several families."

"I know. But sometimes, in the fall, it's nice to know the garden is going to freeze over. It means the frantic food preservation is coming to an end. That greenhouse adds work for a couple of months on either end of the growing season."

"You'd have to keep it warmer for lemon trees, too. They wouldn't do well in January and February in Idaho unless the space was heated."

Sierra dropped her fork and leaned across the table. "We should totally plant a couple in the sunroom! It rarely dips below freezing in there, surrounded as it is by the house and backed by the thermal mass wall. I wonder if that would work. I sure miss lemons."

"We can do some research and see. I don't know at what temperature it's simply not doable."

"Hmm." Sierra carved a tiny flake of meringue off her pie and put it in her mouth, sighing. "Claire uses red currant juice in place of lemon juice in some recipes, as it's kind of tart. But she hasn't tried it in pie that I know of."

Allison shrugged. "So buy a few lemons now and again. The pie mixes are sure to be full of harmful chemicals, but you can make lemon pie from scratch."

"No." Sierra's head was shaking before Allison finished. "It's against our mandate. Everything must be grown locally except for a very few essentials, like salt." She had a nibble of the yellow custard. "Sadly, lemon meringue pie is full of non-essentials."

"Or you get kicked off the island?"

Sierra frowned. "Pardon me?"

"You know, Survivor-style. Claire and Jo would evict you

43

from the farm if you brought lemons home?"

"Well, no. But we've all agreed on our lifestyle." Sierra raised her eyebrows, fork poised above the pie. "As have you, by the way."

Allison sighed. "I know. And I mostly believe in it." She had a bite of the pie in front of her. It tasted of chemicals, and she pushed the plate away. "It can be taken too far."

"Oh, I agree. You've seen our list of things we'll buy, so long as they're organic and fair trade." Sierra lifted her coffee cup meaningfully.

"Right." Allison shifted in her seat. "So I guess it's about time I started taking my turn at cooking. No one has said anything yet."

Sierra grinned. "Claire was figuring on asking you for next week. We all rotate, and the guys do Sunday."

"I noticed that. Together. When is Zach's night by himself? Or Noel's?"

"Ha. You don't want Zach to cook."

"No, I'm serious. You don't know if I'm a good cook. In fact, I'm not. How come he doesn't have to take a regular night and I do? Seems kind of sexist." There, she'd finally come out and said it.

Another bite of pie slid into Sierra's mouth, followed by a swallow of coffee. "I can see how it might look that way."

Right. Because it was.

"Zach is the only one who lives on the farm and has a full-time off-site job. He works more than fifty hours most weeks."

"Uh huh? I'll be teaching a lot of hours once we're operational. Will I get off cooking duty?"

Sierra tipped her head to one side, her blue eyes meeting Allison's gaze. "That's a really good question. I don't see why not. We'll have to see how things go."

Really? They'd bend for her? Whoa. She hadn't expected that.

Her face must have shown her shock. Sierra carried on.

"Claire and Noel both love to cook. They easily do more than half of the day-to-day cooking between them, but when they're hosting backcountry trips, we adjust at home around it. When Jo was pregnant and throwing up every day, we let her off the hook for a while. It's not a dictatorship, Allison. We adapt."

"That's good to know." She managed to get the words out. Dictatorship. That's what her dad had tried to run. It's what her mother and Lori had rebelled against. Allison had been the good girl, trying to toe the line and do everything right. Maybe then Dad would tell her he was proud of her, that she measured up to his standards. She never had, no matter what she did.

All the money he'd left behind, the huge house in Arlington, the vacation house at Cannon Beach, the investments… she'd give it all up in a heartbeat to hear real words of approval from her father.

"Eat your pie," Sierra said. "We bought the pieces. Don't let it go to waste."

Allison blinked the moisture from her eyes. "No, that's okay. You can finish mine if you want."

Sierra's face lit up then slumped. "I really shouldn't. I can't afford to gain any weight. The seamstress has already started my wedding dress."

"Another piece of pie won't hurt." Allison pushed it closer to Sierra. "Go for it."

o0o

"You headed back to Coeur d'Alene for the weekend?"

Brent's head came up and he stared at Noel Kenzie. "Uh, I figured so. Why?"

The other guy shrugged. "Just curious. Zach and I plan on some creek fishing Saturday. I saw you had a fly rod in your truck, and wondered if you'd like to join us."

Brent couldn't help the grin that slid across his face. "Man, I love fishing." It didn't take three more seconds to think through the sterile, lifeless weekend that awaited him in his apartment. They'd brought two company trucks up this week, so the guys could still escape. The town likely had a laundromat, which was the only other thing he needed. "What's running?"

"Cut-throat, most likely."

"You do some guiding, don't you?"

Noel shrugged. "Yes, I do. But this is recreational. Not looking for you to pay me for the day. Just thought you might like to see some of the back country around here."

"It's cool terrain. More mountainous and more rain than back home." He'd learned to slog through the mud and keep the job on track, though. "But yeah, I'd be honored to go with you guys. There's sure no reason to drive back to an empty apartment."

"We can't have that. So let me expand the invitation to include church on Sunday and dinner at the farm afterward." Noel waggled his eyebrows. "It's guys' day in the kitchen, if you're up for that?"

Maybe this wasn't such a good idea after all. It wasn't the fishing so much as getting too friendly with his clients. He kept forgetting that, while Allison might be the lead person, the rest of this gang also had an investment in the project.

"The kitchen doesn't scare me." Though maybe it should. Weren't these people some kind of food fanatics? "It's just... well... maybe it's not a good idea."

"We can make shop talk off limits." Noel grinned. "If that helps."

Had Patrick ever told him to keep business separate? Brent seemed to remember his aunt and uncle joining clients for golf. This wasn't really any different. Besides, fishing was way more fun than golf.

Decision made. "Yeah, sure. Sounds good. I'd really like that."

"Cool. We'll head out mid-afternoon. I'll pack up some sandwiches, so don't worry about going hungry."

"Oh, you don't need to feed me. I can grab something from the deli counter at Super One."

Noel grimaced. "I'm sure you can, but why? I'm offering you real food here, freshly made."

"Well, in that case..." Brent chuckled. "I accept."

Noel cuffed him on the arm. "Good."

Valerie Comer

Chapter 6 --

The Timber Framing Plus truck jounced past the big house toward her house site. Brent waved.

At the window, Allison narrowed her gaze as she lifted her hand in greeting. She recognized the guy in the passenger seat, but where was the third one? And besides, Brent was at least ten minutes late.

She took a deep breath and let it out in a huff. Why did this feel so much like teaching college freshmen who were there simply to party or slide through? These men wouldn't get a single thing done if she didn't ride herd on them.

She certainly didn't trust older men any more than young bucks, but surely Patrick didn't know what was going on. She fingered her cell. She could call him. Oh, so tempting.

There couldn't possibly be a reasonable explanation, could there? But previous conversations with the company owner filtered into her mind. Patrick would only stick up for Brent. Tell her everything was on the revised schedule. Everything was coming together just fine.

As if.

Allison grabbed her coat and headed onto the deck. Right, she needed that stupid hard hat or Brent wouldn't even talk to her. At least her hair was flat anyway. Wearing the dumb thing didn't mess up her hair, just the rest of her style. She reached inside to grab it before striding in the wake of the pickup truck.

Brent and Curtis stood looking up into the beam structure of her little house, pointing and nodding as she approached.

She plunked the glaring yellow hat on her head and stepped up beside Brent. "Hey, what's up?" Casual was hard when all she wanted was to rip a strip off his hide.

"Good morning, Allison." If eyes could smile without any mouth action, his did so as he glanced at her hard hat.

Nice he was amused. She glared. "Aren't you missing part of your crew? Did Franco have to wait for the doughnuts to come out of the fryer or what?"

Curtis gave her a scathing look. He gritted his teeth, sent some sort of telepathic message to Brent, and stomped away.

Good. She didn't like him anyway. Useless kid.

"Franco is in Spokane." He held up his hand before she could respond. "His mother is in the hospital, and it's not looking good."

"Oh." Compassion. Surely she could find some somewhere. "I'm sorry to hear that."

"Hopefully he'll be rejoining us in just a couple of days. Curtis and I will accomplish what we can without him this week."

Allison wrestled her conscience. None of the things that had happened were personal slights. She hadn't spared much thought for all the families affected by the fire in Milwaukee or the young driver who'd scarred some of her timbers in his stupidity. Franco's mother certainly hadn't fallen ill just to spite her, either.

Lord, please help me. I don't want to be a witch. "I hope she'll be okay."

Brent shot her a surprised look.

What, he was shocked she had a human side? Man, this wasn't the kind of person she wanted to be. But she didn't want to think of these people as having real three-dimensional lives, either. She wanted them to be like actors in a movie, just playing their parts and going home at the end of the day, contented.

She realized he was speaking. "Pardon me?"

"We are all certainly praying for her, that God will either heal her or let her slip away peacefully… and quickly."

So he was a Christian? Another dimension to a man she wanted to keep 2-D and at a distance. But she couldn't let the implied challenge rest. "God answers prayer."

"You're a woman of faith, then?" His eyebrows vanished behind the hard hat's brim.

Allison nodded. "Yes." She hesitated. "God has seen me through many challenges in life."

Brent nodded with a grimace. "Me, too. My life hasn't always been an easy one, but God has been faithful to me and brought me through. He is good."

Surely this was enough bonding. She didn't want to know what problems he'd had in life. They couldn't be as bad as being raised by her parents. She stepped to one side and pointed toward Curtis, setting up scaffolding. "You'll miss Franco."

"If you're worried that your structures won't go up in time, his absence for a few days won't make that much difference."

The old Brent. The one with a chillier voice. Better. She could deal with that more easily. She glanced at him, noting his clenched jaw. "How do you figure that?"

"We'll be ready for the windows long before they arrive."

Right. The windows. "Have you found another supplier?"

He nodded. "Patrick has them on order."

Did she have to drag every word out of him? "And they're expected when?"

Brent removed his hard hat, ran his fingers through his black hair, and replaced the hat. "End of June."

That long? She closed her eyes, forcing her first reaction back. They'd be lucky to have the buildings completed by the end of summer at that rate. "I'm sure he did the best he could." Only because he knew she'd call him on it if it seemed they were slacking.

Brent let out a long breath.

Relieved she hadn't blown her top? Was she really that hard to work with? Probably.

"Yeah. He separated the orders and placed your house order first because there are way fewer windows on that one. That should get them here a week or two before the windows for the classroom building."

He could have asked before making that decision. But still, she'd have agreed. The sooner she got out of Sierra's pastel pink spare room the better. The rest of her hostess's suite was even worse with its emphasis on purple, turquoise, and gold. Way overdone. Allison had picked a calming blue gray for her own home, from top to bottom. Light enough no one could complain it was depressing.

"Patrick will send a few extra guys when the windows come so we can move to completion as quickly as possible."

She nodded. "I appreciate that." There was still no way she'd be out of that duplex before Sierra's end-of-June wedding. What were her options? Moving into a spare room at the big house? Maybe getting an apartment in town. Maybe she should look into it this week, and get a little space for all of them. Then the team wouldn't have to figure out where to put her.

Right. They liked making decisions together. Had she really committed to that kind of lifestyle? She must've been crazy.

"Yo, boss!" Curtis called out. "Ready to start sheathing the roof."

Allison shoved her hands into her jacket pockets and watched Brent stride over. He uncovered a stack of plywood and pointed up at the roof. Curtis nodded.

How could two guys manage this without help? She knew what she could do.

oOo

Brent couldn't believe the gall of this woman. "No, you cannot work on the job site."

Her chin came up. "And exactly why not? You obviously need help. I may not have all the experience you guys have, but I can make things easier for you. I can fetch and carry, and whatever you need done. Like an apprentice."

"I don't think so, ma'am."

She leaned closer, her eyes flashing fire from mere inches away. "Don't call me ma'am."

Brent's grandmother had drilled that kind of respect into him when he was a kid. Allison Hart seemed to take it as a personal affront. Just went to prove not all women thought the same, as if he hadn't had enough life lessons on that one already. But he couldn't back down... or away. He was the foreman here, regardless of what she thought. "I beg your pardon." Never mind that his tonal inflection was the exact opposite of begging.

"Give me one good reason I can't help."

He could give her thirty without coming up for air. "Steel-toed boots." He should make her wear them anytime she put that hard hat on.

"Okay. I'll go put them on." She turned.

No way. She had a pair? He might need a few more of his thirty reasons. "No sweaters with holes in them that can get caught on pegs. No hoods on jackets for the same reason."

Allison glanced back at him with a shrug. "You think I only have one change of clothes?"

He could be pardoned for thinking that. She only wore black, as near as he could tell. It all looked the same to him.

She marched back and plunked her hands on her hips. Not that she had any. "Why don't you say what's really on your mind? You don't want me here because I'm a woman and you don't think I can do the job."

Two could play this game. "I don't want you here because you're a woman and you have no experience. I'd rather watch for falling hammers than watch for someone who's bound to get injured in the first hour." He leaned closer. "I don't have the time or the patience to teach an apprentice."

"You have the time," Allison shot back. "But I totally believe you don't have the patience."

What was that supposed to mean? Brent narrowed his gaze. "Thank you for that character assessment. Now, please leave the job site so Curtis and I can get back to work. I'd like to get your roof sheathed today before the weather turns."

Allison flicked a glance toward the structure not far behind him. No doubt Curtis was over there, all ears, laughing his fool head off. It better be silently. She looked back at Brent. "You think I'm useless."

He had no answer for that one, so he raised his eyebrows. Let her think what she wanted.

She jabbed him in the chest with that pointy forefinger. "I'll have you know I know how to swing a hammer. I'll have you know I'm not afraid of heights. I'll have you know that I have some muscles."

So he was supposed to challenge her to an arm wrestle so she could prove it? Oh, come on. "Time's a wastin', *ma'am*." He couldn't resist drawling out the title she hated. "How about you run back to the house and find something useful to do there?"

"You think this is funny?" She poked him once more then shoved both hands in her pockets. Her eyes blazed, and her mouth tightened into a firm line.

This wasn't personal. He was a representative of Timber Framing Plus, in charge of erecting two buildings. He wasn't here to prod this irritating woman into losing her temper, which was likely to happen any second now.

"Look, Allison. I'm sorry. My remark was uncalled for." How could he have let her get under his skin this much? "But the fact remains that I don't need someone on the job so badly I'd risk a greenhorn on it."

"So if Noel came up the path and offered to help, you'd send him away, too?"

Uh. Probably not. Today really would be easier with a third set of hands.

Allison's finger arrowed for his chest again, but he snatched it before it could make contact. He was already going to have a small round bruise on his sternum.

"You're sexist."

He grabbed both her wrists to keep from getting walloped. How could wrists that thin have any strength at all? "I have too much respect for women to deliberately put them in a place of danger."

She wrenched her hands away and pulled back a step. "That's a load of…"

"Don't prove you're not a lady after all," Brent warned. "Look, I'm not trying to pick on you or start a fight. In fact, sometime I'd love to have a real conversation with you, one where we talk and maybe laugh. Where we're not trying to tear each other's heads off."

Allison opened her mouth, but he gave her a warning glare and she shut back up.

"But you're pushing me—" He almost said ma'am again. No point in setting a match to dry tinder. "Allison. Ms. Hart." Yes, the distance was still a good thing.

She smirked.

He'd like to wipe that look off her face. Why was it all or nothing with this one? Why had Patrick sent him here, to Galena Landing? Why couldn't Brent have gotten the contract for the tourist lodge just over Christmas Pass?

"I'm in charge of this build. There's nothing in our contract that says I have to hire the client if we're short-handed."

"Is there anything that says you can't?" She lifted her eyebrows. "Besides, I'm not asking to be put on payroll. I just want to help and believe I'm capable of it."

Brent threw both hands in the air. "Fine. Have it your way. Work clothes. Boots. Hair done so it won't get in the way. Gloves."

"You're not wearing gloves."

"Wouldn't want you to break your nails."

"I don't know why I even want to work with you."

He didn't know, either. But maybe he'd pushed her hard enough she'd leave and not come back. Was that what he wanted? Yes. Most definitely yes.

"I'll be back in fifteen minutes." She flounced down the path.

Or maybe he'd get the chance to find out if they could converse without flames. That would be okay, too.

Chapter 7 --

No way was she going to give any sign how exhausted she was. Brent was taking her at her word that she could handle anything he and Curtis could.

Well, she'd been wrong. She might jog five miles a day and work out on her home gym three times a week — when she could get it set up again — but that didn't give her the strength of a guy who'd done manual labor for a living for years.

Wrong, but not about to mention it.

She crouched on the scaffold at the roof's edge, the lanyard on her harness clipped to the safety line, and reached down to grab the next four-by-eight sheet of plywood Curtis lifted to her and Brent. Her hand slipped and the sheet hung at an angle for an instant before she could grasp it again. Good thing Curtis hadn't let go yet.

"You don't have to do this, Allison."

Yes, she did. No looking at Brent as he hoisted more than half the weight. If there was sympathy in his eyes, she didn't want to see it. Ditto for laughter. Or for I-told-you-so.

She gritted her teeth. "I've got it."

He grunted.

She'd ignore that.

"Grab the chalk and let's snap a line. You can start attaching the sheets. Ever used an air nailer?"

"No. But I'm sure I can handle it."

"Show me. Be real careful where you point it. I've seen guys shoot themselves through the leg with it."

A monster tool appeared in her line of sight. She couldn't help it. Her mouth dropped open. She couldn't lift that thing. Her jaw tensed as she raised her gaze. To his T-shirt, stretched across his muscled chest. To his chin. To his dark eyes and the eyebrows raised above them.

She thrust out her hands to accept the tool. It was as heavy as it looked, but she managed to keep from sagging to her knees. "I'm not familiar with this model."

His mouth twitched. "It's not your average household tool."

Brent didn't need to add that it was meant for men with bulging biceps. Like his. Not that she'd noticed.

"Here, let me show you." He retrieved the tool and knelt on a piece of plywood.

Allison resisted the urge to rub her arms at the sudden relief. Instead, she crouched beside him as he sent nail after nail piercing through the plywood and into the rafters.

He made it look so effortless.

She should take the nailer from him and finish the sheet. She should. But she watched instead. Watched his muscles barely twitch as he hoisted the tool and added a new strip of nails to the intake. Watched as he glanced her way, expressionless, and resumed the task.

Brent could be chiding her right now. He could be making fun of her or ordering her off the roof. He wasn't doing either.

She felt as big as one of the nails, but each of those had a specific purpose. She didn't. Not on the roof, anyway.

"Want a go at it?" His dark eyes met hers.

Why couldn't he let some attitude show so she could lash out at him? He'd asked a perfectly reasonable question, all things considered.

Allison looked past Brent's shoulder, but his gaze pulled her back magnetically. She clenched her jaw. "I don't think I'm strong enough."

Acknowledgment flickered briefly in his eyes. Maybe even respect she'd admitted it. He nodded slightly. "Okay." He tugged another sheet of plywood into place and checked its alignment before hefting that nailer.

That was it?

She didn't want him to be a nice guy. There were so few of them around. What were the odds of meeting one in the very place Claire, Jo, and Sierra insisted they loved men who were worth it?

Brent made short work of attaching the next sheet of plywood before reaching down for the next one Curtis offered. Allison didn't lean over to help. Brent didn't ask.

She unbuckled her harness. "If there's nothing useful I can do, I'll get out of your way."

"Be careful on the ladder."

Was that the same thing as "Don't let the door slam your backside as you go out?" But his gaze held nothing of that. It held nothing at all, actually.

"I will. Let me know if there's something I can do." She edged her way to the ladder, past Brent. He smelled clean, like wood shavings and musk.

This was ridiculous. He couldn't possibly be a good guy.

Allison's feet found the ladder and she made her way down, mindful of the heavy boots that made her footing awkward.

Curtis shot a smirk at her.

Definitely not one of the good guys.

"Curtis," Brent said from up on the roof.

Both Curtis and Allison looked up. Brent shook his head at his worker, and Curtis shrugged, not looking Allison's way again.

What was that about? A warning to treat her with respect?

Man, she didn't really deserve that after the scene she'd made earlier. Sure, she was still the client. They still worked for her. But she'd made some stupid demands.

She trudged over to the edge of the trees and sat down, her back against a trunk, then removed her hard hat. She undid the clip that kept her French braid spiraled against her skull and let the plait hang down the front. Best to keep her hair contained anyway, just in case Brent found something else for her to do.

Curtis hoisted another plywood to the roof and Brent easily swung it into place.

Like he needed her for anything.

oOo

Brent kept a peripheral eye on Allison. Had he been too hard on her? Could he have handled the situation a different way? He couldn't think how and get the job done she'd hired him to do.

"Time for coffee!" hollered Curtis.

A guy didn't need a timepiece with Curtis around.

"Go ahead," called Brent. "I'll be down in a minute." Just needed to attach the last row.

He descended the ladder a few minutes later and rolled his eyes. Curtis sat across the clearing from Allison, sipping coffee from his thermos with a bag of chips in his hand. *Way to speak with each other, people.*

Brent knew which side his bread was buttered on. He snagged his lunch box and strode over to Allison. "Hi." He settled onto the dirt beside her.

"Hey." Her glance caught him then ricocheted off.

He tilted his lunch box her way. "Want a turnover?"

"No." She stared past him for a few seconds. "Thank you, anyway."

"They're pretty good." Brent pulled one out of its wrapper and took a bite. "Glad I discovered that bakery on the side street. Much better food than from the display case in the gas station."

Her lip curled just a little and her gaze snapped to his.

Brent grinned. "Really. Galena Landing isn't a hospitable place for folks like me who don't have a place to cook."

"You can cook?"

Aha. She used words after all. "Sure, sort of. Can't you?"

Allison hesitated, and she glanced away. "I'm not the best at it."

Now why didn't that surprise him? Little Miss I'm-as-good-as-a-guy. "I got tired of eating out."

She shifted on the hard ground.

Must be tough with so little padding. Brent could feel every pebble he sat on. "Maybe sometime I'll cook dinner for you."

Her eyes grew wide.

Brent could've smacked himself up the side of the head. That was way outside the bounds of foreman and client. Whatever possessed him to let those words escape? To have even thought them in the first place?

"Easy to say. You have no kitchen."

"That's true." He munched a bit more of the cherry turnover, watching her. But the idea had caught hold. "I'm sure you do. Maybe I could use yours." In for a twig, in for a kingpin.

Sheesh. Who let his mouth go for a hike without his brain along?

"You're serious."

Brent tossed the rest of the pastry into his mouth, buying himself a few more seconds to respond. "Why not? When's a good time?"

Allison's gaze seemed focused on his mouth. His gut tightened. How had he gone from thinking about cooking dinner to thinking about kissing? But it was Allison who started doing the looking, not him.

"You've got some crumbs on your lip."

A flush started at his neck and worked its way up. His mouth wasn't the only part of him heading its own direction. Apparently his mind had found the same trail. Brent swiped his face with the back of his hand. "That get it?"

"No." She reached over and brushed his lower lip.

Brent caught his breath. Maybe all of him was on the same path after all, but it wasn't one he should be going down.

"There. Got it." Her gaze met his, no hardness in it. Instead, something akin to vulnerability shone from her eyes for one brief instant before she looked away.

There was a real person behind the barriers Allison Hart had erected. And that person was awakening the real person inside Brent.

Against his will, he reminded himself. Now that he was aware, he could turn himself in a different direction. Get himself right out of that forest. No paths at all.

o0o

"What've we got to make muffins with?" Allison knew she'd find Claire in the kitchen, and she was right.

Claire sat perched on one of the tall stools at the peninsula, flipping through a well-used recipe book. She glanced up. "Muffins? We've got all the basics, for sure. What kind are you hungry for?"

"It's not for me." Allison thrust her thumb in the direction of the work site. "Do you know what those guys are eating? Junk."

"I imagine they are." Claire rested her chin on her hand. "Pumpkin raisin muffins. Or apple raisin. Well, raisins in anything, really, thanks to all those boxes of grapes we got last fall and dried in the sunroom."

Right. Of course they didn't just run to the store and buy raisins. *We* don't, Allison corrected herself. She really needed to get thinking like one of the group. Acquaint herself with their food supplies. Well, baking muffins so Brent — so those guys — had something decent to eat was a good start.

"Pumpkin sounds good." Allison reached for her laptop where it lay closed on the counter. "What's a good recipe site?"

Claire quirked a grin. "Not sure. Most of mine are written down. Haven't you noticed the antique library file box?" She rounded the peninsula.

Allison tagged behind. "Can't say I really did." But it was pretty obvious on the counter in the corner, now that Claire pointed it out. Allison had apparently been avoiding spending time in the kitchen. That was about to end. This thing wasn't about Brent. It was about her need to settle into her new home.

Yeah, she could convince herself, given a bit of time.

Claire opened one of the little drawers. "Muffins..." She flipped through a bunch of 3x5 cards.

Allison eyed the bank of drawers. Three across, four down. How many cards could a thing like that hold? "You really have this many recipes suitable for cooking locally? Sustainably?"

"Lots of these aren't. These contain ideas, notes, and recipes we've adapted." Claire swiped a hand down one column, landing on the open drawer at the bottom. "The next set is for food that's close. The last one, we either haven't gone through or they're old family recipes we can't bear to get rid of." She chuckled and glanced at Allison. "Who knows when pineapple upside down cake might become a locally-grown possibility?"

Had to be a joke, so Allison grinned back.

"See, then they're divided by meal or food types, so if I'm looking for soups or... or muffins—" she tapped the open drawer "—it's easy to find the right collection. You're welcome to add your recipes. I'm always looking for new ideas. So long as you don't mind me tweaking them. I'm a perpetual tweaker."

Allison eyed the cataloguing system. Good thing she wasn't relying on her own two cookbooks. All the possibilities these gals had collected. Well, it was probably mostly Claire. She was the professional chef, after all.

Claire beckoned Allison closer. "Have a look through these and see what looks good."

What looked good would be Brent's face when he realized she wasn't completely useless after all. She pushed the image from her mind. Men were all the same. Users. He just hid it better than most.

Chapter 8 ---

*S*he hated accepting calls from unknown numbers. Where was area code 520 anyway? Allison's finger hovered over the button. Should she let it go to voice mail or answer it?

Three rings. She jabbed the button and lifted the phone to her ear. "Hello?"

"Am I speaking with Ms. Allison Hart?" said a man's voice.

She froze. Did she know this guy? "May I ask who is calling, please?"

"Have I reached the correct number?"

Who could it be? Curiosity won over privacy. "Yes, this is Allison. Who are you?"

"Jason Wong from Social Services in Tucson, Arizona."

"Finnley..." she breathed.

"I believe you have a sister. What is her name?"

"Lori."

"Her full name?"

"Mallory Jill Hart." She clutched the cell phone. "Is my nephew okay?" *Please, God, let Finnley be all right.*

"The child is the reason I am calling. Have the Tucson police contacted you yet?"

She shouldn't have skipped breakfast. The wooziness from the man's words caused her knees to buckle. She sank into the nearest chair in Sierra's kitchenette. "No. Please, Mr. Wong. No more beating around the bush. What happened to my nephew?"

"Finnley is in the pediatric ward at Tucson Medical Center. He has a broken ulna and severe bruising over much of his body."

"Oh, Finn..." Her voice caught as she blinked tears from her eyes. "What happened?"

"Your sister and a man are in custody for child abuse as well as drug trafficking. The little fellow is lucky how little damage happened to him, as the man threatened injury to the child to keep the police at bay during the raid."

"No." Poor Finnley. So much terror at the hands of those he should feel safe with. The little guy had never known safety. Neither had Allison or her sister, but that certainly didn't excuse Lori or John from what they'd done to Finnley. "Please tell me he will not go home with them again. Ever."

"Considering the charges against Mallory, I'd say you have a good chance of your hopes coming true, Ms. Hart. She's awaiting trial. If the judicial system can pin the trafficking against her, she'll be in prison for a long time."

"Oh, good."

The man let out a stiff chuckle. "That's not what we usually hear when a family member has been arrested."

"No, I'm sure. I mean, I'm sorry for my sister. I really am, but her lifestyle has led her to this. Finnley hasn't deserved any of it."

"I agree, ma'am."

She clenched her teeth. What was it with men using that term? "How long will Finnley be in the hospital?"

"That depends on a few things. He's become a temporary ward of the state, and we are seeking a placement for him."

"I'll take him." The words flew out of her mouth so quickly she wasn't sure she'd said them out loud.

"Do you live in Arizona, ma'am?"

"No. I'm in Idaho. But Finnley is my nephew. He belongs with me, not some random stranger with a houseful of foster kids. Please, Mr. Wong."

"There's a protocol that must be followed. I won't release a child into another potentially abusive situation."

"But I'd never…!"

"So you say, Ms. Hart. If you wish to be considered, you'll need to come to Tucson and apply. I can assure you it will be a rigorous procedure, starting with a police background check."

"As it should be," she fired back. "I don't want to see Finnley hurt any more than you do. Even less. He's my nephew, not yours."

"If you'll give me your email address, Ms. Hart, I'll send you the required information." The man hesitated, and his voice softened. "If you truly love your nephew, don't wait too long. The wheels are already turning to have him placed in foster care upon his release. I'd hate to see him moved multiple times."

What was this, Friday? The office was doubtless closed over the weekend. "I'll be there Monday morning. Don't worry." She rattled off her Gmail information. "My next move is to book a flight."

He repeated the address for confirmation. "I look forward to meeting you, Ms. Hart. Do you need a cab to meet you at the airport?"

"No, I'll be fine, thanks."

She tapped to end the call. Was this the chance she'd been praying for? A way to get Finnley out of his mother's clutches? She sighed. Not that she'd wanted to see the little guy beaten on to gain his release. Not that she wished ill for Lori. But if this was what it took, she'd be thankful.

What if Lori was found to be innocent and released? What would happen to Finnley then?

Allison would do her best to make sure the boy was in Idaho before that could happen. But where would she put him? Sharing a small space with Sierra for months was not a way to gain custody of Finnley. And even when her own house was built, she hadn't planned for a child.

She unrolled her blueprints across Sierra's little table. The bedroom at the back of the house was hers. And the loft upstairs was to be her home office. She could probably do without that once the school was built.

Was Finnley old enough to sleep that far away from her?

Who was she kidding? He'd never had safety. He'd never run to his mommy's room and crawled in bed with her if nightmares attacked. Allison would bet anything that he held all the safety he knew within his own small body.

Like her. Hurt in different ways, maybe, but he'd be just like her.

For once, she wondered how to get through to him. How would anyone get through to *her*? She kept them at bay so carefully. But then, she had twenty-seven years of experience with that. Finnley had not quite four.

She'd win him over, but first she had to get him here. He could celebrate his birthday at Green Acres.

Whoa. What would everyone say when she sprang a child into the dynamics? But it couldn't be helped. Finnley came first. She'd walk away from the farm and the construction job if she had to.

Anything to create a safe place for her nephew.

o0o

"Thanks for agreeing to this meeting at short notice." Allison looked around the table at the Green Acres team.

"No problem, Allison. What's happening? Another delay in the building?" Noel helped himself to a muffin from the plate in the middle of the table.

She'd made those. She could take care of a child.

A thump and a shriek came from the great room. Zach's chair clattered to the concrete floor as he leaped to his feet and ran.

See, that's what Finnley needed. Someone who cared for him like Zach cared for his daughter. Allison would be that someone if all went well.

"She's fine. Just toppled the rocking horse." Zach came back carrying Madelynn. He settled into his chair, reached for a muffin, and broke it in half. He handed part to the two-year-old, who sniffled and reached for it.

Jo turned back to Allison. "Sorry about the interruption."

She shrugged. "No problem. I'm trying to remember what I've told you guys about my sister and my nephew?"

Sierra leaned over and placed her hand on Allison's arm. "Has God answered our prayers?"

It took all Allison's willpower not to pull out from under Sierra's touch. "Maybe." She took in the questioning expressions on other faces. "My sister made a mess of her life ever since she was a young teen. It's a miracle she's only given birth once. My nephew Finnley will be four in a few weeks."

Five pairs of expectant eyes watched her.

"He's in the hospital in Tucson." Allison took a deep breath. Best to just spit it out. "Lori's current boyfriend used him as a shield while the cops tried to arrest him and my sister for drug trafficking."

"Oh, no." Sympathy oozed from Claire's words. "Poor little guy."

"A man from social services there phoned me a couple of hours ago. It looks like Lori and John are headed to prison. Hopefully for a very long time." She couldn't keep the satisfaction out of her voice.

"I'm so sorry," said Sierra. "How badly was he hurt?"

"The case worker said Finnley would heal. The physical part, you know."

"I can't believe anyone would do that to an innocent child." Jo surged to her feet and paced over to the fireplace and back. "I should probably be more sympathetic, but I hope they get what they deserve." She grimaced. "Sorry, Allison. I don't mean to encourage ill feelings against your sister."

"No, I understand. I've thought the same for years, and I'm just thankful the law finally caught up with her. But... Finnley..."

Jo's hand cut down. "Bring him here, if you can. At least, if you want to."

"Are you sure? It would affect so many things." Allison's mind still reeled with the repercussions. "It's not what you all have signed up for." Nor had she.

Maddie slipped off Zach's lap and ran back into the great room. Rocking sounds from the wooden horse drifted their way.

Noel slid his arm across the back of Claire's chair, his gaze never leaving Allison's. "What do you want to do? What are the problems you see?"

She closed her eyes for a second and breathed a prayer. "He's my nephew. I can't abandon him if there's anything I can do." Her legs jittered under the table. "But it's a crazy thought. I've never wanted to be a mother."

Sierra bit her lip.

"I'm not the motherly type. And seeing... well, you know what my parents were like." Not that she'd given anyone the whole story. Nor would she ever. "It's just that when I joined you guys, I never dreamed this chance would come. I don't know what to do."

Still standing, Jo pressed her hands on the back of her chair. "Sometimes God's gifts are unexpected. The question is, what are you going to do with this one? Tell Him you don't want it? Or embrace it?"

Allison stared at Jo, everyone else dimming at the edges of her vision. "Do you really think this is a gift from God?" She knew what she wanted. But was that best for Green Acres? Was it even best for her and her nephew?

"We've been praying for Lori and Finnley," said Sierra. "This is God's answer. He's intervened."

"Right. But what does it have to do with me?"

"Excuse me if I'm wrong," said Noel. "On the one hand, I hear your love for your nephew and your desire to help."

Allison nodded.

"On the other hand, I'm hearing your reluctance to get involved. Is that accurate?"

She nodded again.

Noel's fingers massaged the back of Claire's neck, but he watched Allison. "Why?"

"I'm planning a school. Long hours of classes to teach. I can't do that while caring for a preschooler."

Claire opened her mouth, but Allison kept going. "Plus I won't have a home for many more months. Where am I going to put him? Will the social worker even allow me to have custody?"

"Anything else?" Noel's voice remained steady.

"No. Yes. I don't know. It's all so confusing. A detour. I should probably leave. Get a job somewhere near a good daycare center. Get an apartment." Finnley didn't deserve daycare. He needed to be held close. Cherished. She had enough money from the estate to go a few years without a job. Maybe that was best.

Zach broke the other half of Maddie's muffin into pieces. "I don't think it's such a big problem, really. People have kids all the time. We adjust."

Allison refused to look at the barely visible bump on Jo's midsection where another little Nemesek grew. "But—"

"I'd really hate to be a single mom, Allison." Jo slid back onto her chair. "And much as I love Zach, I'm glad I have more support than just him. He works long hours."

"I know, and I'm sorry for calling a meeting for toni—"

"I'm glad you did," Zach interrupted.

"But—"

"We all help with Maddie," said Sierra. "Sure, Zach's parents babysit some, but we all pitch in. It's part of being a community."

"Absolutely," added Claire. "We can make things work with Finnley, too."

"It will be nice for Maddie to have someone to play with," put in Jo. She looked around the table. "Is there anyone who thinks Allison should not bring Finnley here?"

Five heads shook.

"He should definitely come, if you can arrange it," said Sierra.

Noel grinned. "I'll take him fishing."

A heavy load slid from Allison's shoulders. "Really? You guys will accept my nephew here?"

"Totally." Zach popped the last bits of muffin in his mouth. "I'm not around as much, but I'll gladly include him whenever I can."

"We may not be related by blood," said Claire, "but we're a family just the same. When you joined us here, you became part of it."

Sierra laughed. "Whether you like it or not."

Had she been that obvious? "Well, thanks. I don't know what to say."

"But your other point still stands." Sierra folded her hands on the tabletop. "You'll need something closer to a home for you two until your house is built."

"Gabe will be back in a few weeks, right, Sierra?" Claire's eyes twinkled. "Maybe we can find him an apartment and move his stuff into it. That would free up the other half of the duplex for Allison and her nephew."

"That might be a possibility," Sierra said slowly. "But it would only be until the end of June. It's a bit of a pain to get a rental for only two months."

"If it's too much hassle for me to have Finn—"

"Allison, don't jump to conclusions." Jo glared at her. "We're looking at options. Let's hear pros and cons of each idea, please."

Allison held up both hands and leaned back against her chair. Both legs jiggled under the table. This was all going to fall through. She knew it.

"It was fine having Gabe's furniture and stuff taking up space when we didn't need it for anything else." Claire looked at Sierra. "What is he saving all that for? You don't have room for everything in your little place."

Sierra bit her lip. "We could do a storage unit, I guess."

Zach reached for another muffin. "You guys planning to live in the duplex indefinitely?"

Allison couldn't decide if she was happy she was off the hot seat or not, but she supposed Sierra's answers reflected on her own situation.

Sierra took a deep breath. "For a year or two, maybe. We've talked briefly about building and leaving the duplex for other uses."

"Speaking of keeping things from the group," said Jo caustically.

"Hey." Sierra glared. "There's no hurry to decide. Or there didn't seem to be until now."

Allison tapped her fingers on the table in time to her jiggling legs. This was crazy. They'd all but admitted cleaning out the other side of the duplex had always been a possibility. Why had they jammed her in with Sierra, then?

Claire gave Allison a sheepish grin. "You must be wondering..."

Allison raised her eyebrows and nodded.

"It's not just that we were too lazy to deal with Gabe's stuff. We wanted to get to know you and give you plenty of opportunity to interact with all of us. It seemed better to have you room with Sierra for a few months to facilitate that."

73

When she would have killed for some privacy. Allison clenched her jaw.

"There's another temporary option." Sierra looked pensive.

Allison raised her eyebrows. "Oh?"

"With Claire and Noel's permission, I can move back into the big house for a bit."

Bad idea. Allison's head started to shake before she could pull words together, but Jo beat her to it.

"I don't think so. That's noble, but the duplex is your home. I already feel badly for how many times you've moved since we got here four years ago. From the musty trailer to the straw bale house to the apartment in town to the duplex. I'm sure there's another solution."

"Besides, your spare room is painted pink." Noel's eyes twinkled. "We can't make a little boy suffer through that."

Sierra lifted both hands. "It was just an idea."

"There's not *that* much stuff in the other side, is there?" asked Zach. "Maybe Allison can use the furniture for a few months, and we can stack the rest in your spare room, Sierra. You're already not using that space because Allison is in it now."

A whole two-bedroom duplex to herself? And if the state of Arizona allowed her to bring Finnley back with her, even better.

"That might be the best plan." Jo nodded decisively. "What do you think, Sierra?"

"That could work..."

"When are you going to Tucson?" asked Noel.

"I booked flights for late Sunday so I can be at the social work office first thing Monday morning."

"I guess you have no idea how long you'll be gone?"

She shook her head. "Not really. A week, maybe?"

"Let's see what we can accomplish tomorrow, then, and the gang will do the rest while you're gone," said Noel. "I can swing by the construction site a few times a day and see if the crew needs anything."

"Thanks. I'd appreciate that." It seemed weird to think of someone else keeping an eye on Brent Callahan. Allison took a deep breath. "Speaking of which, you all know progress has slowed because of the window situation."

Heads nodded around the table, and Sierra leaned forward. "Allison and I talked briefly about trying to manage a few classes in the house or pole barn, but maybe we should simply cancel the summer session."

"We only have five people signed up for it." Allison let out a long breath. "I'd hoped for more, but we need to figure out better advertising, I guess."

"If your nephew comes, you'll be busy settling him in over the summer, too." Jo's face scrunched up in thought. "Rescheduling might be best. When Gabe gets back with that shiny marketing diploma, we can put him to work on a campaign. By then we should have a better idea of the timeline, right?"

Whoa. "Just like that? Everything can be changed?"

Claire chuckled. "We're an adaptable bunch. It's not that we're lazy, but between the windows and your nephew, delaying sounds like the best thing. Want me to contact the students while you're away?"

Relief washed over Allison. "If you would? Thanks." The gang at Green Acres? The best.

Chapter 9 ---

*S*orry, man. We're not going fishing after all. I didn't have your cell number to let you know."

Brent stood on the deck of the straw bale house, fly rod and tackle box in hand. "Uh. Okay." Now what was he supposed to do with his weekend? He'd given up going back to the city for this fishing expedition.

Noel stepped aside and beckoned Brent. "Come on in, anyway. We've got breakfast on."

He really shouldn't, but the smell of sizzling bacon nearly made his knees weak. The Sizzling Skillet served okay food, but he was tired of their three breakfast specials.

"Don't stand on the step all day." Noel jerked his chin, grinning. "You're letting all the warmth out of the house."

"Thanks." Brent followed the other guy inside. He hated being stood up, but Noel was right. They hadn't exchanged numbers.

"Throw a couple of more eggs in the pan," hollered Noel. "Brent's here for breakfast." He looked at Brent. "Want a coffee, man?"

Allison turned from where she'd been sitting at the peninsula counter, pecking away at a laptop. "I'll pour you a cup. What would you like in it?"

"Just black, thanks." *If you're going to drink coffee, drink it like a man*, his grandfather used to say. The Callahan one. The Korean one was into ginseng tea.

Allison rounded the peninsula into the kitchen.

He watched her reach for a mug from above the sink then fill it with steaming black liquid. That'd go down great.

"Have a seat at the table," Claire called. "Food's on its way."

"I'll give you a hand, hon." Noel pointed at a chair then strode into the kitchen, passing Allison on her way out with Brent's coffee.

Brent figured that's where he was supposed to sit at a table set for five. "I thought Zach and Jo ate here, too?" he said to Allison as she handed him the cup. His fingers brushed hers.

Her gaze jerked to his face as she relinquished the handle. "Uh, not usually for breakfast on account of Maddie." She backed up a step.

Somehow Brent's fingers felt chilled after Allison's touch. "Thanks for the coffee. And for the muffins yesterday. I can't remember when I've ever had pumpkin before."

"It's Claire's recipe, but I think they turned out pretty well."

Right, she'd told him she didn't cook. Then why had she gone to the trouble of baking muffins and bringing a few up to the building site at afternoon coffee time?

Miss Priss had done it for him. She was warming up a little. Or maybe that was just him doing some wishing. Whoa, Callahan. She was a client. In a few short months he'd be back in Coeur d'Alene or wherever Patrick sent him next.

Noel set platters on the table as Sierra whisked in the door and took her place at the table beside Claire. Allison reached for the chair next to his.

"Allow me." He pulled it out and seated her.

She cast him a puzzled glance.

Well, his mama had taught him how to treat a woman, though he'd done his best to forget for many years. He couldn't undo the past, but he could do better in the future, so long as he kept his mind corralled. He had a past he couldn't saddle on any God-fearing woman, and he wasn't going back to the other kind.

Case dismissed.

Allison slid a poached egg onto the little mound of sautéed kale on her plate and passed him the platter.

No fingers touched. Good.

She added one slice of bacon and handed him the plate.

"I fixed two for you, Allison," Claire said from across the table. "You'll need the energy today."

Allison shook her head. "This is plenty. More than I'm used to for breakfast."

The girl didn't eat enough to keep a bird alive. No wonder she had no padding.

"About today," Noel said after he'd given thanks for the food. "Zach and I will be moving furniture and boxes around for at least a few hours. I feel bad that I couldn't let you know."

Brent's confusion must've shown on his face.

"Allison is trying to get custody of her nephew, so we're rearranging the duplexes," Sierra said. "Really, you guys can probably go fishing in an hour or two. There's not that much heavy stuff."

The door opened and a whisper of cold air accompanied Zach into the dining room. "Any food left?"

Claire set her napkin down, looking like she might get to her feet. "Want a coffee?"

Zach waved a hand. "I'll get it if there's some made."

"Sure, and there's food," Noel said as Zach passed the table. "Grab a plate and help yourself."

"Where are Jo and Maddie?" asked Sierra.

"Still asleep. Maddie was up half the night screaming over some tooth, I guess. They're both exhausted."

The guy didn't look that rested, either. He brought an empty plate and a fork along with a cup of coffee. His fork poised over the platters of food. "Everyone had enough?"

"Allison?" asked Claire pointedly.

"Go for it, Zach." Allison stirred the kale around on her plate. She'd eaten about half the egg, Brent guessed. And a few bites of bacon.

The Sizzling Skillet did the average decent breakfast, but their eggs had no color and their bacon tasted fake. This meal, however... "Thanks for the invitation, guys. This food is amazing."

Zach's fork, loaded with egg, stopped halfway to his mouth. "I didn't mean to do you out of food, Callahan."

"No, this will be lots. Really. It's just that I've eaten in restaurants too much lately."

"Mostly the Skillet, I imagine," Claire said. "There's not much else in town."

Noel chuckled. "There's always the diner."

Brent shook his head. "I can handle that no more than once a week."

"Poor guy." True sympathy oozed from Claire's voice. "I don't think they have any ingredients besides salt and grease."

"Potatoes. Something that's related to buns. A meat look-alike." Noel reached for his coffee cup as Claire jabbed him in the ribs. "Hey, I had to eat there a couple of times back in the day. When I wasn't talking to you."

Sounded like there was a story in there somewhere.

Claire shook her head and grabbed the coffee pot. "Anyone want a refill?"

Brent nodded when the pot poised over his cup. "Thanks."

Zach pushed his scraped plate away and had a sip of coffee. "How long do you think moving that stuff will take?"

Allison leaned forward. "Look, I can probably manage..."

"It will go faster with all of us. No problem. I thought we'd settled that last night."

They'd said something about Allison's nephew. Brent turned

to her. "Your nephew is coming?"

She nodded, gaze fixed on her plate where most of her food sat cut in tiny pieces. "I hope so, anyway. I'm flying to Tucson for a few days to see if I can make it happen."

"That's cool." Silence all around. Okay, he was on his own. "What's the situation? If you don't mind my asking." He didn't know any young woman who went around seeking custody of someone else's kid.

"My sister and her boyfriend were finally arrested for drug trafficking," she said with satisfaction. "It's my chance to get my nephew out of a bad environment if everything works out."

Brent should be glad she'd be off the job site and out of his hair for a few days. Instead, he suspected he'd miss her frequent visits. And the whole drug thing sounded rough. He'd dabbled too close to the edge himself, back in the day. He glanced her way. "I'll pray for you and your nephew. How old is he?"

"Not quite four." Allison's face clouded. "He's been through so much. Used as a human shield during the police raid."

Brent felt sick to his stomach to think of anyone using a kid that way.

"Are you a Christian, Brent?" Zach asked.

"I am. God pulled me from a pretty bad place. I'm thankful He loved me enough to claim me."

"That's great," Sierra said. "We've all joined forces to pray for Finnley in the past few weeks, and already God is doing big things. I'm sure it's just a matter of time before he's here, safe and sound."

Brent glanced at Allison. "Finnley?"

She shrugged. "That's his name, yes."

"I'm happy to join my prayers with yours."

Allison glanced at him from below long eyelashes. "Thanks."

"In fact, why don't I give you guys a hand with whatever needs moving?"

Noel chuckled. "We'll be out along the creek in no time. You're on, buddy."

oOo

Why had Brent insisted on helping? Allison made herself small in the corner while the three big guys hauled boxes and arranged furniture at Sierra's direction.

She should be thankful, probably, but he made her uncomfortable. She'd gotten a bit used to having Noel and Zach around the farm. They were safely married and didn't seem to be headed in a bad direction yet. But Brent? He'd admitted he had big problems in his past. No one else may have caught that, but she had. She'd be watching for his relapse.

"Where would you like this dresser, Allison?" Noel asked. He and Brent each stood at one end of a long low piece.

The thrift store sounded like a good destination. On a good day she'd call this motley excuse for a style "Early Salvation Army." She'd go through her parents' house before she sold it and bring the best pieces here for her little house. Provided the thing ever got built.

Right, the guys were waiting. "In my room, I guess. I doubt Finnley has much stuff. He can have the smaller one."

"I feel badly that we never painted the walls in here." Sierra hooked her long hair behind her ear. "It's so ugly."

No kidding.

"Well, we still could," Noel said. "Allison will be gone for a few days. I mean, you and Jo and Claire can. You don't want me with a brush."

Sierra's face brightened. "You're right, we could. Put the furniture in the middle, guys. Leave room to get around."

"Really?" The word tumbled out before Allison could rein it in. "You'd do that for me?"

"Sure. Painting is fun." Sierra rubbed her hands together. "What colors do you like? There are some cans with leftovers somewhere."

How could Allison gently tell her how much she disliked the vivid tones on Sierra's walls? "White is good. Or maybe a light gray. I can leave money for new cans."

"You're not serious."

Allison had a feeling her comment wasn't about the cash. "Very. I like things clean and bright."

Sierra looked about to keel over in faint.

Brent set his end of the dresser down and brushed his hands together. "Sounds good."

Allison narrowed her gaze at him. He was going to be busy enough building her house. There wasn't time for him to get involved in the duplex too. Was there? And if so, why?

He grinned at her. "The little guy might appreciate some color for his room, though."

Who knew what a four-year-old would like? One who'd been shuffled around and abused? Probably everywhere they'd lived had been beige. Allison shrugged. "If anyone has any ideas for Finnley's space, go for it. I have no clue."

Sierra's face brightened.

Allison pointed at her. "No purple. No turquoise." Oops, had she said that out loud?

Her friend laughed. "I wasn't thinking the purple, but the turquoise wouldn't be so bad for a little boy. Honestly. Gabe liked it on his apartment walls."

"Whatever."

"I'll go see what there is in the storage room." Sierra bounded to her feet. "I'll be back in a few."

"I need to go check on Jo and Maddie before we go fishing." Zach strode to the door. "We still up for that?"

Noel nodded. "I'll make some sandwiches."

There was no way this little apartment could be a welcoming space in the few days it would take her to get back to Idaho with Finnley. If she were able to, of course. Even so, it had to be better than where he had been living. He'd be safe here. She was Queen of Safe.

"This is a good thing you're doing."

Allison jerked and focused on Brent's face. Hadn't he left with Noel? Apparently not. "Uh, well, he's family." About all the family she had left. She didn't want to count Lori.

"Family doesn't matter to everyone." His dark eyes drilled into hers.

What was hiding in his past?

He lifted a shoulder. "Don't worry about the construction while you're gone. We'll keep things moving just fine."

Of course he would. He was the site foreman, after all. She nodded. "Thanks."

He quirked a grin that reached his eyes. "You'll see. You'll be impressed by the progress when you get back."

She couldn't help smiling at him. "I guess we'll see, won't we?"

Chapter 10 --

*A*llison followed Jason Wong down the corridor at Tucson Medical Center. He pressed the buzzer at the double doors of the pediatric ward. A moment later a plump middle-aged woman opened the door, her face wreathed in a smile. "Jason." Her gaze shifted to Allison then back to the social worker. "What may I help you with today? Are you here to see Finnley?"

He nodded. "This is Finnley's aunt, Allison Hart. We've run a preliminary background check on her and, so far, she seems clean. There is a lot more paperwork to go, but it looks like she may be taking Finnley home with her when he's released."

Marge's eyes narrowed as she took Allison in. After a bit she nodded and put the smile back on.

Did that mean she'd passed preliminary inspection by the head nurse, too? Allison could only hope.

"Physically, Finnley is healing well. Did Mr. Wong tell you the damages?"

Allison nodded. The little guy's left shoulder had been dislocated and the ulna in that arm broken. Two broken ribs. And bruises.

"Children's bones heal quickly. Finnley's cast should be off in a few weeks. We'll send his records to your doctor, so do leave that information at the desk."

Allison thought quickly. "I haven't lived in Galena Landing long, but I'll ask a friend for a recommendation and make sure to get that to you in the next day or two."

"Sounds good." Marge looked her in the eye. "The bruises to his body are already fading. The bruises to his soul will take much longer. Are you certain you're up for it?"

Show no weakness. "Of course, I'm sure. He's my nephew, and I've been wishing since the day he was born that he could have a secure home. That my sister would smarten up and see what she was doing to herself and to her child." A two-by-six across the skull would have been nice. Maybe this arrest was God's version.

"It's not going to be easy, Ms. Hart." Marge ambled ahead of them down the bright hallway. "He's got some issues. His imaginary friend is the most obvious manifestation."

Allison choked back a snort before it could erupt. "Plenty of children have secret companions."

"Indeed they do, Ms. Hart." Marge lifted an ample shoulder. "You'll see." She paused in front of a door on the right. "Do you want to meet him now?"

Jason nodded. "That's why we're here."

Whoa. Allison had thought she was ready. The avenging princess swooping in to save the child in distress. But what was she really signing up for? Could she do this? Once the step had been taken, her life would never be the same. Everything would revolve around this boy she'd only met a few times since Lori moved back out of the house after his first birthday. She couldn't mess this kid up further. Would a foster home be better for him? More secure than a single aunt with issues of her own?

"Are you ready, Ms. Hart?"

Sierra had prayed for Finnley, for God to intervene. She'd

been joined by Claire and Noel and Jo and Zach. Even Brent said he was praying. Allison straightened her back. God had this. She had to believe it and step forward.

"Yes, please, Marge. I'd like to see my nephew." Allison looked in through the open section of the Dutch-style door. A bright playroom contained a dozen children or so. A few sat in wheelchairs with IV bags attached. A woman sat on a green sectional and read a book to several wan faces. And off in the corner, near a tree sculpture leaning out from the wall sat a little boy in striped pajamas and a cast, pushing a car back and forth.

His bowed head revealed a mass of black hair in need of cutting, and his repetitive action reminded Allison of her leg jitters. Finnley didn't look like he was playing on purpose. If she could see his eyes, she had no doubt they'd be staring at nothing.

She caught her breath. He looked so alone. So defenseless. *Please, Lord, help me. Give me what I need to make this little guy's life better.*

Allison looked at Marge. "Can I meet him now?"

The nurse nodded in understanding and opened the door. The three of them walked through. Several children looked up, and Marge had a big smile and a pat on the shoulder for them.

Marge managed to get her bulk onto the polished floor beside Finnley.

The little guy didn't look up.

"Down, Rover. Stop growling. I'm here to see Finnley, not hurt him."

Say what? Allison stared at the nurse. There was no dog.

"That's a good boy, Rover. I'm glad you're taking care of Finnley. He needs you."

The car swished back and forth.

"Finnley's Auntie Allison is here to see him. May she see him? I won't let her hurt Finnley. She's nice."

Imaginary friends were one thing, but an imaginary guard dog that had to be placated? And she was expected to play along?

Yet the little boy's solitude tore at her heart. How long had he imagined a protector? Why did he still believe, even when Rover obviously hadn't kept John from hurting him?

She'd never been one for drama, for acting out. Except with her father. She shoved the thought into the recesses of her mind and covered it up with pleasant thoughts, like imaginary guard dogs. She could do this.

Allison crouched down beside Marge and pretended to stroke a dog she couldn't see. "Hi, Rover. I brought you a bone. We have a really nice dog on the farm where I live. His name is Domino because he's all black and white."

Marge shot her a nod of approval.

Where to go from here? "Domino loves to run and play on the farm. He likes to herd the sheep and the cows. And he takes care of a little girl who lives there. Her name is Madelynn, and she's only two years old, so she needs a dog to take care of her."

The car stilled. Progress? She'd take it.

"Have you ever had a whole farm to play on, Rover? There are mountains nearby, and a river, and a lake." Not that she'd spent all that much time looking at the scenery. Who had time for stuff like that? "There is a big garden where we'll soon plant vegetables, but I have to tell you that dogs aren't allowed in the garden. That's because Domino likes to dig holes. I bet you wouldn't do that, Rover. They probably wouldn't mind if *you* went in the garden. If Finnley wanted to, that is."

In her peripheral, Jason Wong settled into a chair across the room. The adult reading the story deepened her voice. A wheelchair squeaked against the linoleum.

Allison wracked her brain. What else could she say? She'd expected this conversation to go more like, "Hi, I'm your Aunt Allison and I'm here to rescue you." And he'd be happy.

"There are kittens on the farm, Rover. Domino gets into trouble sometimes for chasing them. And sometimes they hiss and smack his nose. They don't care he's so much bigger than they are. They keep themselves safe from him. You wouldn't chase kittens, would you, Rover?"

Finnley's head shook slightly.

Was it time to talk about what little boys might do, not imaginary dogs? "I have a house just the right size for an auntie and a little boy and, uh, a dog." Well, she'd always intended to get a dog when she was settled, right? So it was true. "It's a place where children and animals can play outside and be safe. It's a place where the grownups are nice. They work together and make good food together and go fishing together."

Why anyone would want to go fishing, she had no clue. Though the trout had made a tasty addition to Sunday dinner. Was that only last week?

Marge cleared her throat. "That sounds like a very nice place. Would you like to see it, Rover?"

The little boy's head just barely nodded.

Allison's heart swam with longing to gather this kid up and give him a hug he so badly needed. Even though he didn't know it. Weird. She'd never thought about needing hugs. Like Finnley, she'd built a wall. But never with a pretend dog.

Marge laid her hand, palm up, on the carpet in front of Finnley. "Rover, can Finnley come and meet his Aunt Allison? Would that be okay?"

The boy nodded and he looked up. Not to meet Allison's gaze, but somewhere in her midsection.

"I'm so pleased to see you, Finnley." The words choked in her throat. "Maybe you don't remember me, but I remember you. I've always loved you and prayed for you."

His gaze lifted a bit more. His sweet little round face. No smile. No hint of animation. Dark eyes focused on nothing.

"Are you safe?" The words were so faint, Allison wasn't sure she'd heard them.

Her heart swelled. "I promise you, I'm safe."

And somehow, she'd make sure she was, for his sake. For always.

oOo

"You don't need to do this, Brent." Sierra stood in the doorway of what would soon be Finnley's bedroom.

He shrugged and dipped his artist brush in the brown paint. Sampler sizes of many colors lay arrayed behind him. "She's doing a good thing. I want to help." Why, he didn't know. This whole crew had welcomed him in. He felt more like family here at Green Acres Farm than at any Callahan or Lee gathering. Yeah, no one had abused him or disowned him, but only Patrick had any time for him.

And Patrick had wondered why Brent hadn't come home for the weekend. Was a bare apartment with cheap furniture even a home? It had no life, no soul. No family.

He would never have a family. Didn't look like Allison had expected one, either. But she was stepping up to the plate, and he could help make things easier for the boy. Make him feel cared about.

When Rosemary had brought a length of fabric from next door with red barns, black-and-white cows, and white fences on it, Jo, Claire, and Sierra had got to work making a curtain and blanket cover.

Which had given Brent the idea to paint a farm scene on one wall. He was a fair hand with a brush, having dabbled in art before realizing he couldn't make a living at it.

Sierra edged closer. "You do know this is just a temporary room for him." Translation: "You're crazy to put this much time and effort onto a wall."

"I know. But don't you think this is the most important time for him to feel welcomed?"

She sighed. "Yes. And thank you. It's just, I don't get why you're doing this. You barely know any of us, and none of us knows Finnley. He might hate dogs." She pointed at the mutt he was painting in the corner. "He might hate cows."

"He might. That's a risk I had to take. Can't you see? I think it's better to try and fail than not do anything at all."

Wait, had those words really come out of his mouth? A great sentiment, but not one he lived by. He pushed the thought aside. He had tried. He had failed. What he didn't need was to air his failures and try again. Vulnerability brought pain. Period.

He flexed both shoulders to loosen the knots. "If you're worried about the house and school construction falling behind because of this, it won't. I'm on my lunch break. I'll come back when the guys head back to the hotel at five."

"Allison is bringing him home tomorrow."

"I know. I'll have it done. Nearly there."

She sighed. "If you're bound and determined to finish this tonight, I'll run a plate of supper over for you."

"You don't have to. I'll find something."

"It's Thursday. Even The Sizzling Skillet closes at nine. I'll bring you food." She chuckled. "Claire's cooking, not me, so don't worry. It'll be good."

"Well, thanks, then. I accept." He rocked back on his heels and looked over the wall. He wished he had time to add more detail. But it just didn't exist.

The child was not quite four. He didn't need a Grandma Moses painting in his room. Just something to offset all the white and pale gray paint in the rest of the duplex. It looked great. The girls had worked hard. But the space seemed too chilly for him and for the little boy he'd once been.

Suited Allison, the ice princess. But there might be a crack or two in her facade. Big question, how much did he care if there was?

Chapter 11 --

*F*innley stood beside her — close, but not too close — as she loaded her luggage and the Superman pack she'd bought him into the trunk of her Camry. She hadn't picked up a lot of clothes yet. There had been little time in Tucson. She'd snagged a few outfits, a warm jacket, and a pair of shoes that turned out to be too large from a Target near the hospital. And tossed in a teddy bear at the last minute.

He clutched the bear. That was a good sign, right?

One last thing. She lifted the car seat and locked it into place in the middle of the back seat. The device came with good directions, and her car was a new enough model to make the seat secure. She'd have to adjust the harness once he was in it.

Allison slid out backward and nudged Finnley's shoulder. "Up you get, and I'll buckle you in."

His little face froze in fear and he backed up, shaking his head. He had the teddy bear in a death grip around the neck.

It was only a car seat. Surely he'd seen one before. "It's okay."

"Rover."

He wanted her to pretend to buckle in the dog? They'd been traveling all day with three hours to go, and she didn't want to get in late. She bit back the terse command that nearly exploded from her mouth. Both Mr. Wong and Marge had emphasized how she had to build Finnley's trust. She had to go slow. But how slow? Walking all the way to Galena Landing slow?

She crouched down at eye level and patted the air beside Finnley's hip. "Hi, Rover. Good dog." Seriously? This was crazy. Hopefully no one would come right now and claim the car next to hers. They'd report her for sure.

"See that seat, Rover? It's so Finnley will be safe in my car. Nothing bad will happen to him while he's in that seat, even if there's an accident." Maybe she shouldn't have said that last part. "There's a law in Idaho that says kids his size need to be buckled into seats like that one if they're in a car. And we can't get to the farm without driving in the car. See, Rover? Finnley's Superman bag with his new pajamas and his jeans and Toothless T-shirt are in the back already. They're coming along."

Why couldn't a woman find cute clothes for a kid that didn't have some trademark label on them? She hadn't had time to look through all the racks, though.

"Can you tell Finnley it's okay to get into the car seat, Rover? Can you tell him it is a safe place?"

Finnley shook his head.

Most of the bruises had faded into his darker skin, but that didn't mean they'd faded from his mind. Had someone tied him in a car seat and abused him there?

If Allison ever got a hold of Lori or John, she had a thing or two to say. Jason Wong had offered her the opportunity to talk to Lori, but she'd refused. She didn't trust herself not to pour out all the anger she felt after seeing the battered boy.

She reached for Finnley's shoulder, but somehow it shifted slightly out of reach. "Remember what I told you about the farm? We have to get in this car to drive there. You'll be sitting right here where you can see out the front window and both sides. I'll be up there—" she pointed at the driver's seat "—wearing my own seat belt and driving. Rover can sit on the seat beside you and take care of you. Does that sound okay?"

He glanced around as though seeking a place to hide. Surely a parking lot couldn't be appealing to a little guy not quite four. A tear trickled from his eye before he nodded. His lower lip trembled as he climbed into the car awkwardly with his left arm in the cast. By the time she touched his shoulder to adjust the harness, he'd closed his eyes. That didn't stop tears from dribbling down his little cheeks.

Allison talked to him while she buckled him in, telling him how the straps worked and asking him to move the teddy bear to his other hand so she could finish.

He obeyed silently, his body stiff against her touch.

Her tears matched his as she slid into the driver's seat and clicked her own belt into place. Was she really up for this challenge? Did the gang at the farm have any idea what she was bringing home?

One thing was sure, she was hitting the drive-through for supper, much as she hated to. There was no way she was unbuckling her nephew before they got to the safety of the farm.

oOo

"Hey, buddy, here we are. It's home." Allison pulled up in front of the duplex. Home? Not hardly. Not when someone else had painted it, cleaned it, and moved her things in.

Sierra'd texted Finnley had a bed and a dresser. That's all she said when Allison asked about his room. Oh, well. Whatever it was, it had to be better than what he'd had in Tucson.

She glanced in the rearview mirror as she shut off the car. Dusk settled around her like a cloak. "You awake, Finnley?" Not that she'd seen his eyelids droop once when she checked on him throughout the trip.

He gave a bare nod.

Domino bounded up as Allison opened the back door to release her nephew from his car seat.

Wonderful! She'd forgotten all about Rover. Finnley would love Domino if he already had an imaginary canine protector. Went well with her own plans to get a puppy once the house was move-in ready.

She set Finnley's stiff body on the ground and Domino licked the boy's face. Finnley screamed and flung himself back into the car.

Whoa. "Hey buddy, this is Domino. He's a nice dog, just like Rover."

Finnley scrambled over the car seat clear to the other side of the backseat.

Okay, so Domino wasn't exactly like Rover. Allison took a deep breath. "Come on, Finnley. Domino is just being friendly. He's excited to have a little boy here to play with." Inspiration struck. "See, he and Rover are touching noses. That's what dogs do when they like each other. If Rover likes him, Domino must be safe, right?"

The boy pressed against the far door, staring at Domino, holding his cast arm like a shield.

That single scream was nearly the only sound Allison had heard from him. Anger at her sister clawed up Allison's throat. Had Finnley been beaten for making a sound? What had his short life been like? She blinked back tears and patted the real dog at her knee. "Domino, go home."

The dog looked up at her.

"Go home." She pointed up the hill toward Jo and Zach's log cabin.

He trotted off with frequent glances back over his shoulder.

Time to try this again. She turned back to the child. "The dog is gone, buddy. Come on, let's go in our house, okay?"

He shuddered. After a few more seconds, he navigated the backseat to the open door. Ignoring her outstretched hand, he slid to the ground, his eyes still fixed on the spot in the distance where Domino's black tail had last been seen.

Allison popped the trunk, gathered their luggage, and headed for the door. She shouldered her way in and flipped on the light with trepidation. The sight of a sparkling clean apartment with white and two shades of gray on the walls met her eyes. A bundle of brightly colored balloons drifted from the doorknob of one bedroom.

"Hey, buddy, have a look at that!" She stepped aside to allow Finnley entrance.

He stood in the doorway staring out. Her gaze swept the area as she wondered what it looked like to him. The garden area across the driveway still lay dormant. In the dusk, the buds of leaves and blossoms on the fruit trees were invisible.

She inhaled deeply. It had rained recently, and the daffodils beside Sierra's door were especially fragrant this evening. A rooster croaked in the distance. A lamb bleated.

It was all going to be okay. Away from the smog and clamor of the city, away from skyscrapers and crowds, away from syringes and addicts sleeping on cardboard. This was a good place to raise a child. To give him a fresh start.

Her, too. The peace of Green Acres Farm soaked into her soul. *Thank You, Lord. Please bless Finnley.*

She turned back to the apartment. The little boy had reversed direction and now eyed the interior. If she wasn't mistaken, he'd spotted the balloons.

Allison set down her bag and closed the door, shutting the quiet farm out. She slung the Superman pack over a shoulder, walked over to the balloon-clad door, and bumped it open.

A different world met her eyes when the light came on. A brightly patterned farmyard quilt lay on the bed, its white frame pushed up against pale green walls. A small shelving unit beside the bed held several books and a Fisher Price barn. But the wall at the end. *Oh my goodness.* The pack slid to the floor as she stared at the farmyard scene spread out along the wall. Where on earth had this come from? Who'd done it? She'd never seen anything like it. No one had even hinted they had mural-painting skills.

"Finnley, come see!"

No movement behind her when she glanced back. Ah, right. "Rover, come see your new room." Her gaze landed on a black and brown and white mutt painted in the corner, lying in front of a little blue doghouse. "There's a special place just for you, Rover. See? Is that you?"

Allison walked in and sat down on the bed. Maybe Finnley would follow her in if she weren't blocking his way.

Indeed, there he stood, paused in the doorway, taking it all in with solemn dark eyes.

She held her breath as his gaze roved over the entire mural from barn to a garden with kittens prancing across it to the doghouse in the far corner.

He took a step closer.

The lack of screaming or fleeing had to be a good sign. "Does that look like Rover?"

He gave a bare headshake as he sidled within touching distance of the wall. After a moment he turned and took in the whole space again.

"Doesn't this room look nice and cozy, Finnley?" Allison still couldn't believe they'd pulled this off in five short days. "It's for you. This is your new home, here with me. Tomorrow you'll meet Maddie. She's littler than you, and I think you'll like her." If the loud, busy toddler didn't intimidate him first. "And my other friends, the ones who helped get your room ready for you."

To think she'd nearly taken Finnley and headed back to Portland rather than impose. Look what she'd have missed.

She set the Superman pack on his bed, pulled out his meager supply of clothes, and opened the top drawer of his freshly painted white dresser. The drawer had two pairs of pajamas and several pairs of socks and underwear already in it.

What?

Allison opened the next drawer. A couple of pairs of pants and a short stack of neatly folded T-shirts lay inside. She held her breath as she opened the bottom one. Empty. But hey, that was okay. Whoever had tucked these clothes into Finnley's dresser had bought her a little more time. She set the clothing from his Superman pack in with the others, spread one pair of pajamas on the bed, and tucked the pack itself into the bottom drawer.

A tap sounded at the door, and Finnley's head jerked up as he edged down the wall further from the sound.

Allison smiled at him as she walked past. "It's okay, buddy. Just one of my friends." She opened the door to Sierra, who stood with a tin of chocolate chip cookies, so warm the sugary smell engulfed the air.

"Welcome back, Allison! I brought you and Finnley a treat." Sierra glanced around then looked back at Allison with a puzzled frown. "Where is he?"

Allison accepted the plate. "He's very shy." She kept her voice low. "I think tomorrow will be soon enough to meet him."

Sierra hesitated, hand on the doorknob. "Okay, then. I hope you had a good trip?"

All she wanted to do was get Finnley tucked in and collapse in bed herself. She hadn't even had a moment to see what they'd done to her bedroom. Hopefully no murals. She mustered a grin for Sierra. "One time zone, a stopover, and way too many hours of travel. I'll catch up with you later."

Sierra peered toward Finnley's room, where balloons floated in the doorway. "Does he like his room?" she whispered.

"I think so." Allison let out a deep breath. "It's hard to tell, though. Talk to you tomorrow."

Sierra gave her a swift hug before she could resist. "Glad you're home." Then she whisked out the door.

"Hey, Rover, can you smell these yummy cookies?"

Valerie Comer

Chapter 12 --

*B*rent drove into the Green Acres driveway midmorning Saturday. He'd been all the way to Wynnton last night before turning around and driving back to Galena Landing and his hotel room. Thankfully Patrick paid for it by the week. There'd been no reason to go back to Coeur d'Alene. His uncle would've been glad enough to see him, but the Timber Framing Plus offices were closed on the weekend. They could talk on the phone anytime.

All Brent could think of was whether the little boy liked his bedroom. Whether Allison liked it. Would he even be able to tell if she did? She held so much in.

He'd snap his measuring tape around the job site for a bit, take some meaningless notes, and hope someone came over to talk to him. Noel, maybe.

Or Allison.

But why? Was he so enamored of this communal living set-up that he couldn't stay away? Had he noticed her because she was the only single one? Sierra was engaged, after all, though Brent had never met her fiancé. But Sierra didn't catch his eye anyway.

Just Allison.

Which was ridiculous. She certainly had no use for him or any other guy. Maybe he just liked a challenge? Also ridiculous.

He slammed the hard hat on his head and strode over to the school building, its timber frame structure all that stood yet. As soon as they finished roofing Allison's house, they'd start sheathing this one. Patrick would send a couple of extra guys for a few days.

Brent whistled under his breath as he pretended to do something useful.

A soft clop-clop and a jangle caught his attention. Noel led two Percheron horses in harness around the side of the straw bale house. He waved when he saw Brent.

What on earth?

Claire skittered down the house steps and joined Noel. Together they headed toward the garden. Some contraption — a plow, maybe? — dragged behind the horses. The animals stopped in the garden and Claire pulled a lever, lowering the device. Noel clucked to the pair and guided them to the end of the garden patch. Soil turned up behind them, a rich hummus-filled odor reaching Brent's nostrils.

Life on this farm wasn't normal. Surely they had a tractor. How many acres had Zach told him they farmed? Eighty? A hundred? Too many for horses, though Brent supposed the pioneers had done just fine.

He set his clipboard and tape measure in the truck and strode over to stand beside Claire. His wish had come true. Someone had come outside before he went crazy from solitude.

"Hey, Brent. I didn't expect to find you on the job over the weekend."

He could keep this vague. "I had a few things I wanted to check out."

"I didn't get a chance to tell you how amazing Finnley's bedroom looks, thanks to you."

Brent grinned, refusing his eyes the chance to see if Allison or the little guy were in sight. "Do they like it?"

Claire shrugged. "I haven't heard anything yet. Sierra stopped by last night to bring them cookies when they arrived, but Finnley didn't come out to meet her." She glanced toward the duplex. "When Allison emailed from Tucson, she said Finnley was emotionally withdrawn, so we decided not to overwhelm him with everyone crowding around him last night. Hopefully we'll get to meet him soon."

"Poor little kid."

"Yeah. I can't imagine what all he's gone through."

Footsteps sounded on the gravel behind them. Brent turned, keeping his face neutral.

"Allison!" said Claire. "How was your trip? How's Finnley handling things?"

"Okay, I guess." Allison glanced from him to Claire and back. He held her gaze for a moment.

She wrapped her arms around her middle. "This isn't going to be a walk in the park, just so you all know. I hardly know where to start with him."

"Is he okay by himself in the house?" asked Claire.

Allison let out a short laugh. "The door is open. He can come out if he wants. As for being alone, I'd hazard a guess he's spent much of his life that way. And I'm guessing when he wasn't alone, he wished he were."

Her words crushed Brent. How could anyone treat a child like that?

"I don't know who all to thank for Finnley's room. It's amazing." Allison's voice caught. "The quilt, the toys, even the clothes. I barely had a chance to pick up anything for him. Whatever he had is gone, it probably wasn't much to start with."

How had Brent ever thought Allison cold? He wanted nothing more than to touch her right now, hold her, maybe, and let her know she wasn't alone. Which was silly, since he would be gone in a few short months. And because he wasn't ever getting involved again.

He'd done enough damage in the past. He didn't need to saddle a good woman with it.

"You can thank Brent for that." Claire's voice interrupted his reverie.

He blinked. "What did I do now?" He tried to keep the tone light, but his dark college years still grabbed at his ankles.

Allison turned to him. "You painted it?"

"Uh…"

"Allison asked about the mural," prompted Claire. "Your mind must've been a million miles away."

A flush burned up his neck. "Uh, yeah. Just wanted to do my part to welcome him home."

Allison met his gaze. "It's amazing."

The warmth spread throughout his body. "You like it? I mean, does Finnley like it?"

She gave a short laugh. "Who knows what Finnley likes? Not me. But he didn't run screaming from it, anyway." She glanced at Claire. "Unlike when Domino came running up to the car when we got home last night. Finnley totally freaked."

And he'd painted a dog into the mural. Never even thought a kid might be terrified of dogs. Weren't they supposed to be a boy's best friend?

"Funny thing is…" Allison rocked back and forth. "He has an imaginary friend. A dog named Rover. With Finnley it's like 'talk to the hand.' He usually won't respond to a direct request, but if I explain things to Rover, Finnley may go along with it." She shook her head. "Or not."

"An imaginary dog?" Claire's face drew into a quizzical frown. "That's a strange choice."

"And yet he's afraid of a real one?" asked Brent.

"Terrified." Allison shuddered. "You should have heard him. It's just about the only sound I've heard out of him all week. You know how excited Domino can get, but he wouldn't hurt a fly."

"If you want me to paint over the dog, I can." Where had those words come from? He didn't have time to fiddle with it. Not really. Though he'd enjoyed being part of team evenings last week as they readied Allison's new home.

She shook her head. "It's really a sweet puppy. Finnley just stared at it thoughtfully for the longest time, so I think it's okay." She looked at Brent with sober eyes. "Thank you."

"Can I get a hand over here with the disc?" called Noel.

"Oops!" Claire scooted over to the horses to see what her husband wanted.

Brent turned to watch. "I can't believe they plow with horses."

"It's not a plow. It's a disc."

Uh... what was the difference exactly? "Whichever. The horses look neat. If I'd known, I'd've put them in the mural."

"Brent." She rested her hand on his arm.

He stared down at her manicured fingers as warmth spread. Then he lifted his gaze to hers.

Allison swept her hair behind her ears with her other hand. "I can't say thank you enough. This... this means an amazing amount. No one's ever done anything like it for me."

His hand covered hers. "Then I'm happy I could. You're doing something pretty amazing, too, taking in your nephew. And I think it's cool how your friends pitched in to get things ready. I wanted to be a part of something big like that."

She searched his face for a moment then extracted her hand. His arm chilled where her touch had been.

"Want to meet Finnley?"

oOo

Why had she invited Brent in, of all people? Why not Claire, who looked less intimidating than the contractor and would at least live on the same farm? But no, it was Brent matching his stride to hers as they crossed the gravel driveway. Brent who glanced over at her quizzically as they approached her open front door.

This whole talking to Rover thing was going to sound really dumb to a grown man.

"Hi Rover! I've brought somebody here to meet Finnley. Somebody who painted that special farm picture on his wall. Would you ask Finnley if he'd like to meet Brent?"

The door to Finnley's room stood open, and she peered inside. No little boy.

Her heart seized. Had Claire been right? Maybe Finnley had wandered out of the house while she'd been across the way. He was so quiet he could be anywhere by now. Had he purposefully run away?

Maybe in the bathroom. "Finnley?" she called. But that door was open, too, with no child in sight. A quick glance around her bedroom did not reveal him, either. Where could he be?

Allison's vision dimmed. Her hands grew clammy as she twisted them together. Voices screamed in her head. What had she been thinking, taking in a child with such severe needs as her nephew? She should have listened to Jason Wong, who thought Finnley needed a home with a psychologist, not an aunt who instructed farming.

Farming, of all things.

But where was the boy? Was he out on the hillside behind the house, wandering with only an imaginary dog to keep him safe?

Safe. There was no safe. A sob wrenched out her throat.

Strong arms came around her, held her close. A hand rubbed up and down her back. "It's okay. We'll find him."

Brent?

She pushed away, but he didn't let go. Not completely.

His hands cupped her shoulders, warming them. Concern filled his eyes, so dark they were nearly black. "You okay, Allison?

We'll find him. He can't have gone far in only those few minutes."

She had to get a grip on herself. It was nice to pretend for a moment that someone cared, but it wasn't realistic. She was on her own. She always had been. She'd been strong before. She would be now.

Allison backed up a step, and Brent's hands dropped to his sides. His facial expression shifted. What had she seen there for a moment? Something like caring? For her, personally, not just because he was a nice guy?

That was ludicrous. He was foreman on her job, hired to build her a school and a home. Nothing more.

But wouldn't it be nice to have someone in her life who focused on her and on her happiness? Like Noel was there for Claire. The more she'd watched the two of them together, the less she could imagine Noel cheating on his wife. Allison's dad had certainly never treated her mother that way. But Mom had never treated Dad with any kind of respect, either. Neither of them had ever once tried to make the other one happy. If they had, the impulse had been gone the next second before any evidence remained.

Allison took a long breath and let it out very slowly. Good, she was regaining some control. Other than continuing to stare into the depths of Brent's eyes. "Where could Finnley be?" Her voice cracked only a little.

"He can't be very big," Brent answered. "Might he fit under a bed, do you think?

Allison dropped to her knees and lifted the skirt of her own bed. Nothing. The place was so new there wasn't even a dust bunny. She looked around her bedroom with new vision. She slid open the closet door and peered in. Only her rack of shoes sat on the floor beneath her clothing. And the luggage she'd taken to Tucson, but it was fully zipped.

She looked around the room. He couldn't get in a dresser drawer and then shut it. There were no other possible hiding spots in her room.

"I'll check his room." Brent turned.

Allison entered the bathroom. Checked behind the shower curtain. Peered into the little cupboard under the sink.

"Allison?" Brent's voice was quiet.

"Yes?"

"Come."

She ran the few steps into the happy farm-themed room.

Brent crouched in front of the closet door, open just a crack. "It's okay, squirt. I won't hurt you."

"Finnley?" Allison dropped on her knees beside Brent and stared into the dim recess of the closet. Without his white cast, she might not have spotted him, crouched in the very back with his knees drawn up to his chin beneath wide black eyes.

"Thank God you're here. Thank God you're all right." She held out her hands. "Come to Auntie Allison, buddy."

He didn't flicker so much as an eyelash.

Right. "Good boy, Rover. I'm glad you're here with Finnley, helping him to feel safe."

Brent shifted beside her, but she didn't dare spare him a glance.

"Why don't you and Finnley come out, Rover? I'll get you a bowl of dog food, and maybe Finnley would like some breakfast. What do you think?"

A statue couldn't hold anymore still than her nephew. What had Lori and her string of boyfriends done to this precious child? "Rover, tell Finnley he's safe. No one is going to hurt him."

Finnley's gaze shifted to Allison's right.

"This is my friend Brent. He's the person who painted the farm on your wall. Who painted the puppy and his little house just for you."

The boy looked back and forth between them.

108

"He did it because he cares about you. I care about you, too, buddy." Those tears were starting to slide down her cheeks again. She took a swipe at them. Felt Brent's arm around her shoulders.

"I painted the cows and the sheep and the dog because I wanted to welcome you to your new home," said Brent. "I did it because your aunt is a very special lady and she loves you."

Allison's knees wobbled and she lowered herself the rest of the way to the floor. Away from Brent. She didn't dare look at him. What was happening here?

Focus on Finnley. He was the only important guy in her life. "I made some oatmeal. I'll go in the kitchen and put it on the table for you. Your tummy must be hungry. You didn't have much to eat yesterday."

His arms slid down his legs a little. The boy might actually be considering moving.

Allison rose from the floor, Brent's hand right there to steady her. It would be rude not to accept it, but she let go as soon as she stood vertical. She didn't feel all that steady as she made her way into the kitchen and scraped Finnley's oatmeal into a bowl. Her hand trembled as she spooned in a dollop of honey. Then she turned to set the bowl on the table.

She nearly ran into Brent.

He gripped her shoulders and looked into her eyes. "Why didn't you tell me your nephew was Korean?"

Chapter 13 ---

*A*llison stared at him, her brow furrowed. "What?"

It was all Brent could do not to give her a little shake. "Your nephew. Why didn't you tell me he was Korean?"

"Oh, is that what he is? My sister never knew." Allison grimaced. "She slept with a lot of guys, and I guess she didn't bother to ask questions of their heritage."

"But..." But what? He'd been just as bad once. Questions hadn't played a significant part of his vocabulary back then. They'd been more like, "Want to hop in bed? Great, let's do it."

Somehow he'd assumed Allison's nephew would look like her. Caucasian. Yeah, her hair was as dark as his, but women dyed their hair, so a guy couldn't tell from that. And her skin was definitely pale. So seeing a little guy with straight black hair and darker skin — not tanned from the sun — caught him off guard.

"Sorry. It's not a big deal to me." Allison stirred the oatmeal some more.

He doubted it needed stirring.

"He's my nephew. He could be black or... or purple for all I care." She shrugged. "It doesn't matter."

Didn't matter? She hadn't grown up with a different ethnicity. "It mattered to me as a kid. Growing up. People can be mean."

"Trust me, I know."

Yeah, right. "You're white. What would you know about it?"

"Brent, stop trying to pick a fight. I don't care what color your skin is or where your ancestors are from any more than I care about Finnley's."

"Oh, so you're one of the few brought up in a bubble where it didn't matter?"

She raised her eyebrows and dropped her hands to her hips. "My father was definitely racist. He did not accept—" She jerked her head toward the boy's bedroom. "Obviously, my sister didn't care who she slept with. There's no chance this was a one-time incident. In fact, I think she picked guys that would send Dad ballistic all along. Lori is that kind of person."

"So she was the rebel."

"You could say that." She glanced over to where Finnley stood in his bedroom doorway. "Come on, Brent. This is no time to argue about something so stupid. Let's go sit down in the living room and let Finnley eat without us hovering over him."

Now she wanted him to stay? Today was strange. All week had been strange. Surreal. But he followed her, no doubt just like the invisible Rover followed Finnley as he side-walked to the table, keeping an eye on him and Allison.

Allison settled in a rocking chair. "I can't wait until I get into my own place so I can bring my own furniture from Portland." She patted the arm. "I think this chair is on loan from Zach's mother. I'm not sure where they came up with all of it."

Brent crossed to stand by the window. Just when he was loosening his guard around her, she had to jab again? "I'm doing the best I can."

"That's not what I meant." She shook her head. "My, someone's touchy today."

Yeah, he was. And why? All because her nephew looked different than he'd expected? Stupid. An inkling there was more to his discomfort than that niggled the back of his mind. It was

Allison herself. She was the total opposite of any girl he'd ever noticed in his life. He'd been all over the flirty girls. Literally.

Just the thought deepened the flush on his cheeks.

Allison wasn't like that. He'd bet she couldn't flirt if she tried. She wouldn't know how.

Refreshing. But his attraction — oh, man, was he admitting it to himself? — had nothing to do with that. He'd noticed her even before she'd gotten into nephew-custody mode. He'd been determined to bring a smile to her face.

Because she was a challenge? Because she was a client?

Didn't matter why anymore. He'd seen something in her from the first day they met and, no matter how porcupine-prickly she was, he couldn't shake his… okay, yes, attraction to her.

"Penny for your thoughts."

He jerked and blinked the room back into focus. Allison back into focus. Her dark hair, pulled forward and flowing nearly to her waist, covered much of her light gray fitted hoodie. Her legs, clad in dark gray stretch pants, kept the old wooden rocker moving ever so slightly.

A clink came from the table, and Brent glanced over. Finnley cradled the bowl with his cast and made short work of his breakfast while keeping his watchful gaze firmly fixed on Brent and Allison.

Poor little man. He deserved a whole lot of stability and love. He deserved his aunt's undivided attention for a long time, until he relaxed and settled in.

Besides, Brent wasn't going to drag any God-fearing woman into the nightmare he'd created of his life. And he was done with the other kind of woman. Which meant he had no business dreaming about a relationship with Allison. It wasn't fair to her. It wasn't fair to Finnley.

He met Allison's gaze. "I need to get going." This from the guy who'd stayed in Galena Landing for the weekend because nothing seemed more important than the woman and child in this room? "I, uh, drove out to take some measurements on the building." Measurements he didn't need for anything. He nodded toward Finnley. "I thought I'd check in on the little fellow while I was out here anyway."

She didn't look convinced.

Which wasn't surprising, since he wasn't, either.

Allison glanced at Finnley then back at him. "I'd love it if you stayed a bit longer, Brent. Have a seat? Maybe we can go for a walk after and show Finnley around the farm."

Something in her eyes caught at his. Uncertainty? "You'll want the people who live here for that, won't you? People who will be part of his life." The child needed stability. Brent couldn't deliver that.

He almost missed her slight shrug. "Maybe. But you're here, and I asked you. Unless you're too busy."

He should say he was. He should glance at his watch, claim to be late for a meeting, give her a glimpse of his to-do list. But it was a lie. He had nothing but free time today and all weekend, really.

Brent turned so Finnley couldn't see him. "Is it wise to let him get attached to me, even a little?" he asked, barely above a whisper.

Allison surged to her feet, leaving the chair rocking in her wake. She stepped close to him.

A floral essence filled his senses. He barely needed to look down at all to see directly into her dark brown eyes.

"Please?"

Somehow his hands cupped her shoulders, her warmth spreading from his hands through his body. Oh, man. He was a sucker for a lady in distress. Allison didn't know how to deal with a little boy. Neither did he. She probably figured that, but thought there was safety in numbers.

Problem was, at this exact instant, he wanted to forget the vows he'd made to himself. He wanted to bend ever so slightly and kiss the lips mere inches from his.

What he really ought to do was walk out, get in his truck, and find something else to do today. Like go swimming in a lake barely melted from winter ice.

Still he stood there. Still he looked in her eyes as they widened slightly.

He caught his head tipping and managed to make contact with her forehead instead of her lips. He loosened his grip on her shoulders and dropped his hands. "I can stay for a little while."

Mistake. But what else could he do?

oOo

His lips still seared her forehead as he backed up a step. Then another. His dark eyes begged hers for understanding.

Heat crept up Allison's neck and across her face. She hadn't meant to come on to him like that. She'd been asking for help with her nephew. That's all she needed from Brent. Not kisses.

Right?

Right. It was all about Finnley. It was all about her learning to cope with a silent, hurting child. Brent was right. Finnley was nothing to him, just a kid who happened to share a racial gene pool. Finnley shouldn't get attached to Brent.

She shouldn't get attached to Brent.

She was tough. She knew what happened to women who trusted men. Every. Single. Time.

Noel's face swam into her mind's eye, and she pushed it away. Even Noel wouldn't be exempt forever. He was male. That's all it took.

She forced the words from her lips. "No, on second thought, it's okay. Finnley, Rover, and I will be just fine."

Brent ran a hand through his black hair. "Look, I'm sorry. I shouldn't have done that. I said I'd stick around, and I'm going to." He angled his head toward Finnley. "For his sake."

Allison glanced at her nephew. He sat in front of an empty bowl, eyes wide as he watched them. It was all about Finnley. It had to be. She took a few steps toward him. "Are you still hungry, buddy? I can get you a cookie or two. Remember the yummy ones Sierra left us yesterday?"

He looked down at his bowl and gave it a little nudge with his cast.

Right. The imaginary dog. "Rover, would Finnley like a cookie?"

The boy's head nodded so slightly Allison might have imagined it, but she'd pretend it was real. Just like the dog. She crossed over to the cupboard and lifted out a plate and the tin. The cookies still smelled amazing. She set two on the plate and slid it in front of Finnley.

Her nephew glanced up at her. Something flickered in his eyes before he looked down. He lifted a cookie and took a wee nibble.

Allison held out the tin to Brent. "Want one? Sierra went on a baking binge yesterday."

He reached past her for two more plates and set them on the table. "Only if you are. Homemade?"

She took a deep breath. "Want a coffee?"

"Sure. Just black, please."

A little grin poked at the corners of her mouth. "That's good. I think that's all they supplied me with for starters." She poured two cups while he shifted two cookies to each plate and sat down across from Finnley.

Brent took a bite and his eyes widened. "These are awesome, aren't they, squirt?"

Allison slid into the other chair and raised her eyebrows at Brent. "I bet Rover likes them just fine."

Finnley sneaked a peek at each of them. He took another bite and nodded.

If that was progress, she'd take it.

"You know, when I was a little guy, I had an imaginary friend named Kefir." Brent leaned back in his chair and popped the rest of his cookie in his mouth.

"Oh?" Allison resisted the impulse to look at her nephew. "What was Kefir like?"

"I made my mom set a place at the table for him. Once my sister tried to sit in that chair and I yelled at her. I didn't want Kefir squished."

Allison grinned. "I'm sure she was very understanding."

He rolled his eyes. "Not so much." Brent grabbed another cookie. "Kefir was braver than I was. He could ride a bike before I could. He could climb a tree. He led me into all kinds of scrapes."

"Did your parents buy your excuses?"

"My mom. No dad in the picture. And no."

Interesting. "I didn't know your parents were divorced." She shouldn't have said that. What if his dad had died?

Brent's words were clipped. "My father wandered through once in a while when he wanted something of my mother."

Didn't that sound just like a man? But maybe things like that were best not spoken of in front of Finnley. "Tell us more about Kefir."

"He was a little boy, like me. Only he was white." Brent glanced at her.

Allison felt the burn of his eyes. Had it mattered so much to him? Would it bother Finnley, too? She looked down at the cookie on her plate and broke it in half. Then again.

"He had blond hair and blue eyes and was always getting me in trouble. I don't know what happened to him. I guess eventually I didn't need him anymore and he stopped coming around."

"I wonder how many little kids have imaginary playmates." Or imaginary guard dogs.

Brent inhaled the rest of his cookie and glanced toward the tin.

Allison bumped it closer to him. Let him have a few. She certainly didn't need them.

"I've always thought of Kefir as an angel sent by God, actually," he said casually as he helped himself to another.

"An angel?" She blurted the words out before she could censure them.

"Why not?" Brent grinned. "God gives us imaginations, right? And when a child needs comfort or encouragement, why wouldn't He nudge that imagination to think up a secret friend? Someone who is always there, someone who understands." His gaze flicked to Finnley then back to her. "Maybe someone who protects."

That made an incredible amount of sense, actually.

Was it a good sign that Finnley sat at the same table as her and Brent, calmly eating a cookie? She sent a silent prayer thanking God for Rover. Whatever the dog was.

Chapter 14 ---

Noel, Claire, and the horses were long gone by the time Brent stepped back outside Allison's doorway. Inside, she suggested to Rover that Finnley put on his jacket, saying it was colder outside here than in Arizona. How was she ever going to get through to the hurting child? That anyone could abuse a little one like had happened to Finnley made Brent's gut churn.

Some people simply shouldn't be parents. It was more than biology. More than sex. It was about nurturing life and putting someone else's needs first. Obviously the little boy's needs had come last, if at all.

A cat twined around Brent's ankles, its rumbling purr filling the air.

He crouched down and rubbed its back. The cat put both front paws on his knee, revealing milk-filled teats.

This little thing was a mama? Where were her babies? Movement over by the stack of lumber at the school caught his eye. Several little fur-balls tumbled and played.

Brent lifted the cat and stepped back into the duplex. "Finnley, look." Oh, right, the dog. "Rover, I want you to meet a cat. No chasing her, okay? She has babies."

"Don't bring it inside, Brent."

Right. Miss Priss wouldn't want a single cat hair to drop on her floor. He backed outside, holding the rumbling cat against his chest. She couldn't weigh an ounce over four pounds.

Finnley, wearing an oversize hoodie, followed Brent, eyes fixed on the feline.

Brent lowered himself to the concrete stoop and set the cat further out on his knee, but she was having none of that nonsense. She wiggled closer, still purring like an incoming train.

"Want to touch her? She's really soft."

Finnley reached out and patted the cat's back. He pulled his hand away quickly and glanced at Brent.

"It's okay, squirt. She likes to have her head rubbed. Like this." He demonstrated. "Here, want to sit down and hold her?"

The little guy sat at the other end of the concrete pad.

Brent set the cat on Finnley's lap, and the boy's fingers tangled in her long fur. The cat bumped her head under Finnley's chin, and he pushed her away.

Something that minor wasn't going to slow down this attention-starved feline. She shifted around Finnley's hand and pressed against him again.

"It's okay. She really likes you, I think. Can you see over there?" Brent shifted closer to Finnley and pointed. "There are her babies. Want to go closer and see them?"

The boy nodded slightly, pushing the cat away again as he stood.

Brent rose, too, only then becoming aware of Allison in the doorway behind him. She leaned against the doorjamb, watching. She gave him a nod and a little smile when their eyes caught. *Thanks*, she mouthed.

Finnley sidled toward the playing kittens.

Brent held out his hand. "Come on. Does the cat have a name?"

She tucked her hands inside her sweater pockets. "Jane Eyre, I think. After the classic. I knew she'd had babies but hadn't seen them playing before this." She ambled beside him.

Had he really expected her to take his hand? Of course not. Up ahead, Finnley had stopped several feet away from the roughhousing kittens. The mama, Jane Eyre, was still more interested in the boy's ankles than in her offspring.

"Wonder if I can catch one," he murmured as he and Allison came abreast of the child.

Allison settled on the ground and the fickle Jane Eyre homed in on her, setting her paws on Allison's knee.

Finnley's gaze twitched between the cat, Brent, and the kittens. Allison must have realized how important the moment was. She allowed the cat to climb on her lap. Her nephew edged closer to her.

Brent couldn't help the grin. Didn't look like Allison was comfortable, but she'd do nearly anything to soften the relationship with her nephew. He glanced over to the lumber pile only to see three kittens scampering toward their mama.

Allison set Jane Eyre in front of her. The cat flopped onto her side and the three babies nuzzled into her belly.

So much for catching kittens. Brent dropped to the ground beside Allison, bracing himself on an arm that just so happened to brush her shoulder.

"See, Finnley? See what a good mommy cat she is? She's letting her babies drink milk from her. She's taking care of them."

Brent scratched Jane Eyre's head, and the rumbling purr returned. She stayed put for the kittens, though. "Good mama."

Domino appeared as though from nowhere. He jumped around the scenario with little sharp barks, daring Jane Eyre to run so he could chase her. The cat opened lazy eyes but did not twitch. Even the kittens ignored him.

Finnley sidled closer to Allison, gaze fixed on the dog.

Right, she'd said the boy was terrified of the Border collie. Brent snapped his fingers. "Domino, come."

The dog danced to his side.

Brent pushed his rump to the ground. "Sit. Stay."

Allison pulled her phone out of her pocket and tapped a message.

He raised his eyebrows at her.

"Asking Jo to call him in. I know the dog was on the farm first, but…" She shrugged. "We need a little time."

Brent jerked his chin toward Finnley. "I think we're doing okay. Domino is no more traumatizing than Jane Eyre." Really. Who named a cat something that stupid?

"You didn't hear him last night."

"But this is a new day. See?"

A whistle sounded from up the hill. Domino's ears perked up then he took off running.

The boy watched the dog disappear before turning his attention back to the kittens. Apparently a snack was all they'd needed. They now took to wrestling with each other again, rolling around on the ground. One little orange and white kitten bumped up against Finnley's foot.

Finnley crouched down and held out a hand.

The kitten smacked it then darted away. A second later it was back, dancing around the boy's hand and jabbing it with ninja paws.

Brent peered at Finnley. Was that really the ghost of a smile on the little boy's face? He leaned closer to Allison, his shoulder brushing hers. "See that?" he breathed.

She nodded so slightly he felt it more than saw it.

Finnley settled on the ground and the kitten jumped in his lap, attacking the dangling string from his hood. The boy sat very still, his hand moving slowly until he touched the kitten's fur.

The kitten leaped backward, twisting to land on its feet, then bounced back to attack Finnley's fingers.

That was definitely a smile. Brent leaned a tiny bit closer to Allison, his hand braced on the ground behind her, her shoulder touching his chest. Her perfume begged him to close the gap.

The immense satisfaction he felt at this little victory rocked him. This was Allison's victory. Finnley's. He was nothing in the grand scheme of things, but he couldn't resist the lure. He shifted even closer so Allison's long silky hair brushed his cheek.

She pulled away slightly, a startled look on her face as she glanced at him.

Brent nestled back in. "Just enjoying the view." He kept his eyes on the child though he could feel Allison's gaze. Let her think what she wanted.

In that instant, he felt her relax against him, ever so slightly. Two victories in as many minutes.

He was a goner.

o0o

Wouldn't it be nice if she could really rely on someone? Brent almost made her think it might be possible. She'd always stood alone and prided herself in it. Seeing the mess needy Lori had made of her life only added incentive, even when Dad... No, she was not going there.

Brent was a guy. He couldn't help it. And Finnley, too. No matter how Allison raised him, he was going to turn out like all other men. But that couldn't be. If she really believed that, wouldn't she have left him in some foster home in Tucson? Why bother getting attached to someone who'd only become a selfish abuser himself someday?

Noel. Zach. Brent. All men? What about the grace of God? But this line of thought was going to get her in more trouble than holding firm in her all-men-are-in-it-for-themselves belief. If she opened up her mind, who knew what would swarm in?

Allison had been deriving altogether too much comfort from the slight contact of her shoulder against Brent's chest, his arm touching her back. How could she allow it and remain true to her convictions? And yet she didn't move. She didn't want to startle

Finnley, after all, or Jane Eyre or her kittens. Best to remain still.

In the distance, she heard Maddie yelling, but the kiddo didn't sound upset. She just lived life out loud. Opposite of Finnley, that was for sure. Maddie's voice sounded nearer, then nearer yet.

Allison shifted away from Brent, the contact spots immediately chilling. She turned to look toward the house. Indeed, Jo walked toward them, Maddie running at her side and singing some unrecognizable song at the top of her lungs.

Finnley froze, his hand still in the kitten's attack zone. He turned slightly to take in the approaching pair. Appraising them for safeness, no doubt.

"Hey, buddy. That little girl is Madelynn. We call her Maddie sometimes. She's younger than you, but she can be your friend."

Finnley's gaze slipped to Allison then back.

So far, so good. She hadn't even had to go through Rover to talk to him this time. "The lady's name is Jo. She's Maddie's mommy." Hmm, that might not be much comfort. "She loves Maddie very much and would never hurt her."

"Yoo-hoo!" hollered Jo. "You found the kittens. We wondered where Jane Eyre had them holed up."

"Right here," Allison called back. "Want to come see them, Maddie?"

"Kittens!" Maddie let go of her mom's hand and charged toward them.

Finnley flinched. The kittens scattered. Only Jane Eyre stayed put under Brent's stroking hand.

Allison raised her eyebrows and shook her head. Who'd have guessed that one?

"Maddie, you're scaring the babies." Jo chuckled and sat down beside Brent. She glanced over at Finnley. "Hi there, little guy. My name is Jo."

Maddie saw Finnley for the first time. She ran toward him, stopping mere inches from his knees. The boy reared back, bringing up his cast arm in front of his face.

"Whoa, Maddie!" Allison snagged the toddler and tugged her sideways out of her nephew's bubble. "This is Finnley. He's here to be your friend. Finnley, this is Maddie."

Maddie tipped her head and considered the boy. "Friend?"

"Yes. Someone to play with and have adventures with."

The tyke nodded eagerly. "Play. Maddie share toys."

"Good job, kiddo. Right now Finnley wants to play with the kittens."

Maddie swiveled to see them. They were back to pouncing on each other near the pile of lumber. "Kittens soft?"

"Yes, they are." Allison grinned. "Except for their teeth and claws. You have to be gentle with them."

"Gentle. Kittens soft." She pulled away from Allison and ran toward the lumber. The felines fled.

Brent chuckled. "That went pretty well."

A sidelong glance at Finnley revealed his wide eyes staring at Maddie, his arm no longer in a defensive position. If anything, the boy looked a little curious.

Well, Maddie had that effect on people. Impossible to ignore. Impossible not to love. Allison should know. She'd only been here a month herself and already the toddler had her wrapped around her little finger.

Allison leaned toward Finnley. "Maddie is sometimes very loud."

"Loud!" yelled Maddie, running around the lumber stack.

It would be good for Finnley to have Maddie around. Kind of like a little sister for him, or a cousin. Jo's kids — and maybe Claire's, someday — were as close as the little guy would ever have to cousins. Allison certainly wouldn't have any.

The image of newborn Finnley popped into her mind. She'd have a baby that looked a lot like him if she married Brent. One happy part-Korean family.

Right. So not going to happen.

Allison pulled to her feet and stepped out of the semi-circle. "Come on, Finnley. Let's go back to our little house."

Her nephew looked at her then at Maddie, who hadn't yet stopped running and hollering for the kittens to come to her. Because chasing them would help.

"Finnley."

His little jaw set firm.

Oh, man. She was doing it, wasn't she? But this was too much closeness. Too much pretending there was a future. There wasn't. Just her and Finnley, and he was already more attuned to Maddie and Jane Eyre than to her. She could make him come, but that was the worst idea she'd had all week. The boy didn't need someone else telling him what to do — or else.

Allison swallowed the anger that wrestled with panic in her throat. She was the adult. Finnley needed safety. He needed to matter. The time to demand obedience would come, but later. Not just because she'd had a panic attack.

Brent's worried gaze lifted to hers. "You okay?" he asked, so low Jo was unlikely to hear.

She blinked back tears. "Maybe." She closed her eyes and breathed a prayer. Breathed some air, too. In and out. In and out. "I guess we can stay here a little longer." She walked around to the other side of Finnley before settling back onto the ground.

Brent was addictive. Best to keep a distance. She couldn't allow herself to depend on him.

Chapter 15 --

*H*e could understand why Allison thought she'd better wait
another week before taking Finnley to church. The boy had
made considerable progress yesterday, not quite smiling at
Maddie, but not cowering from her again, either. He'd solemnly
eyed everyone on the farm as Allison introduced him, clutching
his teddy bear behind his cast and a kitten in his other arm, and
had even managed dinner with the group.

Brent parked his truck beside the two from Green Acres
Farm that he'd followed home from church. Back from church.
Not home. As appealing as this place was, he needed to
remember he was only a visitor. Only temporary.

Once he knew Finnley had settled in and Allison had
adjusted, he'd back off again. Stick to getting her house and
school built and driving back to Coeur d'Alene every weekend.
To his lonely, cold apartment.

Moths that insisted on circling a flame generally got burned to
a crisp. The warmth he felt inside and out in Allison's presence
wasn't worth the eventual scorch marks on his soul.

He could tell himself that all he wanted. Still, he kept circling.
Right now it was a wide circle, as he walked beside Noel and
Claire to the big house steps with Allison nowhere in sight.

"So glad you could join us today." Noel's eyes held a wicked gleam.

"Hmm?" Brent hadn't been looking at Allison's duplex, had he?

"We can always use another hand in the kitchen on Sunday."

From behind them, Jo laughed. "Did Noel forget to mention the guys cook Sunday lunch most weeks?"

Brent scratched his head. "Uh... so long as I'm told what to do it should all be good. I've been in a kitchen before."

"Oh, telling people what to do is one of Noel's talents." Zach reached past Brent for the door, holding it open as everyone trooped in ahead of him.

Noel draped an apron proclaiming him *King of the Kitchen* over his neck then grinned and pointed at a door behind him. "There are more where that came from. Help yourself."

Brent followed Zach across the kitchen and into the adjoining room. A pantry? Wowzer. He'd never seen so much food in one place outside a supermarket. "You guys are prepared for the apocalypse."

Zach laughed. "Pretty much. But we've gone through a whole lot over the winter. See the empty canning jars? All once full of food."

Row upon row of sparkling glass jars spread over several shelves. The room must have looked amazing when all of them were full. Brent could barely imagine the work of preparing all that, but he'd bet it tasted great.

"Which do you want?" Zach looped an apron over his head.

Brent read the front. "World's Okayest Chef?"

"Yep." Zach chuckled. "I know my limits. I can't claim a higher title than that."

"What else is there?" Brent had seen some mighty suggestive ones when a former girlfriend had once dragged him into an x-rated shop. Surely these guys would have cleaner taste.

Your Opinion is Not on the Menu.

Stand Clear. Man Cooking.

Real Men Cook.

Brent shook his head and reached for *Dude with the Food.* Sounded all right. He followed Zach back into the kitchen.

"Hey, man, can you shave that cheese paper thin?" Noel pointed to the far side of the large Green Acres kitchen. "There's a meat slicer over there. Then run the ham through."

Brent shrugged. "Sure." He washed his hands in the kitchen sink. "What are we making?" This whole cooking-with-a-bunch-of-guys thing was just weird.

"Chicken Cordon Bleu." Noel placed waxed paper over an array of chicken breasts. "Don't worry, we use the legs and backs for other meals."

Uh. He'd been expected to fret about that?

Zach dumped a small bag of potatoes into the sink. "We raised the chickens ourselves. Nothing goes to waste around here."

Half a dozen adults ate here regularly. "It must take a lot of birds to feed a crew this size."

"You have no idea." Noel began whacking the breasts with a mallet.

"We eat more beef, pork, and lamb. Especially beef." Zach grabbed a scrub brush and turned on the faucet. "More meat for less labor."

Brent picked up the chunk of cheese from the butcher-block island and crossed to the slicer. "So I should be honored you're sharing chicken with me."

Noel laughed. "I guess so."

The zing of the electric motor drowned out the other guys' conversation. Brent set the cheese slices on the plate and switched to cutting ham. A minute later he turned off the slicer and returned the food to the island. "What now?"

Zach opened the oven door in the massive rock wall and tucked a slew of whole potatoes onto a rack.

"A layer of cheese, a layer of ham." Noel set a plate of crumbs beside the meat. "If you can get that, Zach will roll, and I'll start cooking."

Brent nodded and began assembling the parts.

It didn't take long before Noel had two cast iron frying pans full of sizzling roll-ups. "Into the oven with them." He suited action to his words then began cleaning the butcher-block island. "Get some green beans out of the freezer?" he asked Zach. "We'll stir-fry them."

Brent tried to think ahead. "Do we serve at the table or cafeteria style?"

"At the table." Noel pointed at open shelving above the peninsula. "If you want to start setting it, there's what you need."

He remembered the seating arrangement from yesterday. He'd sat on the same side of the farmhouse table as Allison, with Finnley between them. Like Zach and Jo sat on either side of Maddie. Like a family.

Dangerous territory. This hanging out with the guys who lived here, acting like one of the crew... this wasn't a good thing any more than dreaming up reasons to be near Allison or trying to coax a smile onto Finnley's face. Though God knew Allison needed someone, and so did her nephew.

Only not him. Someone pure, someone with a solid Christian walk stretching back to birth. A man of God. A leader. So many things Brent wasn't. Yes, God had forgiven him. Yes, he'd been devoted to following Jesus for several years now, but his past still haunted him.

He set plates around the table and arranged the cutlery the way his mama had taught him.

The door opened and Allison entered with Finnley. For an instant she stood framed against the brightness of an early spring day. Like a halo around her. No doubt she'd find that thought distasteful.

"Hey, squirt." Brent couldn't bring himself to speak to Allison. He'd choke on his words for sure. "Did you bring Rover with you?"

The boy, dark eyes so much like Brent's own, looked up for a moment before shaking his head slightly.

Brent grinned at Allison. A win!

She gave him a pensive smile in return before guiding Finnley to the great room where Maddie set out rows of wooden farm animals.

Brent was wedged between a truss and a kingpin. He'd spent too much time dreaming lately, and too little praying. Surely if he asked God for direction, he'd receive it?

oOo

Finnley sat on the rock hearth and watched Madelynn, who paraded one toy or book after another in front of him. "Maddie share." She thrust a wooden sheep at his face then pulled it away.

Well, the little guy hadn't reached for it, so Allison guessed that version of sharing was fine for the moment. Still, she couldn't help but think that was how she gave problems to God, too. *Here you go, God. You can have this mess. All my problems. Now I'll take them back. Thanks, anyway.*

"What day is Gabe getting home?" Claire asked Sierra.

"His last exam is next week Thursday. He'll drive home Friday."

"Gives us two months to finish planning the wedding. How are you at decorating, Allison?"

Allison jerked her gaze to Claire. "Me? Not really my thing." She managed a small smile. "I don't think Sierra wants everything in black and white and gray." She'd seen the dress the maid-of-honor was to wear, a frothy lilac-colored thing. It would look great on Sierra's sister, Chelsea, who loved everything girlie.

131

"Sounds perfect to me," Claire deadpanned. "A wedding is a solemn affair." She ducked the decorative cushion Sierra tossed at her head.

Finnley's eyes grew wider as the women laughed.

Allison would bet dollars to Dobermans he'd witnessed many flying objects, all of them intended to do more damage than a pillow between friends.

"You're one to talk, you with the Christmas wedding. You totally cheated, making use of an already-decorated church."

Claire laughed. "We brought in a ton of extra poinsettias. Besides, I like red."

Sierra scrunched up her face. "Red schmed. Not for me."

Jo lowered herself to the arm of an easy chair. "The nursing home enjoyed those plants. I know Zach's grandmother adored the ones we put in her room."

Allison had never met the old lady before she died, but everyone spoke of Mrs. Humbert so fondly.

"Still seems strange to see someone else in two-twenty-four." Jo sighed and twisted her wedding rings. "I miss her."

Maddie patted Jo's leg. "Mama sad?"

Jo slid to the floor and gathered her little daughter in her arms.

Allison's eyebrows went up. That was about the most snuggling she'd seen the little whirlwind do. She glanced at Finnley, who watched, a puzzled frown on his face. Someday soon — please, Lord — she'd be able to hug him, too.

"I'm glad we have photos of your great-grandmother holding you, baby girl. Did you know her name was Grace, just like your middle name?"

Maddie squeezed Jo's cheeks between pudgy hands. "Madelynn Grace."

"That's right."

Maddie extricated herself from Jo's arms and ran to Finnley, poking his chest. "Finnley Grace."

Allison chuckled. "More like Finnley Daniel. Not sure where my sister got either of his names from. There are no Finnleys or Daniels in our family. Not that she'd have wanted to name him for our father."

"I'm a sap for family names," Sierra said. "But Gabe says his is one we won't saddle a kid with. Ever."

Jo's hand rested on her belly. "Gabriel is a great name. Zach thinks that's what we should call our baby if it's a boy."

Sierra chucked another cushion at Jo's head, and she toppled over, laughing.

"Mama owie?" Maddie leaned over her.

"No, I'm fine, baby girl. Auntie Sierra keeps throwing things at Mommy."

Maddie put both hands on her hips and glared at Sierra. "No, Auntie Sera. Stop."

Little knots inside Allison loosened. Unraveled. To think she'd been invited to join this sisterhood. This family. Well, she'd invited herself, but they'd received her with open arms. Her, and now Finnley.

She walked over and dropped beside him on the hearth. Not too close. "How are you doing, buddy? Is your tummy hungry?"

He gave a wee nod.

Allison leaned a bit closer and whispered. "I'm so glad you came to stay with me, Finnley. I love you."

He glanced up at her, dark eyes bright, and his little lips twitched.

The Grinch had nothing on Allison. Just like the Christmas story, she could practically feel her heart growing a few sizes. And it encompassed not only her nephew but all the women in this room.

"Food's up!" called Noel.

Finnley was on his feet before she was, and she followed him to the farmhouse table, lured by the delicious smells.

"Hey, squirt, I found something for you in the pantry." Brent stood behind the chair Finnley had occupied at supper last night. "See? A booster seat. Then you can keep your chin out of your plate."

Finnley craned his neck to see as he moved closer, and Brent picked him up — just reached down and picked him up — and swung him into the seat then pushed it close to the table.

And there was no response.

Allison closed her mouth. She hadn't dared touch Finnley beyond the absolutely required. She'd never have dreamed of simply lifting him.

"Is that okay, Allison?"

Brent's gaze met hers over Finnley's head. He looked a bit worried that he'd overstepped or something.

She found her voice. "No, that's great. Much better. Thank you." She rested her hand on Finnley's shoulder. The boy shifted slightly, but not like it really bothered him.

Maybe that heart expansion she'd just experienced included Brent Callahan. But that was possibly the most dangerous direction she could stretch.

Chapter 16 --

*F*innley Daniel Hart.

The name had chewed at Brent's consciousness ever since he'd overheard it before Sunday lunch. Finnley Daniel Hart.

Hart was a common enough surname, but Brent couldn't remember ever knowing a Finnley before. Daniel, however, was his own middle name. Coincidence? Probably. He didn't remember a Lori Hart, but then, there were gaps in his memory. More like chasms.

He opened the email from his mother on his tablet in the privacy of his own room at The Landing Pad. The paperclip symbol told him she'd done as she asked. Sent him a few half-remembered photos of his own childhood.

Brent's finger shook as he tapped the icon. An image of a little boy riding a tricycle sprang onto the screen. Brent expanded the photo so the child's face enlarged. His face. Finnley's face.

Did they share more than Korean blood?

Brent closed his eyes and took a deep breath. "Oh, God. What do I do now?"

He swiped to the next image. Then the next. In each case, it was like someone had taken photos of Allison's nephew. This couldn't be. No way.

Hart. Lori Hart. If it were true, he should have a clearer memory of someone who looked like Allison. He hadn't spent all his time drinking. Too much, but not all.

Mallory Hart. Mid height, white-blonde, brown eyes.

Brent dropped the iPad to his bed and paced the small room. She'd lived with him, what, two or three months? When had it been? He'd been flunking out of school, working part-time, struggling to pay his rent.

She was a drug addict... oh yes, it all came back now. He'd dabbled in her scene but knew better than to go all in, even though she shared his bed.

Even now, Brent's face burned with memories he'd tried to suppress. Mallory hadn't been the only one, but she had been the last. She'd stolen his rent money for drugs, and he'd kicked her out in a scene the entire neighborhood probably still remembered. Because he couldn't pay his rent, he'd been evicted, too. That had sent him back to Coeur d'Alene where Patrick had taken him in, straightened him out, and set him back on his feet.

He'd always been thankful he'd hit rock bottom. That God had used those circumstances to work in his heart and draw him to a saving faith in Jesus.

Brent dropped back in the chair and covered his face with his hands. That had not been rock bottom after all. This was.

He'd fathered a child. Never knew. Never guessed. He had memories of condoms on his nightstand, but he couldn't swear he'd always used one. And besides, he'd heard it said those things were not foolproof. He always figured he was lucky.

Or not.

Mallory called him Danny Boy. She'd simply dismissed his first name, saying it didn't suit him, and shortened his second. That had been that.

Finnley Daniel Hart. Fourth birthday next week. Brent could do his own math. There was little chance of a mistake.

In the recesses of his mind, he'd always known he couldn't get involved with a good Christian woman. Allison might have a temper like a whip, but she loved that little boy and treated him like porcelain. And Brent was falling for her.

He had three choices. Tell her everything, or revert to a fully foreman-client relationship. Or he could ask Patrick to re-assign him. No, his uncle would demand reasons. Brent couldn't tell him. Which meant he couldn't tell Allison, either.

She already despised men. Thought they were strong in body but weak in every other way.

He'd proved her correct.

God had saved him, all right, but hadn't removed the results of his actions. All Brent could do now was pray for Finnley every day for the rest of his life. Pray that Allison met a great Christian guy she'd fall in love with, so Brent's son could have a daddy.

He didn't want to think what the child had gone through. Neglect. Abuse.

Tears streamed down Brent's face and dropped onto his clenched fists. "Lord, I didn't know. I didn't know! Please forgive me. I didn't know."

o0o

Allison hadn't seen Brent for over a week, except from a distance. She heard hammers pounding, drills screeching, and saws buzzing from up at her new house. She'd ventured up there once with Finnley, before his cast had come off, but Curtis had stopped her. "Kid needs a hard hat to come closer."

Of course. Brent and his rules. Yeah, yeah, she knew it made sense and was probably even a law. But how else was she supposed to see Brent when he never stopped by? His truck zoomed past the duplex several times a day, but he didn't so much as wave.

137

"You're skittish, Allison. What's up?" Jo worked beside her, digging barely-emerged dandelions out of the greening lawn while the two children stalked kittens nearby.

"I'm fine."

"Sure you are. Every little noise has you looking over your shoulder."

"Checking Finnley."

"He's on the other side of the garden. If I didn't know better, I'd think you were watching for that Timber Framing Plus truck."

Allison managed not to glance at Jo. She tossed a nonchalant shrug. "I can't help but wonder how the house is coming along. I don't have a hard hat for Finnley, so we can't check."

Jo snickered. "I'm sure there's a spare hard hat somewhere. Or you can leave Finnley with me for a few minutes if you want."

Now there was an idea she could have thought of herself. "Maybe."

"You guys have a fight?"

Allison kept her voice even. "Me and who?"

"Brent, silly." Jo tossed a dandelion at Allison's arm.

A fight would explain his sudden coolness, but there hadn't been anything at all. "Brent? He's too civilized to fight. And there hasn't been cause." He'd been rather quiet at Sunday dinner last weekend and had made himself scarce ever since. Try as she might, she couldn't think of a single thing she might have said — that anyone at Green Acres might have said — to shut him down so thoroughly.

"He seems to have eyes for you."

"Guess you'd be wrong, then. Not only that, but I'm never getting married. Men are a bunch of jerks."

Jo snorted.

"No, seriously. They're not worth the effort."

"And I thought *I* had a jaded upbringing."

Allison added another dandelion to the basket. Soon they'd have enough greens for tonight's pesto. She glanced at Jo. "Oh?"

"My dad disappeared when I was young. I don't even know if he ever found out he was a father."

"Same as the guy my sister was sleeping with. Who knows who fathered Finnley? Except in Lori's case, it was probably she who left the guy. Or a mutual parting." She couldn't imagine any man in his right mind sticking with Lori for more than two minutes. Even that was a generous time frame.

"My mom married when I was old enough to care. If I only had Brad and his sons to go by, I'd have to agree on the whole men-are-idiots thing."

Allison knew all along she'd like Jo.

Jo sat back on her heels. "Though he's put up with a surprising amount from my mother, all things considered." She swept her hand. "But then there's Zach's dad. You've met Steve, haven't you?"

Allison nodded. Zach's parents lived on the farm next door, and his dad'd had some kind of random neurological disease that limited his physical movement. But the man did seem to have a gentle spirit.

"You'd be hard put to find a nicer man than Steve. And there's Ed Graysen at church, too."

Ed. Ed. Allison thought through her two visits to the Galena Gospel Church. "I don't think I've met him."

"He's an older man. Seventy-something if he's a day. He's such a sweetie, though. Seriously."

What, Jo wasn't going to go on and on in praise of her own husband?

"Pastor Ron is another example of a man who's been a terrific husband and all-around good person for eons. And Sierra's dad." Jo chuckled. "He is the greatest. Even Sierra's little brother is pretty cool. You're a friend of their family, right? Have you met him?"

Allison shook her head. "I heard a lot about him from

Chelsea, but he was away at college during the months we hung out."

The girls dug in silence for a few minutes. Maddie made enough noise that keeping track of her and Finnley wasn't a problem. Finally Allison couldn't stand it any longer. "I keep waiting for you to tell me how awesome Zach is. Isn't that who you're supposed to be bragging on? Your own husband? Or maybe he isn't all that great."

Jo chuckled. "I figured you've seen Zach around enough to have a good impression of him." She lowered her voice. "You nailed it, though. He's not quite perfect."

Allison's eyebrows shot up as she swung to meet Jo's gaze. "Really? Isn't that disloyal to say?"

"I could give you a list of things that drive me crazy each and every day. Trust me."

Allison settled onto her rump on the damp lawn and gathered her knees under her arms. "You guys are getting a divorce?" The little Green Acres bubble quivered like it was about to shatter.

Jo reared back and skewered Allison with a look. "Who said anything about a divorce?"

"But you said he drives you crazy."

"Of course he does. He's a man. I'm a woman. I'm pretty sure God made both genders then laughed His head off."

"But — but I don't understand."

Jo's voice softened. "There is no perfect guy, Allison. The only flawless man ever to walk this planet was Jesus."

"But—" Allison shook her head. This conversation was so not what she'd expected. "Zach seems pretty nice."

"Sure he does. But he can't seem to find the laundry hamper with his dirty clothes, never mind knowing how to turn the washing machine on. He works way too many hours at Landing Veterinary and gets tired and cranky. And sometimes, especially when I'm pregnant, I like a little pampering, and I don't really get it."

Allison opened her mouth and closed it again. This was stuff she didn't want to know about Jo's marriage. Until now she'd thought these gals were all perfectly happy… or at least portraying that publicly. Hearing these things made her want to plug her ears.

"I suppose you're wondering why I'm telling you all this."

"Yeah." Allison glanced at Jo. "It's not like we know each other that well."

Jo chuckled. "But you know me better than you did half an hour ago. We're doing life together here on this farm, but we're not perfect. None of us. We have to give each other a bit of grace. Sometimes a whole lot of grace."

Now that was a new angle. "I'm not sure what I was thinking."

"You mean by joining us?" Jo put her hand on Allison's arm. "My thinking is God sent you here. You've got a lot to offer, and I'm not just talking about the farm school. I'm talking about you as a person."

"Me?"

"Yes, you. Allison Hart. A woman who's been very alone for how long now?"

"All my life, really." The words spewed out before Allison could stop them.

"I understand better than you think. Until I met Sierra and Claire in college, I had no one."

Allison had another ten years of alone beyond that. And surely Jo's father hadn't — no, the other woman didn't even know her father. "I had to be strong." Whoa. She had to get a grip on her voice. No trembling. No teary stuff.

"But you don't anymore. We accept each other, warts and all. We know you're not perfect." Jo patted Allison's arm again. "And you know we're not. But we all love Jesus and believe He's called us to do something really cool here at Green Acres. Together."

141

The words made sense. But Jo didn't know everything, and Allison wasn't about to fill her in. Some memories were best left jammed in a dark closet with the key thrown away. "It's not just for my sake. I have to be strong for Finnley."

Finnley.

It was too quiet. She whipped her head around. The children and kittens had disappeared.

Chapter 17 ---

*L*ooking good," Brent said to the electrician.

The man nodded at the wires running through the studs of the interior walls. "Should be outta here by the end of the week. Then let me know when the drywallers are done so my guys can come back and do the final."

Brent grimaced. "That's not going to be for a while. The windows won't be here for at least two months. There's no point in exposing drywall to the elements. We can get some driving rain in this region."

The older man pursed his lips. "We have a full summer booked up, but I'm sure we can fit it in when you need us. Let me know as far in advance as you can."

"Currently the windows are scheduled to arrive for the house the last week of June. We separated the order from the farm school's windows so we could get a head start. They'll be probably two weeks later."

"You'll need a few days to get them in and the drywallers and such. Got anyone lined up for that?"

Brent shook his head. Something he couldn't bring himself to talk to Allison about. Along with too many other things. "We did have, but they fell through on account of the schedule taking a whack." Who'd done the duplexes? He should ask Noel about that. The inside of the straw bale house was plastered, but Zach's place had some interior walls that weren't log. Who'd done those? But the school for sure was way too large without an experienced crew. "My boss is still looking for a crew."

"This here is an interesting design for a house. Packs a lot of punch into a small footprint."

"It does." Every step Brent took through the space as it took shape, he could imagine Allison taking. Could visualize the finished product. Could see Finnley running down the stairs or perched at the counter. They'd changed the great room layout as Allison wouldn't need a full kitchen. This bunch cooked and ate most meals together in the big house where Noel and Claire lived.

Big house indeed. It really wasn't that large by today's standards, but it had a professional kitchen and a good flow to the public spaces.

Everything about Green Acres Farm drew Brent in. The camaraderie with Noel and Zach for one. He hadn't had that many close guy friends. The whole farm-and-food thing attracted Brent more than he'd have guessed. The peacefulness of country living. The heady scent of spring unfurling in the forest behind Allison's house.

Allison.

Finnley.

The electrician looked at him strangely.

Brent shook his head. What had they been talking about? Right. "It's a great layout."

But not big enough for a growing family. Allison had asked him to nestle a computer space under the staircase. She'd intended to use the upstairs as an office. Now the small bedroom and loft area would be Finnley's.

His son.

In the distance, he heard little Madelynn's squealing grow louder. She and her mama must be headed back to the log house.

That kid was so loud she was practically a beacon. Brent couldn't help grinning as he crossed the space to look out a hole in the wall where one day a window would be fitted.

Jane Eyre trotted up the path, with Maddie in hot pursuit. It's a wonder the mother cat let the child get as close as she did, given Maddie's penchant for hauling her around by the neck. Behind Maddie came Finnley.

Brent tore his gaze from his son — his son! — to search for Allison and Jo, but there was no adult with the children. He frowned. These two were too young to wander the farm by themselves. Maddie had just turned two, and Finnley would be four next week.

Where were the women?

He strode for the gap that would be occupied by a set of French doors one day. The cat veered toward the hillside behind the house.

"Jane Eyre!" yelled Maddie. "C'mere, Jane Eyre."

Brent crouched down to intercept the toddler. "Hey, Maddie. Where's your mommy?"

She pushed past his arm. "Mine kitty."

"Does Mommy know you're chasing the cat? Where's Mommy?"

Maddie peered around Brent's shoulder, but he didn't let her past. "Jane Eyre gone," she announced sadly.

Lucky cat, this time.

Brent looked past Maddie to Finnley, and his heart clenched. He'd managed to avoid a close encounter since his revelation last week, but now that the boy stood in front of him, he wondered how he'd ever missed the connection for even a moment.

Finnley looked up the path the cat had taken, not seeming to notice that Brent knelt in the way of his and Maddie's pursuit. The little guy wore jeans and a navy T-shirt not that dissimilar from Brent's current attire. Bright red sneakers peeked below the jeans.

Brent couldn't help the grin. He'd bet someone besides Allison had picked those out. "Hey, squirt. Looks like you got the cast off your arm. Is it feeling okay? How are you and Rover doing these days?"

The boy's gaze shifted to Brent's face for a moment before looking down. The red shoe scuffed the dirt.

"Is Maddie your friend?" Brent asked softly.

A tiny nod.

"And the cats?"

A bit bigger nod.

"Where's Auntie Allison? And Auntie Jo?"

Finnley's little shoulder rose slightly and fell.

Brent's arms craved to press that little body close against his own. To soothe away the pain in the deep brown eyes. His son. How could Mallory have ruined this boy's life?

How could Brent have ever participated in creating a child with someone he barely knew?

He forced his gaze back to Madelynn then stood, taking the toddler's hand in one of his. "Let's go find your mother. I bet she's wondering where you are." He reached for Finnley, but the boy shifted just out of easy reach and didn't seem to notice.

Brent would bet Finnley noticed everything. "Come on, squirt. Let's go."

oOo

"Madelynn Grace Nemesek!" yelled Jo.

Beside her, Allison's guts froze solid. Those children better have stayed together. What if Finnley hadn't kept up? What if something else caught his attention?

There was no point in hollering for her nephew. He'd never answer if she did. In two weeks, the most animation she'd seen was how he held the kitten tight and watched Maddie.

Kitten. Jane Eyre and her troop were nowhere to be seen.

Allison hurried after Jo. "Do you think they followed the cats? Where does Jane Eyre consider home?"

Jo set her jaw and shook her head. "There's a box on our deck stuffed with old rags. Let's check. I can't believe Maddie disappeared out of my sight."

Allison couldn't believe she and Jo hadn't heard the deafening silence. She'd counted on Maddie. To what? Babysit a boy two years her elder? If Jason Wong ever heard about this he'd know Allison wasn't fit to have custody of her nephew.

She swallowed her panic — again — and jogged after Jo. Maybe they should split up. Would that give them a better chance of finding the children quickly? After they'd checked Jo's deck. Then they'd need to get help. Call Claire and Noel. Get Zach home from the veterinary clinic. Brent would help. And his guys, probably. There were hours until dark, but the mountain was huge and the nights still dipped below freezing.

Brent. He'd know, too, that she was irresponsible. Whatever went through his mind about her would be even worse. She still didn't know what she'd done wrong, but it had been a good thing he'd pulled back. She needed to focus on Finnley. To remember her vows about not getting involved with a man. She hadn't expected to ache to see him. Hadn't expected Jo to tell her that men weren't perfect, and it was worth it anyway.

Jo hadn't stopped calling, but this time there was an answer.

"They're right here!"

Brent's voice. There wasn't enough air in the entire outdoors to breathe as he neared. Allison could hear Maddie's high-pitched chatter now. What about her nephew? No, Brent had spoken in plural. Finnley must be there too.

She took off at a run behind Jo on the footpath, shorter than the gravel driveway that followed a longer, shallower grade.

Jo dropped to her knees and Allison nearly ran her over.

"Madelynn Grace!" Jo grabbed the child and crushed her to her chest. "Don't run off without telling Mama. Auntie Allison and I were so worried about you and Finnley."

"Tell Mama?"

But Allison only had eyes for the man and the boy standing side by side only an arm's length apart. Both regarded her with dark brown eyes beneath a shock of straight black hair. No wonder Brent knew the boy's nationality at a glance. The resemblance between them was remarkable.

Allison crouched on the path a few feet from her nephew and held out her hand. "Finnley? I was worried about you."

Behind her, Jo went on and on, trying to get through to Maddie, who kept saying, "Jane Eyre? Kitty?"

"They followed the cats up here."

Allison looked up into Brent's eyes. A woman could get lost in those deep, dark pools. She blinked. "I'm glad you found them."

Brent reached over and gave Finnley's shoulder a little nudge with the hard hat in his hand. "The little man is sorry he ran off. Aren't you, Finnley?"

Her nephew glanced at Brent then over at her before staring down at his red shoe poking in the dirt. He nodded slightly.

If only she could gather him in her arms like Jo had done with Maddie, but didn't he have to make the first move? She'd held out her hand, and he'd only ignored it. Allison swallowed hard. If she were lucky, it would happen before he turned into a sulky teenager. She had time.

She stood and patted Finnley's shoulder. He slouched from her touch. "Well, thanks, Brent."

"I just saw them a minute ago, out the window." Brent's eyes kept their focus on Allison's face. "Following the cat. I got them turned around to bring them back to the farm."

Allison's shoulders warmed with the memory of the times he'd held her. Her forehead remembered his light kiss. Why on

148

earth did she respond to this guy? But more to the point, why had he been avoiding her the past week? Everything in his eyes, his mannerisms, told her it wasn't because he didn't care anymore.

For the one million, eight hundred and forty-five thousandth time, she racked her brain over what had happened that day in the big house. When he'd started the day carefree, grinning, and winking at her then turned into a cold, distant stranger. Almost as still and unrelenting as Finnley.

A thought flickered through her mind, but she dismissed it. What did she really know about Korean culture? It might all be just part of their heritage. A bit stoic. Finnley certainly had reason enough to learn to hide in plain sight, to avoid being touched.

What had happened to Brent?

Expressions she couldn't quite catch flickered across his face, through his eyes. Then he set the hard hat back on his head and nodded. "Glad it ended well." He turned and strode back up the path.

Finnley watched him go. Then his mouth quivered, and he glanced at Allison.

Whatever that was supposed to mean. "Come on, buddy. Let's go home. It's almost time for lunch, and then Maddie gets a nap."

"No sleep. I be happy."

Jo chuckled and swept her daughter into her arms. "You need a nap anyway, kiddo. And so does Mama. Auntie Sierra made soup for lunch, so let's go get some."

Maddie wiggled to get down. "Biscuits?"

"Probably."

Allison winced as the toddler ran down the path, nearly tripping over a root but recovering her balance in time. Finnley followed Madelynn at a more sedate pace, while Allison and Jo brought up the rear.

"Something is definitely up with Brent." Jo glanced over at Allison. "You can deny it all you want, but I'm not blind or stupid."

Did everything have to be on public display at Green Acres Farm? No wonder Sierra had kept her cancer scare to herself last fall. Once the others got wind of any hint of a juicy tidbit, they were as relentless as hounds.

If she thought there was a chance Jo could figure things out, she'd be all over dumping the details on her. But there was nothing to go on.

Allison shrugged. "It doesn't much matter in the end." Not if he kept avoiding her. Closing her out.

Or were there clues? Puzzle pieces she could put together if she only knew what the resultant picture was supposed to look like? She'd turn the thoughts off if only she could, but it didn't seem possible. Her brain was going to worry those pieces around, testing a bazillion ways to fit them together, without any conscious effort on her part. Whether she wanted to or not.

Chapter 18 ---

"Nice to meet you again, Allison. How are you settling in?"

It amazed her that Gabe Rubachuk had presence of mind for anyone besides Sierra. After all, they were engaged to be married in just eight weeks, and he'd been away at college for several months. Plus the guy had driven all night to surprise Sierra by arriving early.

"Doing fine, thanks." She offered him a smile. She'd been here for two full months herself, and she really was doing fine. It amazed her to realize it, remembering the first few weeks and how hemmed in she'd felt. "I'd like you to meet my nephew, Finnley."

Gabe crouched to her nephew's eye level, dragging Sierra down with him. She hadn't let go of him since he'd driven up to the duplex. "Hi Finnley. I'm Gabe."

"*Uncle* Gabe," Sierra corrected.

He grinned, shaking his head. "I kind of like the sound of that. Do you like it here at the farm, Finnley?"

The little guy gave a tiny nod but didn't look up.

Rover seemed to have disappeared, and Allison hadn't brought up the subject. Other than Finnley's reluctance to speak or be touched, he seemed okay. He even tolerated Domino so long as the Border collie kept his distance.

Gabe didn't give up. "What do you like best?"

Finnley peeked at the man. "Kittens," he whispered.

"Really? There are kittens? Can you show me?"

Finnley's head twitched affirmatively.

If Sierra didn't have that guy all wrapped up, Allison would be tempted to snag him for herself. Finnley needed a man around who treated him with this much respect. Having Gabe for an uncle would be the next best thing.

Who was she kidding? She didn't want a man. Not for herself. Just for her nephew.

Unless he happened to be Brent Callahan, whom she hadn't seen since the children had wandered up to the building site several days ago.

Gabe kissed Sierra and released her, turning to Finnley. "Come on. Show me the kittens. Do they have names?"

Finnley glanced up at Allison, and she nodded permission for him to leave her side. He went off, Gabe at his heels. "Jane Eyre," he said softly.

Sierra linked her arm through Allison's. "Whoa. Isn't he great with kids?"

And Sierra had severe endometriosis and would likely never conceive. Allison patted Sierra's hand. "Thanks for sharing."

Sierra chuckled. "It only goes so far."

"That's not what I meant." Allison pulled away.

"It was a joke." Sierra rolled her eyes. "No need to get jumpy."

Allison took a deep breath. She knew that. Why had she reacted? That Brent. He'd muddled her thinking. She'd been able to completely block any hormonal urges before she met him. He'd turned her all soft then stopped talking to her without so much as an explanation.

For the first time in her life, she wanted to have kids. She wanted the experiences that would get her pregnant. Even that realization made her face flush. Those thoughts were off-limits.

Totally. She was glad Brent had stopped hanging around and touching her. She'd shoved those hormones down before, and she could do it again.

"Looks like Finnley will handle his birthday party okay," observed Sierra, watching the pair disappear up the path toward the log cabin, Domino bounding ahead.

"It's just the people he already knows, all at one time." Rosemary and Steve were joining them for dinner.

"True, but everyone will be singing to him. Think he'll handle the attention okay? Blow out his candles?"

Allison shrugged. "If not, Maddie will help him. Or I will. If he's okay with the party, I'm planning to try Sunday school tomorrow. Do you think Marnie will mind if I sit in the preschool class?"

"I was wondering when you'd think he was ready. I'm sure Marnie won't mind, and it will be a comfort to Finnley to have you there."

It was hard to tell if anything comforted him. He was still so aloof and stiff, like he waited for someone to hit him or yell at him. Still, there'd been a lot of progress, and she'd take it. Maybe one day he'd crawl up on her lap and give her a squishy hug. One day before he got too big to fit.

oOo

Brent glanced out a gap in Allison's house at the sound of voices. A man he didn't know walked beside Finnley up the steps of the log cabin next door.

"Rubachuk!" Zach exited his house and the two guys exchanged a back slap and a fist bump. "When did you get in?"

Finnley watched then crouched over the cat box beside the door. He pulled out his favorite, the kitten with orange and white markings. He held it out to Zach's friend, who immediately knelt down to receive the boy's gift.

Behind Brent, a plumber drilled for the hot water line, drowning out any words the guys might be saying.

The other man sat cross-legged on the deck, cradling the kitten and talking to Finnley, whose back was to Brent. The boy's hands moved slightly. Was he actually responding to this new man?

A surge of jealousy coursed through Brent. This was his son. He should be the one talking to him, playing with him, naming kittens with him. Yet he had no right to do any of those things. No way would Allison accept him. No way could he hurt Finnley further by revealing himself then disappearing again. Mostly, though, he couldn't imagine telling Allison his sordid story. She deserved so much better than him. It would be better if she never knew who Finnley's father was.

"Callahan!" Zach beckoned him over.

Well, why not? Brent could soak up a little bit of time near his child without anyone cluing in. He waved back and wove through the building and out the French door opening.

"I'd like you to meet my best pal growing up, who also happens to be Sierra's fiancé. Gabe Rubachuk. Gabe, our resident timber framer, Brent Callahan."

Resident, huh? Didn't sound so bad. Brent grinned and reached out to shake Gabe's hand. Firm grip. Direct gaze. Good things to have in one's best friend. Zach was lucky. Brent didn't even want to think about the direction his school friends had taken. "Good to meet you."

"Likewise." Gabe eyed the partially completed house. "Now that's an interesting design. You offering tours?"

"To anyone with a hard hat. I've got a couple of extras in the truck. Want to have a look?"

"Maybe later." Gabe rested his hand on Finnley's shoulder.

Wonder of wonders, the boy didn't flinch from the touch.

"I promised this guy's aunt I'd take good care of him."

154

"Hey, if Brent has two hard hats, there's no reason you and Finnley can't go through together. I get regular chances, but I'm not sure when he's last been on the job site."

Never? Brent had been so busy avoiding Allison he hadn't told her he had a hat the boy could wear. Yeah, it'd be big on him, but it met requirements.

Still clutching the kitten, Finnley glanced over at the house.

That settled it. "Sure. Let me grab them." Brent strode over to the truck and pulled two yellow hats out of the backseat. He dropped one on Finnley's head.

With a little imagination, Brent could believe the kid looked smug as he reached up with his free hand and touched the hat. No letting go of that kitten, though.

Brent handed the other hat to Gabe as they walked across the space between the two houses. "The front door is actually on the other side. A set of French doors will go here."

"Sierra mentioned there had been a delay."

Brent nodded. "So this space is the great room. Kitchenette here to keep plumbing lines in one wall. And enough space for an eating area, a sofa, and a computer or TV area."

He pointed across the room to a staircase of half logs, each wrapped in plastic then cardboard. "Trying to keep the rain off everything until the windows get here."

"They usually go in early in the process, don't they?"

"Yeah. This is definitely messing up the timeline. Usually we raise the beams, put on the roof, pop in the windows and doors, clad the exterior walls, and then do the outside finishing and all the inside work, safe from the environment. As it is, the interior studwork is complete and the electricians and plumbers are finishing up the rough-in. We'll soon be at a standstill."

"That's too bad."

Yeah, it was. But he still had work to do on the school building before he was truly stuck.

Gabe pointed to the far corner. "Hallway? Where does it go?"

155

Brent led the way. "Bathroom here," he said over the plumber's drill. "Bedroom beyond." Allison's room. He would make sure the finishing was perfect here and everywhere. If he couldn't be at her side, he could at least make sure her home was everything she could want.

"Just one bedroom?"

"Down here, yes." Brent glanced at the top of Finnley's hard hat. "There's another one upstairs she was going to use as her office, but now that's going to be Finnley's domain. Want to see?"

He was speaking to Gabe primarily, but the boy's head nodded, too. He really was settling in. Starting to interact with everyone around him. Good to see.

Finnley looked up and headed for the stairs.

"Careful up there. There's no railing."

The caution didn't slow the boy down any. A framed doorway leading into a bedroom stood at the top of the stairs. Finnley's room.

The boy looked around with a puzzled look on his face.

"What's wrong, squirt?"

"No Rover," he whispered.

"Rover?" asked Gabe.

"His invisible dog."

Finnley's jaw set.

Brent crouched in front of him. "Do you like the farm on your wall where you live now?"

He nodded.

Brent allowed a grin when all he wanted was to thrust his fist triumphantly in the air. "Right now this room doesn't even have walls and windows, but it will." As soon as Brent could make it happen. "Would you like a farm on the wall here, too?"

Finnley nodded. "Rover."

"You've got it, squirt. I'll make sure."

Their eyes met and something he'd never felt before washed over Brent. Pride. Possessiveness. Paternity. Anything in the world that would brighten this little guy's eyes and was in Brent's power would be done.

That powerful feeling clung to Brent as they retraced their steps down the steps and out the door. It's what made him say, "Yes," when Zach asked him to stay for supper to celebrate Finnley's fourth birthday.

However he felt about Allison — and she felt about him, if anything — took second place to feasting his eyes on this little fellow and wishing him a happy birthday.

Chapter 19 --

Relax. It will be fine." Zach's mom, Rosemary, who lived next door, snagged Allison to her side.

Allison looked at the inviting table spread with cat decorations she'd ordered off the Internet. A bunch of balloons hung from the light fixture. Amazing smells came from the kitchen, where Noel worked his magic on festive food. "But I want everything to be perfect." She straightened out of Rosemary's embrace.

"He's four, Allison. This is probably the first time he's ever had a birthday party at all."

"I suppose. I just want him to know how much I love him." It was true. She'd always had a soft spot for Finnley, but her love had multiplied exponentially since he'd come home with her three weeks before.

"Do you think a fancy party will tell him that more than everything else, day to day?"

"Um…" One point for Rosemary.

"You ever hear about the five love languages?"

Allison eyed the older woman. Did she even want to?

Rosemary grinned. "I take that as a no. I'll loan you the book sometime. It talks about the various ways people are wired to give and receive love."

"Sounds… interesting." Did she have time to listen to this? Didn't Noel need help with something in the kitchen?

"One is hanging out with someone. Just spending quality time together makes some people feel loved."

That had to be Sierra. No one Allison had ever known wanted togetherness more than that girl.

"Another way is physical touch." Rosemary glanced over to the kitchen, and Allison followed her gaze in time to see Noel pull Claire into a quick hug as she walked through the kitchen. "Noel's got that one in the bag."

Not as much as Lori. If anyone craved touching, it had to be Allison's sister. Strange. Dad's attention had pushed Allison in the opposite direction.

"Some of us do things for people and want them to do things for us." Rosemary chuckled. "That's me. I figure if you love me, you'll help me when I need it." Her gaze sidled toward her husband sitting in an armchair while Maddie climbed all over him. "I've kind of had to unlearn that one in the last few years. If I were depending on Steve doing things for me since he contracted Guillain-Barré, I'd spend all my time grouching at him. He can't show me love that way anymore."

Maybe these love languages had merit after all. Allison had asked Jo about that disease of Steve's. He'd been a strong, hardworking middle-aged man before the neurological syndrome had attacked him. Now he had a difficult time getting around and lived with constant pain.

"Gift giving is a form of showing love, too. Some people thrive on picking up trinkets for those they care about."

Chelsea had never popped in on Allison without a handful of flowers, a little box of chocolates, or a paperback to loan. Was that her love language? It sure wasn't Allison's. All that stuff seemed like a waste of money to her. She'd been hard put to graciously accept.

"Some people want to be told how special they are and what a good job they're doing. That love language is called words of affirmation."

Bingo. She'd begun to wonder if there was one that pegged her. Well, there it was. It was so true she hung her head, unable to meet Zach's mom's eyes. All she'd ever wanted growing up was her dad to be proud of her. To hear him say it. But she'd never measured up, no matter what she did. A four-point-zero GPA hadn't done it. A scholarship hadn't. Her masters with honors hadn't. Nothing had erased the...

Stop. No crying in front of Rosemary. It was Finnley's birthday, and Dad was long gone. Thankfully. She raised her head and set her chin.

"That's you, isn't it, sweetie? Hear it from me. You're a good woman, Allison. You're smart and pretty and tenderhearted. Finnley is lucky to have you in his life, and we're all so thankful you've come to Green Acres."

About those tears. If Rosemary kept this up, Allison wouldn't be able to stop them. Her mascara would run and her face would get blotchy. She took a long slow breath, managing to keep control of it. "Thanks."

"Now..." Rosemary winked. "I've got a few things out in the car I need help bringing in. If you could give me a hand, it would make me feel loved indeed."

"Sure." Allison gave her a watery smile. "I'm happy to help."

She followed Rosemary out the door. The warmth of the May Day sun eased the tension in her shoulders. Rosemary was right. Finnley had no big expectations for his birthday. He was likely to be overwhelmed as it was. She wasn't doing all this because he expected it, but because she wanted her friends to know how special her nephew was. And, yes, she wanted them to tell her what a good job she was doing both in the party and in Finnley's life.

Was it so wrong to want to hear those words? Words of affirmation, Rosemary called them. She hadn't made it sound like that was the worst love language. Maybe she'd put it last in the list because she already had Allison pegged.

Maybe any of those could be taken to an extreme. Like touching. Noel hugged everyone. He'd even hugged her a time or two when she hadn't run in time. It wasn't inappropriate, and Claire didn't seem to mind. It was obvious he had eyes only for Claire. Allison couldn't even begin to imagine him cheating on Claire any more. Not with the adoration and devotion she saw on his face every time they were together.

But it could definitely become negative, like with Lori, who craved physical touch so much she didn't care where it came from or who gave it to her.

So maybe wanting to hear a *well done* now and then was okay. Where was the line? When was it healthy and where did that change? She'd have to think about it.

Men's voices came from up the hill as she walked over to Rosemary's open trunk. She risked a glance. Zach and Gabe came down, talking and laughing, while Brent walked behind with Finnley. The little guy glanced up, and Brent tousled Finnley's hair.

Allison's heart froze. Her nephew was supposed to get attached to the men on the farm who'd promised to mentor him. Not a contractor who'd be disappearing out of their lives soon.

Mechanically, she reached for the laundry basket covered in a quilt. "Anything else?"

Rosemary shook her head. "I'll get Zach to bring the rest."

The guys trooped over at Rosemary's call. Zach and Gabe lifted the two remaining boxes from the trunk.

"Here, let me get that." Brent reached for the laundry basket, his gaze meeting Allison's.

Those brown eyes. They shouldn't rattle her so much. Maybe it was because of Rosemary's talk about love. Not that Allison

162

loved Brent, of course, nor did he love her. They were just friends. Not even that. They were client and contractor.

He took the load, his eyes never leaving hers as he gave her a lopsided smile. "I showed Finnley around the house."

Wait. Had he asked her permission? No. She narrowed her eyes. "What about a hard hat?"

His gaze grew wary. "I found an extra."

"I wanted to—" She bit off the words. What was done was done.

"Sorry. I should have asked first."

Yes, he should have. She gritted her teeth and glanced at Finnley. His dark eyes swung back and forth between the adults. Allison forced a smile as she crouched beside the boy. "Did you like the house?"

He nodded.

"Mr. Brent is making a nice house for us to live in, but he'll be going away soon."

Finnley looked up at Brent and shifted half a step closer to the man.

This could not be happening. Who had given Brent permission to bond with her nephew?

oOo

Brent's jaw tightened. To think he'd forgotten for one brief moment why he should steer clear of Allison Hart. Reminder times two as both she and Finnley looked at him with singularly different expressions.

Which of them could he placate? Finnley had taken a shine to him, and God only knew how much the boy needed positive influences in his life, the more, the merrier. Brent couldn't push Finnley aside even to please Allison.

But she was right. He was leaving soon. It wasn't fair to Finnley to cultivate a relationship. Even if he was the boy's biological father? Yeah, try explaining that one to Allison, because it wouldn't help. Besides, it would link Brent back to the past he'd done his best to put behind him.

He did the only thing he could. He tucked the basket under one arm and, with his other hand, guided Finnley toward the house. The boy didn't flinch away but nearly leaned in.

The ferocity of Allison's glare stung the side of Brent's face, not that he was looking. He was here for Finnley.

"What are you doing? It's Friday afternoon. Aren't you leaving for Coeur d'Alene?"

"Later." He shot her a glance. Yep, her face was set in stone. "Zach invited me for Finnley's birthday."

She opened her mouth and closed it. Probably a good thing. No doubt she was about to rip up one side of him and down the other. Maybe he even deserved it, but not in front of Finnley.

He beckoned her to precede him up the steps to the deck. Rosemary and the guys had already disappeared inside as Brent reached for the door handle.

Allison's lips pursed as she nudged Finnley inside ahead of her. Not that he paid any attention to her lips. Oh, who was he trying to fool? He'd love to give them a taste. To hold her and care for her.

Wasn't going to happen. Brent pushed the door shut. "Where do you want this?" he asked Rosemary.

"Over by Steve. Thanks for bringing it in, Brent."

He grinned at her. "No problem." He set the basket down and nodded at Steve Nemesek.

"Have a seat, young man. How's the construction coming along?"

Brent guessed he wasn't needed anywhere else. He dropped into a chair near the older guy. "Pretty well, all things considered."

"Finnley!" shrieked Maddie. "Play with me." She slid off her grandfather's lap, ran to Finnley, and hugged him fiercely.

The little man allowed it, holding still until she let go. Then he followed her to the toy box across the room. Talk about progress.

"Too bad about the window factory."

Brent pulled his attention to Steve. "Yes. That set the project back by a couple of months. But we should have the first shipment about the end of June. Patrick separated the order into smaller parts so we'd get regular deliveries instead of all in one. First truckload will be for Allison's house." He poked his chin toward the little boy. "They need to get settled into their home as soon as possible."

Steve's gaze slid to Finnley. "Good call."

"Then the upper floor of the school building should arrive a couple of weeks later and, hopefully, the rest of them not long after."

"So you'll be doing finishing work for a while yet, I take it."

Brent grimaced, but inside he was pretty happy about it. More time for Finnley. More time for Allison. "You won't be rid of me around here until sometime in fall, I'm sure."

"Any call for a timber framer in the area permanently?"

Brent narrowed his gaze at Steve, who raised his eyebrows innocently enough.

"Or I heard you're a talented artist, too. Must be ways a guy could make a living in Galena Landing."

"I'm sure there might be." Brent kept his voice even. "But there's really no reason to. Patrick has enough projects farther south to keep me busy, probably for years to come."

Steve nodded, his gaze slipping past Brent's shoulder. "Well, it was just a thought. The area is in recovery, and a man with a vision is always a good thing."

A man with a vision. Brent could hardly hold back a snort. No one had ever hinted he was such a man before. But Steve was right in one way. The town was growing and a few other new houses were going up nearby. None as nice as Allison's, though they might be bigger.

"Wash up, everyone, and come to the table," called Claire.

Brent couldn't see Allison anywhere, but he knew Finnley's hands had been all over those cats. "Come on, squirt. Let's go wash our hands."

Chapter 20 ---

*F*innley's gaze kept going to Brent during the birthday meal. Didn't he remember who'd brought him to safety? Didn't he know who'd invited everyone over for his birthday party?

Not that Allison had invited Brent. Why should she? He'd been keeping his distance for a couple of weeks, proving that he didn't really care about her or Finnley. And no reason he should, of course. Contractor. Client. The lines were drawn.

But then he should leave her nephew alone. Shouldn't give the little guy false hope.

She didn't even want to consider what kind of expectations Finnley had. If he thought for one little minute that Brent was going to be a father figure in his life, the boy had another think coming.

Allison didn't need anyone. She never had. She'd been tough all her life, and Finnley had sprouted from the same soil. He didn't need Brent or anyone else. Besides her, of course. He was just a little kid. He needed clothes and food and shelter. Security. Love.

Down the table, Brent laughed at something Noel had said. His elbow rested on the back of Finnley's chair and, when the boy looked up, Brent grinned at him and tousled his hair. While replying to Noel.

Finnley didn't draw back.

This couldn't be happening. She needed to win Finnley back for his sake as well as her own. Brent was leaving. Her nephew was going to get hurt.

Like her.

Allison shoved the thought aside. Conversation buzzed all around the table, but she heard none of it. She scurried to the kitchen for more homemade fries. Claire had made those, using up the soft remains of last year's potatoes that hadn't been set aside for seed. She passed more rolls for the burgers Noel had grilled and filled another bottle of ketchup from the quart jar in the fridge. Made sure the raspberry vinegar pitcher stayed topped off. Hoped the sautéed asparagus held out.

"Sit, girl," said Rosemary. "You're wearing me out."

Allison glanced down the table at Finnley. "Just making sure everything's perfect."

Rosemary grabbed Allison's hand and tugged her into the chair she'd barely sat in. "It *is* perfect. We don't need you hovering like a hummingbird. You need to eat, too."

Eat? She probably should. She forked a beef patty to her plate but shook her head at the rolls. Too heavy.

A pair of tongs dropped fries beside the burger.

She hadn't planned to eat that many, but one couldn't simply say no to Rosemary. She added a few spears of asparagus and held her hand up when the older woman encouraged her to take more.

Maybe she should've sat beside Finnley and let others serve both of them. But then she'd be vying with Brent for her nephew's attention. Better to be at the opposite end of the table where it wasn't so obvious.

"He's settling in really well. "

Allison jerked her head to take in Claire on the other side of her. For an instant she wondered which *he* Claire meant. Finnley. Of course, Finnley.

"Yes, he is."

168

"He might like the baby chicks almost as much as he does the kittens. I loved the look of awe on his face when you put that yellow fuzz ball in his hands."

"The kittens are sturdier." Allison managed a smile. "I fear for the chicks when Maddie's around."

"I can't wait to hear him giggle," Claire went on. To start telling tales. To lead Maddie into trouble instead of following."

What? Allison stared at her friend.

Claire winked. "You know, be a normal kid." She flicked her gaze toward Finnley. "It's coming, I think."

"Isn't the goal to raise a kid that *won't* get into trouble?" Allison had tried to be that kind of child. It had found her anyway.

"He needs to have fun. He needs to grow some wings and not be afraid of being hit if he moves or opens his mouth." Claire grimaced. "Learning those boundaries in a healthy environment will involve making mistakes. Him, you… all of us. It's reality."

Rosemary leaned over. "You should have seen some of the scrapes that Zach and Gabe got into as boys. I sometimes despaired of keeping them alive to adulthood."

Zach? Jo had mentioned he wasn't perfect. Now his mother admitted it, too?

Claire's eyes brightened. "Do tell!"

"There was the time they went into the sheep pen to play with the lambs, and didn't latch the gate tightly when they came back out. By the time we noticed, the pen was empty."

"Oh, no." Allison could imagine the panic that must have caused.

"Sadie and Old Pete rounded up the sheep and lambs, but one of the lambs wasn't found until the next day. Poor thing barely survived a cold night alone in the rain."

"Sadie and Old Pete?" She hadn't heard the names of Zach's siblings before. Old Pete was a strange thing to call a boy.

"Our Border collies. Domino's parents. I raised and trained sheep dogs for years."

That made more sense.

"And then there was the time those boys decided to weed the garden for me. Their hearts were in the right place, bless them, but they didn't know the weeds from the seeds. We were low on vegetables but big on dandelions and other weeds that year."

Allison had to protest. "Dandelions aren't weeds, though. We've been enjoying the young greens sautéed."

Rosemary chuckled. "Weeds are any plants growing where they're not wanted. A daffodil would be a weed in the carrot patch, and onions are weeds in the rose garden."

"True." She hadn't thought of that before. Even good things could be negative in the wrong setting.

Like little boys looking up to a good man when the good man would never be a permanent part of his life. That was a weed she needed to dig out. But how? Maybe she'd have to let the weed wither of its own accord. It wouldn't last long once Brent had finished all he could do without windows. He'd be back later in the summer, though.

Her heart clenched. She'd never wanted a man to share her life with. She'd never wanted to fall in love. That was for insecure women, not her. Good thing Brent had walked away before she'd done something stupid. Like fall in love.

oOo

Along with everyone else, Brent watched Allison carry a lit birthday cake around the table toward Finnley.

"Look at that, squirt." He leaned closer to the little man. "Want to blow out the candles?"

Finnley cringed, shaking his head.

"That's what we do for birthdays. See? Four candles because you are four years old." No one needed to know where Brent had

170

been four years and nine months before.

The kid looked terrified. Even Allison noticed. She paused a few feet away, watching Finnley. "It's a birthday cake, buddy. To celebrate you're four now."

"Cake!" yelled Maddie. "Want some."

A few people chuckled.

Finnley glanced at Maddie then focused back on the flickering flames.

"Want me to take away the candles?" Allison asked.

Brent massaged the little guy's shoulder as he nodded, leaning closer to Brent.

"Okay." Allison's narrowed eyes certainly noticed his hand on her nephew, but she turned away and blew out the candles in one go.

"What, no boyfriend?" teased Noel.

Brent took a deep breath. Birthday candle lore said the number of candles left aflame after one attempt signaled how many boy-or-girlfriends the birthday person had. That wasn't going to go over well.

Allison's jaw clenched and her lips pursed. She tugged out the candles and set them in Jo's outstretched hand before glancing at Finnley again and all but running to the kitchen.

Silence.

"Oops," murmured Noel.

More than oops. If only Brent could follow her, but it was best if someone else did. Best if he stayed put and didn't draw further attention to her. Besides, he needed to stay with a worried-looking boy.

Claire followed Allison into the other room, followed by Rosemary.

Brent could hear low voices, then the clinking of cutlery on a plate. A few minutes later Claire emerged with a tray of plated cake slices, each with a scoop of ice cream.

Smiling, she set the first in front of the birthday boy. "Happy birthday, Finnley."

The boy glanced up at her then stared at the cake.

Brent caressed his shoulder. "Hey, that looks great. Look at all that chocolate. Can you say thank you to Claire, squirt?"

Finnley whispered, "Thank you."

If that was victory, he'd take it.

Claire passed the second slice to Brent then continued around the end of the table before going back for a second tray. Still no Allison or Rosemary. Man, he wasn't trying to hurt her by luring the boy away. A kid needed more than one adult in his life.

Brent pulled his hand away from Finnley and focused on having a bite of the cake in front of him.

What the boy needed was a daddy. Not his biological father, but some strong guy who could sweep Allison off her feet and love Finnley like his own. Surely that man existed. With all his heart, Brent wished it could be him, but there was no way.

Low chatter resumed around the table as forks clinked against plates. Even Finnley dug in. The cake tasted amazing, sweet and rich. This definitely hadn't come from a box.

After a while Allison reappeared and slipped into her chair with a sliver of cake in front of her. Her face was pale, and her red-rimmed eyes focused on her plate.

Brent's heart clenched. She'd been crying. Was it his fault, or only because the boy had seemed afraid of the candles? Had that pushed her over the edge?

Sierra leaned closer to Finnley from the other side. "Isn't that yummy cake?"

He flicked a glance at her and nodded, his fork poised for another bite.

"Say, that little orange striped kitten seems to really like you."

Another little nod.

"Does that kitten have a name?"

"Danny Boy," he whispered.

Brent froze. Somewhere deep inside he'd clung to the unlikelihood of this child belonging to him. Oh, he'd known, but that was different than *knowing*.

In the vague distance he was aware of Sierra exclaiming over how nice that was. "Where did you think up that name?"

A wave of nausea rocked Brent.

"Mama," Finnley whispered. "Sometimes she called me that."

Danny Boy. Mallory's sweet voice when she wanted something. Mockery when he put his foot down. Had it been a term of endearment after all?

"Daniel is his middle name." Allison's voice echoed through a week-long tunnel. "Finnley Daniel Hart."

Brent pushed back from the table, his chair grating on the etched concrete floor. Buzzing surrounded his head, whirled through it, clouding his vision and his thoughts. "Excuse me, please."

Was every eye fixed on him? Probably. He couldn't help it. He needed air. Escape. He'd known coming for birthday dinner was a mistake from the beginning. He'd been wrong. Much more than a mistake, it was a disaster.

He managed to get out the door and shut it without creating a scene. He gulped vast amounts of air as he hurtled up the path toward Allison's house where his truck was parked.

Be sure your sin will find you out.

Wasn't that in the Bible somewhere? But he'd repented in tears before the Lord. He'd been gut-wrenchingly sorry for the lifestyle he'd led for those ugly years. And God had forgiven him. He'd felt that soothing peace of being right with God. Forgiven. Redeemed. A fresh slate.

How could this be happening now? Would he rather be in ignorance of the results of his sex life? Yes. No. Finnley was a person, a sweet little boy who'd been abused and neglected. He wasn't a result. He was a human being.

And Brent was responsible for the fact that he existed.

His hands trembled so hard it took three tries before he could line the key up with the ignition slot. The truck rumbled to life. He shoved it into gear and jounced down the driveway between the trees. He only needed to get past the house and out on the road. Where would he go? Would he ever return? No clue.

He handled the curve at the bottom of the hill and slammed on the brakes. In the middle of the track stood a tall thin woman huddled in a long black cardigan.

Chapter 21 ---

*H*ad he even seen her? Was he going to run right over her?

Allison jumped to the side of the driveway. For a second she was sure he'd careen on by and disappear down Thompson Road with a diminishing roar. Instead he slammed on the brakes, skidding to a stop beside her. Dust billowed from under the tires.

His eyes looked at her wildly. His hands clenched the steering wheel so hard his knuckles were white and, even in those few minutes since he'd escaped from the house, he'd obviously run his hands through his hair enough times to stick it out all over.

She reached through the open window and touched his arm. "Brent? Are you okay?"

He flinched in the same way Finnley used to.

What on earth had happened in there? One minute he'd been laughing and talking with Noel, his fingers toying with Finnley's hair, and the next, he'd gotten a crazed look on his face and run.

He took a deep breath, but it didn't seem to help. "I'm leaving."

Like that wasn't obvious.

"What happened?" It couldn't all be about her anger at him showing Finnley the house without her. He'd seemed completely relaxed after that. It'd made her even madder.

Brent shook his head so hard she had to wonder what he was trying to dislodge. "Nothing I want to talk about," he choked out.

Her temper flared. "If it's about the house—"

"No. It's not you."

"Right."

He focused on her, but the wild look hadn't completely left his face. "It's true." He swallowed hard, and his Adam's apple bobbed. "There are more important things."

Allison reeled back. After all the talks they'd shared, the touches, the hugs? Now all of a sudden she wasn't important? She forced her hands to her sides. Forced her chin up to meet his gaze. "You bet there are more important things. If that's how you're going to be about it, you might as well leave."

Wait, was she firing her contractor? She couldn't do that. She jerked her head up the driveway. "Stay out of my way while you finish my house." She leaned a little closer to the truck. "And leave my nephew alone. No good can come of him looking up to you."

"We're agreed on that."

Show no shock. But it was impossible. This was the guy who'd slid into a relationship with Finnley without even half trying, from what she could tell. Now he agreed to ignore her nephew, just like that?

She jerked her chin. "Well, good, then." Allison stared at Brent.

He stared back. The craze faded from his eyes. Something washed across his face she couldn't catch — regret? — then his jaw tightened and his gaze hardened.

"Look, I—" Whatever he'd been about to say broke off when he shook his head. "No."

"What do you mean, no? If you're taking back leaving Finnley alone, I'll fire you." Oh man. How could she even do that? She leaned closer to the truck window. "Don't mess with my nephew." *Or with me.* But she couldn't say that.

Brent's head flicked from side to side. "Not that. You're right. I should've stayed clear of him. Getting him used to me, l-liking me... not a good idea."

The words made sense, but the reason he stated them did not. Why were these thoughts even going through his head? He'd never declared lo — affection for Allison. Why was Finnley such a big deal to him?

He closed his eyes as though in prayer. A moment later he looked at her again from those deep brown eyes. Haunted eyes.

Why?

"The guys and I will be done what we can do on both buildings in a couple of weeks. Then we'll be about six weeks before I'm back with the first batch of windows. From there, we'll be full blast until both are completed."

Allison nodded. Okay, back to contractor-client. She could do this.

"I'll do my best to stay out of your way. And, uh, Finnley's way. But when we're working on the school, it will be up to you to distract him. It's right there in plain sight of your home."

Something crossed his face again. Something was terribly wrong in Brent's world. Had he dropped a hint she'd missed?

She kept her voice as professional as possible. "I'll keep him busy."

Brent swallowed hard. "Okay. That's all we can do."

Wait a minute. "Why?" The word burst from her lips. "Why is this such a big deal? With Finnley, I mean."

She knew why it was for her. She'd been half in love with Brent Callahan. Maybe more than half. But he was making this all about Finnley, not about her. And that didn't make a lick of sense.

"Brent?" Oh, no. Maybe she'd softened her voice too much. Maybe he'd read something into that. Was there something to read?

He shook his head. "No."

For a brief, piercing instant she saw through his eyes and into his soul. She stepped closer, barely aware she did so, and rested her hand on his arm, locked into that gaze.

His right hand covered hers. Warm. Caressing. Possessive?

A breeze rippled across the farm as the sun dipped behind a cloud, chilling every part of her except the hand cushioned against him. Those eyes. Magnets. She sidled closer.

His breath warmed her face. "Allison."

She'd never wanted this. She tried to remind herself of what men were like. Unfaithful. Selfish. Overbearing. But not Brent. He was a rare breed. A man of honor. Someone she could trust, if only she could figure out what he was thinking. But that could happen later. She pressed against the door of the truck, she was so close.

His fingers swept the hair from the side of her face, and her hand cooled where his touch had left her. She leaned into his hand as it cradled her jaw. Then he slid his hand to the nape of her neck and tugged her closer yet. "Allison." This time her name sounded like a groan.

Their lips met with a gentle touch. Allison quaked. Leaning against the truck door barely kept her upright. She tangled her fingers in his shock of black hair as his left arm snaked around her, holding her. She angled her head to meet his lips more fully, to revel in their taste, to feel the hunger evoked in that simple touch. Her eyes fluttered shut so she could block all distractions and focus on the sensations cascading through her body.

She'd never imagined welcoming a kiss — from Brent or anyone else — but now she didn't want it to end. Ever. Whatever had made Brent run like Jane Eyre chased by Domino had galloped on by. There was only this moment. This perfect moment.

Other than the thick truck door separating them. She shifted again, as though that would remove the barrier, still clinging to him. "Brent," she murmured against his lips.

His grip tightened and for an instant his kiss grew more insistent. Then he released her. All of her.

The truck door held her up as she opened her eyes to gaze into his. But he wasn't looking at her. Both hands scrubbed his face as he bent over the steering wheel.

"Brent? Are you okay?"

o0o

Was he okay? Not even a little bit. It'd been years since he'd kissed a woman. He'd gleefully allowed passion to overwhelm him time and time again, not caring about the consequences.

One of his consequences sat in that straw bale house not far away. Close enough all the occupants had probably glued themselves to the wide windows and watched every moment since he'd nearly run Allison down.

Now he felt like he was the one who'd been hit by a truck. Oh, his body wasn't bruised. Not this time. But his lips surely were. And his heart. His soul.

Allison reached through the open window and captured his fingers. "Brent, talk to me."

Was there any way to keep his past swept under the rug and pretend it hadn't happened? He'd been doing that for over four years. But the past was still there, even when hidden. Ignored.

And a mature honorable man couldn't enter a relationship while living a charade. He couldn't. He forced his gaze to meet hers, and his resolve nearly vanished like a wisp of a spring breeze.

The wariness, the hardness that had always guarded her had fallen away. In her brown eyes he saw only trust. An awakening. He was going to send her back into that dungeon she'd lived in, where men were untrustworthy jerks.

Whether he left or stayed, whether he told her everything or not, the result was the same. He couldn't be the man she needed.

"Allison, I-I'm not the man you think I am."

She tilted her head to the side, her gaze still warm. But her jaw began to tense.

He couldn't resist touching it, trying to wipe away the tension, but she stepped back.

"What do you mean?" Her voice was soft, but the wariness had returned.

How could he do this to her? He thought of Finnley. He had to. He couldn't live with himself if he dragged Allison through this. And then she wouldn't be able to live with him, either.

There was no middle ground. He'd tried to find it, but there was nothing but a sand trap. A sinkhole. "Allison, I—" Was he really going to say this? But he had to. "I love you." He choked on the words. The only time in his life he'd understood what they meant and hadn't used them glibly. "But it can't work. You need someone stronger. Someone better."

Her arms crossed in front of her in the classic Allison move that portrayed she held herself up. Didn't need anyone. How well he knew her. How much more he longed to know her.

"I don't know what you mean."

He couldn't really say anything more without giving it all away. The end result would be the same regardless. He knew it with complete certainty. The only difference would be that then she'd *know*, and now she didn't. This way was better.

"I wish things were different." Different enough he could exit the truck and kiss her properly. Where they could plan a future together. "But they're not. Allison, I don't want to hurt you more. I-I love you too much." Loved Finnley too much.

"What's that supposed to mean?" The edge had returned to her voice. The softness left her eyes.

Ice crept into Brent's veins from his fingertips, from his toes, toward his core. "It means you're better off without me. Much better off."

Her chin rose. "What if I disagree?"

"You have to trust me." What a laugh. If she could trust him at all, these words — this parting — wouldn't be necessary. There was nothing to trust.

Her jaw flexed. She looked so alone, so vulnerable.

"I never meant to fall in love." He nearly managed to keep his voice steady. "But I have. I'm sorry, Allison. You deserve so much better." He shifted the truck into Drive.

She inhaled sharply. "Brent, no."

"I'll see if Patrick can come and finish the job." *Brilliant idea, Callahan. Seriously.* "Take care of that little man." He moved his foot to the accelerator, and the truck rolled forward. "Goodbye, Allison."

If he looked in the rearview mirror, she'd be standing there, arms tight around her middle, staring after him, with hurt and anger in her eyes.

He didn't look back.

Valerie Comer

Chapter 22 ---

f or two weeks, Allison tried not to watch Brent and his
workers saw, hammer, and drill their way around the school
building not far from her duplex. For two weeks she ignored
the quiver of Finnley's chin as he, too, watched from a distance,
obeying her, clutching the kitten to his chest. For two weeks, she
avoided talking to the other people who lived at Green Acres
Farm. Anything beyond, "yes," "no," and "thanks for dinner."

How could she have fallen for that man? He said he wasn't
the right guy for her — that she deserved better — but he didn't
know what she'd gone through. What her dad had done. The only
person who deserved better was Brent.

Then why didn't it feel like anyone was being done any
favors?

oOo

For two weeks, Brent tried to keep his gaze from slipping
toward the duplex beside the construction site. It nearly killed
him. Which was worse, seeing Finnley sitting on the stoop,
watching him with, Brent imagined, vulnerability in his brown
eyes, or seeing Allison shepherding Finnley into the duplex, into
her Camry, into the straw bale house?

The worst was that she didn't even glance his direction when she did it. She held her head high and looked anywhere but at him.

"You guys need to talk."

Noel's voice caught Brent by surprise. He didn't even bother asking who Noel meant. He knew. Everyone knew. They might as well have taken out an ad on the front page of the Galena Herald.

Brent shrugged. "We talked." At volume. And kissed. He'd relived that kiss a hundred times a day for two weeks.

"I don't like being caught in the middle. By rights, Allison should be the one over here going over the project with you and making decisions. Signing off."

"I know." He would not look toward the garden, where she weeded beside Claire. With her back to him, incidentally. "Sorry, man. It's just the way it is. Better this way."

Noel chuckled. "I doubt it's better. Do you want to talk about it?"

Wasn't the first time the other man had asked. The first time, Brent had hesitated. He was used to saying "no" now.

"Today's the last day for a while. Patrick refuses to let one of the other foremen take over once the windows come." He grimaced. "So I'll be back."

"Smart man." Noel ran his fingers along a post that Brent had planed with his own hands.

He wanted to see the school bustling with eager students in the worst way. Wanted to see Allison's joy in her new home. See Finnley slide down that banister. See his son grow up. Not just watch from a distance, but experience it. Dwell within it, every single day.

"Being as you won't tell me what's going on, let me tell you a bit about myself." Noel dropped onto a giant roll of electrical wire.

Like Brent didn't have anything to do to wrap up the project? He crossed his arms over his chest and surveyed the other guy.

"It seems to me your faith is solid."

Brent nodded, even though it felt anything but. Yes, he clung to God every single day, but only because the waves of despair threatened to wash him away. God was his anchor. If he let go, all hope was gone.

Noel picked up a pair of electrical stripping pliers and turned them over in his hands. "I didn't have that. My mom took my sister and me to Sunday school when I was a kid, but I bailed as soon as I could. Wanted nothing to do with an old peoples' religion, you know?"

"Yeah, I kind of did the same. It didn't seem relevant in the face of football or parties."

"I wandered. A lot. I lived for myself. Whatever felt good at the time. After I started Enterprising Reforestation I realized I needed to make some changes or I was going to end up on the streets like my father. A guy couldn't run a business if his head was muddled with alcohol."

"Yeah." Brent had heard bits of Noel's story before.

"So I quit drinking. Gradually pulled back from the whole scene. Some of it just wasn't fun anymore when I wasn't half-smashed."

Brent grimaced. "I can relate."

"I was pretty proud of myself. Still didn't need God. I'd done it myself. The self-made man and all."

That's where his story and Noel's diverged, then. Obviously Noel's path hadn't been as wrong as Brent's. Brent had known beyond a shadow of a doubt that he couldn't save himself from it. He'd thrown himself at the mercy of a loving God. God had forgiven him.

Forgiving himself was harder.

Facing consequences was harder yet.

"It wasn't until after I met Claire that I began to see Christianity as something other than an escape hatch from eternal damnation. I was determined not to believe for her sake, you know?"

Brent knew, all too well.

"But it was God reeling me in." Noel chuckled. "Like a big sucker fish on a line. He let me pretend I was free, but the lure had been set and, sooner or later, He'd reel me in." Noel met Brent's gaze. "I'm so thankful He did. Changed my whole life, and I don't just mean selling my business, marrying Claire, and moving to Green Acres. Those might be the biggest outward changes, but inside... that's where the magic happened."

"I get it, man. I do." Brent had to choose his words carefully. Not give away too much to this man he could see being a real friend. A brother.

"Allison's changed a lot since she came three months ago. She's softened."

Brent leaned over, grabbed a hammer off the concrete floor, and jammed it into his tool belt. "Softened?" He couldn't keep the bitterness out of his voice, even while he knew Noel spoke truth. He'd seen the vulnerability. She'd tried to open up to him.

Noel chuckled. "Yeah. You notice she's wearing some color these days? Finnley told her his favorite color was yellow."

Yearning flooded Brent. "Finnley's talking?"

"More every day, but I doubt he'll ever be as loud as Madelynn."

Brent forced a grin. "Hard to imagine that."

"The two of them have picked nearly every dandelion on the property, until Sierra is protesting there's no blossoms left for the honeybees. There are flowers in jars and vases all over the farm."

Several times Brent had arrived in the morning to find two or three dandelions on the school floor. They'd been droopy. Dead. Had they been meant as a gift from a small boy who looked up to him? Who looked up to a man who, while he was his father, didn't deserve to be looked up to?

Brent closed his eyes. Yes, God forgave, but sin still had consequences.

What had Noel said? Oh, yes. About the children picking dandelions. "That's cute."

Noel's brows furrowed. "What?"

"The dandelions."

"We're having them for dinner."

Brent couldn't stop the guffaw. "You're what?"

"I promised Finnley. We're making dandelion pesto." Noel's eyes twinkled. "Adding leaves to the salad. Digging up some roots to dry and make tea."

"They're just weeds, man."

"That's where you're wrong. There's no such thing as just weeds. Every plant has a purpose. Claire's been teaching me that. Sierra, too. She's the herbalist, after all. A weed is simply a plant that grows where it's not wanted."

"Yeah, okay. But dandelions?"

"A French delicacy. They breed them. Grow them commercially."

"You've been in the sun too long."

Noel laughed as he stood and stretched. "Not so, Callahan. It's the truth."

"That's crazy." He'd have to look it up online. Not that he suspected Noel was purposefully lying to him. But pulling his leg, maybe.

Noel socked him in the arm. "There's a lesson in that."

Brent raised his eyebrows.

"There's no such thing as a weed. Even all the stuff in my past I wish I could undo, it's just like dandelions."

Best not let this get too deep. "You can cook them and eat them?"

"Maybe." Noel laughed. "But they all have a purpose in my life. For me, they were ugly mistakes. I didn't care who I hurt there for a while. It was all about me. But God was still in control, you know? Romans eight twenty-eight."

"All things work together for good..."

Noel nodded. "Grab hold of it, man. Whatever happened between you and Allison, believe that God can work it out for good."

That would be easier to do if what had happened was between him and Allison. But not with Mallory in the mix. Not with Finnley.

oOo

Every place at the farmhouse table was marked with a small jar of dandelions. The kids had been busy. Many of the stems were nonexistent. Maddie's work, no doubt.

Allison laughed. It felt freeing. Noel had handed her the signed-off papers on the house and school. She now had six entire weeks of not seeing Brent. This was good. Finnley would get over him. She'd get over him. Life would be normal for a while.

Without her classrooms built, but normal. Everything would come together in its own good time.

"Hello the house!"

Allison, being nearest, went to the door and opened it. A scruffy man with tied-back red hair stood on the other side. Wearing bicycle shorts? That was all kinds of wrong.

"Have I found the famed Green Acres Farm at long last?"

She blinked. "Um, yes, this is Green Acres. How may I help you?"

He beamed. "To think I have arrived at long last. So far it is from the City of Angels."

This dude was a certifiable nutcase. Her gaze slid past him to a bicycle with a little trailer hitched on behind. Hmm. She ought to get one of those for Finnley to ride in, actually. Wait. This guy had come from where? "You biked here from Los Angeles?"

"Indeed."

"Are we expecting you?" If so, no one had bothered to tell her, or she'd been so wrapped up in the could-have-beens with Brent the words hadn't registered.

"Alas, no one knew of my coming."

Plain English, buster. This was a farm, not a Shakespearean event.

"Someone at the door?"

Whew. Noel could handle this dude. Allison stepped aside. "Yes. This guy has apparently biked from L.A. looking for Green Acres."

Noel thrust his hand out. "Noel Kenzie. And you are?"

The guy shook it firmly. "Keanan Welsh." His gaze settled on Allison. "And this lovely lady is your wife?"

He was crazy. Had to be. But it was nice to be called a lovely lady.

Noel laughed. "My wife is inside. This is our friend Allison. Come on in."

Just like that? Now they were welcoming tramps off the street? Well, off the dirt road. This guy could be anyone. Some weed-smoking peace-loving convict. Allison snuck him a glance.

His clear green eyes snagged hers, twinkling. Didn't look so drugged. Or like a madman. But still.

"Join us for dinner, Keanan? We're having dandelions." Noel laughed. "And a few other things. There's plenty."

"It would be my great pleasure. I haven't feasted on dandelions since last year. Is there a place I might wash up?"

Her first impression had been correct. The guy was a kook, but at least one willing to be clean. "There's a tap right over here."

Chapter 23

Keanan had pitched his tent up the hillside. He dug a latrine, and he and Noel erected an outhouse over it with scrap wood from the building site. Apparently the guy could drive a team of horses, and Zach had delegated the responsibility of reseeding the north pasture to him.

In the evenings, Keanan sat cross-legged in front of a campfire, strumming his guitar. It seemed he'd moved in, at least for the time being.

"I have an apology to make," he said to Allison one evening when the flames and music had drawn the group together.

"Oh? What's that?"

"My complaint at the great distance from the City of Angels." His fingers danced across the strings as he spoke, the notes speeding up as they climbed. "If Green Acres were closer, it would be more likely to be tainted. Instead it is fresh and pure, the mountain air bracing and refreshing. God's peace abounds here."

Allison locked her fingers together and stretched her arms in front of her until her knuckles cracked. "I understand. I grew up in Portland." The city itself was more peaceful than L.A., but nothing like here. Now that Brent was gone and life settled into a routine of planting and weeding and caring for Finnley, she couldn't wish to be anywhere else.

oOo

"Patrick?" Brent poked his head around his uncle's office door. "Do you have a few minutes?"

Patrick pushed blueprints aside. "For you, anytime. What can I help you with?"

"About finishing the job at Green Acres Farm..."

His uncle sighed. "Haven't we been over this? We'll lose too much momentum on two jobs if I switch you out with Dale. Your crew is used to working with you, and Dale's guys with him. And moving the whole crew is an even worse idea, because then no one will know what's going on. On either job site."

Brent hadn't thought through how much it would cost the company. How much it would disrupt other people's lives.

"You know I love you like my own son. I'd do anything for you." Patrick held up his hand. "But I have a dual responsibility here. One is to Timber Framing Plus and our clients. And the other is to you."

Brent dared to meet his uncle's gaze.

"You need to find yourself a wife, lad. Settle down. Once you've got that taken care of, you'll find these contracts to be mere business. A job to do well. A way to make a living and meet your family's needs."

As though it was simply something a guy could check off a list. Three rolls of electrical wire. Check. Twenty-eight lengths of half-inch copper tubing. Check. One wife. Check.

Allison Hart. Check.

"Maybe this is the one?"

Time suspended. Collapsed. "I wondered that myself for a bit," Brent admitted. "But it's more complicated than that."

"It always seems so."

Brent closed his eyes for an instant and breathed a prayer. "She's taken custody of her young nephew."

"And that's a problem how? You love kids, or so I always thought."

"Her nephew... is my son." Brent's voice choked as he stared at his hands, clenched in his lap.

"Oh." The springs in Patrick's desk chair creaked as he leaned back. "Is this supposition or fact?"

"Fact," whispered Brent. *Danny Boy.*

"Does she know?"

He shook his head.

"That would be a good place to start," Patrick said mildly.

"Allison doesn't trust men. The little bit of trust I've earned was hard won." The memory of that kiss would be forever imprinted on his lips. And his heart.

"So you've decided to make the decision for her. Just walk away before she finds out."

"To protect her. To protect Finnley."

"Look at me, son." Patrick leaned forward. "Is she an adult?"

A full woman in every way that counted. He nodded.

"Why is it your job to shield her by withholding facts from her? Is that really protection?"

Brent's clenched fingers demanded his full attention.

"Or is it your pride getting in your way?"

Ouch. He shot a glance at his uncle, only to discover compassion in his brown eyes.

"I made such a mess of my life, Patrick, and yet it never occurred to me that there might be a child out there imprinted with my features." He swallowed hard. Licked his suddenly dry lips. "What if... what if Finnley isn't the only one?"

"Son, have you confessed your sin to God?"

"You know I have."

"Has He forgiven you?"

Brent nodded.

"Then forgive yourself."

"That's not the problem. It's the consequences. Forgiveness doesn't get rid of the results." What was he saying? That he'd rather Finnley didn't exist? No. Yes? Just thinking about it made his head hurt. His heart seize.

"What's keeping you from telling Allison?"

"What will she think of me?"

Patrick shook his head. "Why does it matter?"

Brent pulled in a long shaky breath. "Because..." He tried again. "Because I could... maybe... love her."

His uncle steepled his hands. "That changes things."

Miserable, Brent nodded.

"Does she know how you feel?"

Did she? Had she felt the passion in that kiss as much as he had? He'd said the words. Not once, but twice. "Yes."

Patrick jerked to his feet and strode to the window. "Brent. Don't tell me you fired that at her on your way out the door."

He closed his eyes. "Pretty much."

"Then you're a fool. You know that? A fool. When you love a woman, you don't walk away just because it's difficult. The love of a lifetime is worth fighting for. If it's going to fail, don't you be the one making it happen."

"She's been hurt so much, already." Whatever had happened in her past to create so much distrust, he couldn't even begin to imagine. But with his son, he knew. "Finnley, too," he choked out. "He's better off without me."

Patrick loomed over Brent's chair. "Do you really believe that any child is better off without his father? A man who loves God and cares deeply for his child?"

"But—"

"Brent, think. Think of all you went through because your father left the family. What did it do to you?"

"It tore me apart." Still did.

"How can this child not deserve to have a relationship with his dad?"

"He's never known a father." Brent surged to his feet. "From what Allison says, his mother had a new live-in every few months." He'd been one of those. The only one, apparently, to implant a child in her.

"I repeat. Does he not deserve a father now? The past is past, Brent. Yours and his both. All there is is the future. He's what, four, you said? He's got a lot of years to go. Years you could make a huge difference in."

"But—"

"And you love the woman who has custody of him." Patrick flung his hands in the air. "You are making no sense to me, boy."

There was no way in heaven or on earth that Allison would listen to his entire sordid tale and accept him anyway. None. He had an imagination. He'd had an imaginary friend like Finnley did. Kefir. But he didn't have enough imagination to see any positive outcome from laying it all out for her.

On the other hand, he'd already lost her. He'd pushed her aside himself. For the first time in two weeks, he wondered what she thought the reason was. Did she suspect? Her only clue was that both were Korean. Far from conclusive, of course. There was no shortage of Koreans in this world.

"Brent, my boy. You've got nothing more to lose."

o0o

Sierra and Gabe's wedding loomed. The pace at Green Acres picked up as the garden needed weeding and the early strawberries ripened. Finnley spent long hours with Keanan, perched on the back of one of the huge Percherons as they circled the field next door.

Allison tried to tell herself it was the wedding she was looking forward to. She'd never been involved in preparation of one before. They'd prepared gallons of rhubarb punch for the freezer. Poured clear golden honey into miniscule jars, topped with tiny paper bees for wedding favors. Baked baguettes, squares, and the bases for petit fours. Nurtured the flowers beside the pole barn where the ceremony was to take place.

What would it be like to prepare for her own wedding? And that's all it took to send her mind chasing Brent again. Wondering what he was doing, whether he was thinking about her, what would happen when he returned to the jobsite, windows in tow, the Monday after the wedding.

Whether there was a chance in the world they could get past this roadblock. Wondering if she wanted to. Changing her mind a dozen times a day.

Was this love? He'd said the words then taken them back. They were still true. Weren't they?

But if she expected Brent to say what held him back, wouldn't he expect the same from her? How could she share the most secret, shameful bits of her past? Become open and vulnerable? He'd already rejected her, even without knowing all that. The knowledge couldn't reverse it. It would only drive a deeper stake.

If only she could block him from her mind, but he'd been gone over a month now, yet was still at the forefront of her mind every minute of every day.

Finnley loved to listen to Keanan's guitar, haul Danny Boy around, play with Maddie, and follow the men around the farm. But when nothing else was going on, she'd find him sitting glumly in the vacant school building, or, once, up at the unfinished house, dandelion stems tufted with white fluff clutched in his little brown hands.

He missed Brent, too.

And when Brent returned, nothing would have changed. He'd do his job, complete the buildings over taunting months, and disappear again, this time for good.

She should consider a man like Keanan. A gentle, poetic guy who didn't demand, didn't argue, didn't make her pulse race. She liked him. So did Finnley.

What had happened to her plans to do life alone, her and a guard dog, until she was eighty? Was it only because Finnley needed a father figure? No. If she were being really, really honest, it was all Brent's fault.

It was Brent or no one. But at what cost, either way?

Valerie Comer

Chapter 24 ---

*I*t is so good to see you again!" Chelsea bounced in front of Allison. "How's farm life treating you?"

Sierra's sister obviously wanted a hug. Somehow, Allison wasn't as adverse to those as she'd once been. She laughed and held out her arms.

Chelsea beamed and gave her a tight squeeze. "And your nephew is adorable. Sierra says he's come a long way since he got here?"

Allison nodded. "He really has." Not that he jumped into her arms of his own volition yet, but he allowed brief hugs and pats on the way by.

"How's your sister doing?"

Allison stared at Chelsea blankly. "My sister? She's in prison."

"I know, but how's she doing on the inside? Does she miss Finnley?"

"How would I know?"

Chelsea searched her face. "You... there hasn't been any contact?"

Allison tightened her arms around her waist. "No."

"Oh. I just wondered. I thought she might like to hear from you. I know you haven't been close like Sierra and me—"

Allison snorted.

"—But she's still your sister."

"Half-sister."

Chelsea shrugged. "Your sister in every way that mattered. You grew up together." She grinned. "Probably stole each other's clothes."

"Not really." Lori had dressed like a hooker as young as she could get away with it. She'd always sought the attention. Allison? She'd rather have stayed hidden. Even that hadn't worked.

"I've been praying for your sister. Do you know if her prison has a chaplain?"

Allison stared at her friend, emotions awash. Guilt that she'd shoved every thought of Lori out of her mind. Hadn't really prayed for her — much — now that she'd gotten Finnley. Hadn't thought to wonder about her sister's spiritual needs.

She used to pray for her. What happened? Had she only cared about Finnley and not her own sister? But Lori had made her choices and dragged Finnley along. It hadn't been the little guy's fault. Only his mother's.

Was there any chance Lori was a victim, too?

Victims came in so many sizes and shapes. Some hid everything better than others. Allison should know. She was a hider.

She tried to imagine telling Brent the real details of her growing up years. He'd rejected her already for far less.

"Allison?"

Her gaze snapped back to Chelsea's concerned face. "I, uh, I don't know if there's a chaplain. I've been rather busy with the building projects and Finnley, and I haven't given much thought to Lori." She stared at the floor. "You must think me a terrible person."

"Of course not."

The awkward silence belied that.

"Where is the little guy, anyway?"

"Out in the field with Keanan." Allison shielded her eyes and looked out past the plum trees, all leafed out now. The team was out of sight at the moment, probably at the north end of the field. "He loves riding on the horses."

"Keanan?" Chelsea glanced at Allison. "Sierra told me a bit about him. So he's living here now?"

Allison shrugged. "If you can call living in a tent anything permanent. He just showed up one day and offered to work for food and a place to pitch his tent."

"Sounds weird."

"He's basically a leftover hippie, I guess. Nice enough guy. We often all gather around in the evening and sing along with him and his guitar."

"Does he spend a lot of time with Finnley?"

"Quite a bit." Allison caught Chelsea's gaze. "Why? Do you think that's a problem?"

"I don't know. Is it? How well do you really know him? And after all your nephew has been through…"

"Trust me, Finnley's radar is better than most. He adores Keanan, and there's no way he'd go anywhere near him if Keanan didn't treat him right."

A grin deepened Chelsea's dimple. "He adores him, does he? How about you?"

"He doesn't show affection for me, really. He—"

Chelsea chuckled. "That's not what I meant, and you know it."

"Huh?" Allison met her friend's gaze.

"Do you adore Keanan, too?" Chelsea's elbow caught Allison's ribs.

The horses plodded back into view in the distance, cutting hay on Steve and Rosemary's land next door. The big man with bushy red hair walked behind them, handling the reins. Did she adore him?

Allison chose her words carefully. "He's really sweet and well-educated. He spent the past ten years working on organic farms around the world, learning and making a difference. I can't tell you anything I don't like about him, but he doesn't make my heart speed up."

She'd caught him looking at her a few times, with something like speculation evident. Not calculating, really. Just wondering. She wondered, too.

"Well, he lives in a tent, so I guess he's not really up to standard anyway."

Allison shot Chelsea a look. "That's not it. Not at all."

Chelsea's eyebrows went up.

"No, really. He's given up the trappings of wealth to make a difference in the world. I admire that in him. And honestly, if I were in love with him, I have more than enough money for the both of us. He's poor by choice, not because he's a lazy bum. Look at him." Allison pointed out across the pasture. "He works hard, but he isn't consumed by work. He takes time to enjoy it."

"He'll probably disappear again in a whim, anyway."

Allison shrugged. "He might, I guess." Was that why she held back from Keanan? No. She simply wasn't attracted to him. Brent, on the other hand... even the thought of his name increased her heart rate, and she hadn't seen the guy in over a month. The only message she'd had from him had confirmed the date of the windows' arrival and his return to the job site. She'd read even that a dozen times, looking for nuances.

"So when are you moving to the farm? I know you wanted to come almost as much as I did."

Chelsea grimaced. "Every time I set a date, something comes up. I get hired to plan a large event or something. Right now I'm trying to set a solid break for September."

Allison chuckled. "Be more like Keanan. He just showed up."

"Yeah. I'm not that kind of impulsive. I'm hoping September will work. Every time I come to Green Acres, it seems to fill a bit of my soul, and I wonder what's taking me so long. You know what I mean?"

Allison nodded. "Yeah, I know." She took a deep breath of the forest-scented air. "I don't ever want to leave."

"Now you sound like Claire." Chelsea chuckled.

"Noel gets her off the farm once in a while. Mostly into the high mountains, though. They have quite a few guiding trips lined up for fall."

"Sierra said they'd turned down a fishing trip with a group of German men for this week."

"Yeah. It would have required them to miss Sierra and Gabe's wedding. That wasn't an option. The German guys hired a company in Colorado instead."

"Well, one day I'll move here, too. Right now I'd have to live with Claire and Noel in the big house with Sierra getting married. That's fine for a few days for a visit, but not long term."

Allison laughed. "I get it. But you could always pitch a tent."

"And freeze to death all winter? I don't think so." Chelsea poked a chin in Keanan's direction. "Dude there will have to make other plans, too. I can't believe someone would just wander onto a farm, uninvited and unannounced, and act like he belonged."

"Methinks you should meet our Keanan." Allison took Chelsea's arm.

"Uh, no. I'm thinking not."

oOo

Keanan's guitar plucked out love songs in the hushed pole barn. Sierra's brother, Jacob, and Noel seated the last few wedding guests that straggled in, then Jacob seated his mother.

Allison's pulse quickened. She'd watched this romance develop last fall when she'd visited Green Acres a few times. Gabe and Sierra'd had baggage, too. Different than Allison's, but baggage all the same. And who knew what Brent's problem was? Could it be worse than Gabe's struggle with mourning his first wife, who'd died in a vehicle accident? Could it be worse than Sierra's struggle with depression and her cancer scare?

And yet, here they were.

Gabe stood at the front of the pole barn with Zach beside him, best friends since childhood, as Chelsea strolled down the aisle as maid-of-honor. Neither Jo nor Claire showed any signs of jealousy that Sierra had chosen her sister for the privilege instead of them.

Who would she choose? Who was she that close to? Certainly not Lori, though Chelsea's words niggled in the back of her mind.

Not that it mattered. She wasn't getting married. There was only one man for her, and he'd pushed her aside.

Of course, Gabe had thought there was only one woman for him. He'd been happily married. He and his wife had been expecting their first child when she died.

The light on Gabe's face as Keanan switched to the strident wedding march could not be denied. Allison stood with the others and watched Sierra walk down the aisle on her father's arm, her white gown barely brushing the gravel path, her gaze never leaving Gabe's.

It was obviously possible to love again. Maybe, in time, Allison could set thoughts of Brent aside and fall in love with a man who loved her and Finnley. Whatever had happened to her vow to remain single? What had happened to her belief that all men cheated like pond scum?

The men in this barn had changed her. Noel. Zach. Gabe. Steve. She didn't know most of the others, but Gabe's parents were here all the way from Romania, where they were missionaries. They'd been together for a lot of years, too.

Keanan's guitar slowed as Sierra and her dad stopped in front of Pastor Ron. The music dwindled and faded.

Allison studied Keanan's face, visible for once as he'd tied his mass of hair back with a leather lace. He wore a white shirt and, Allison knew, his best jeans. Could she love Keanan?

He must've felt the heat from her gaze because he glanced her way. A slow grin crossed his face and one green eye closed in a wink.

No tingle. No spark. Not even a flush of embarrassment.

She grinned at him and turned her attention back to the ceremony as Sierra's dad laid his daughter's hand into Gabe's. Tim Riehl slid into the seat beside his wife and draped his arm around her shoulder. She dabbed her eyes as she glanced at him, then leaned against him.

Yeah, Allison's parents would have been all about the society pages. Who was present. How expensive the whole event was and how much it would raise their standing in society. Dad would have had an apoplectic fit if he'd seen Keanan's wink or the look that passed between him. That was probably why Allison even entertained the thought.

"We are gathered here today to join this man and this woman together in holy matrimony."

Had she ever been to a wedding like this? Not the farm setting, of course. But where everything was tasteful and elegant yet understated. Where the focus was on the marriage before God instead of the societal maneuvering.

Pastor Ron spoke of true love. Patient. Kind. Not envious or boastful or proud. Not dishonoring of others.

Dishonor. What did that even mean? Her father had certainly dishonored her. He hadn't exhibited any of the traits Pastor Ron spoke of, not to his wife, not to his daughters. It had all been about him.

Sierra's mom nestled her head against her husband's shoulder, as his arm snugged her tight. Across the aisle, tears rolled down Gabe's mother's cheeks. She and her husband clutched their hands together. Beside them sat Gabe's former mother-in-law, a widow herself. If that genuine smile on her face wasn't strange, nothing was. Next to Doreen, Steve's arm surrounded Rosemary.

Love could last a lifetime, even in the face of huge changes.

Which of these people could have seen the difficulties ahead? But it didn't matter. The evidence was clear. Trials had brought them even closer together. They faced things as one. United.

Love always protects. Always trusts. Always hopes. Always perseveres. Never fails.

This passage spoke of God's love to mankind, Pastor Ron explained. Yet it gave a standard for human love to stretch for. No one could reach it. Words like "never" and "always" made the goal unattainable, but with prayer and commitment, a couple could come closer and closer to the ideal God had laid out.

Beside Allison, Jo wiped her eyes. Allison caught Zach watching his wife from the front of the pole barn, his own eyes bright. At the end of their row, Noel had slipped in beside Claire and tucked her firmly to his side.

Marriage as an example of Jesus' love for the church was not something Allison had really thought about before. Did she actually love Brent? Her heart sped at the thought of him, at the memory of the kiss they'd shared. But that couldn't be enough.

Which kind of guy was Brent? The kind she'd always believed all men were? Or the rare breed that seemed to hang around Green Acres — a man who could love like Pastor Ron talked about?

To find out, she'd have to risk herself. Be vulnerable. Her gut froze at the very thought. Brent had already pushed her aside. How had she become desperate enough to consider going back for more of the same?

No. Brent wasn't that kind of man. He needed to know how she felt. If he rejected her anyway, well, that was his problem. She'd always know she'd tried her.

Her heart lightened. Yes, it would be hard, and it might backfire. It wasn't that she wanted to bare her soul to him… or to anyone. But, looking around her as Pastor Ron introduced for the first time, Mr. and Mrs. Gabriel and Sierra Rubachuk, it seemed worth the risk.

Chapter 25 ---

*S*ix weeks of working on an eight thousand square-foot mansion overlooking Lake Coeur d'Alene had been plenty long enough for Brent. What did anyone need that much space for, unless they had ten kids or ran a bed-and-breakfast? The client agonized over marble versus granite on the countertops, over walnut versus cherry on the floors, over every chandelier, sconce, and nightlight. Dale Everly treated the client with all the deference of a good foreman with Timber Framing Plus.

Maybe Patrick had done Brent a favor, sending him to Galena Landing and Allison Hart.

Brent knew he had.

He left his room in the Landing Pad early Monday morning, telling Franco and Curtis he had some things to check at the building site. The guys smirked at each other.

Brent would ignore that. Yeah, the windows wouldn't arrive for another hour or so — Patrick had called when the truck left Coeur d'Alene — but Brent couldn't wait that long to reacquaint himself with Green Acres Farm. To catch a glimpse of Finnley. And Allison.

Would he get up the nerve to tell her everything? He'd try.

207

He pulled into the farm driveway. So many extra cars. Several motor homes. Even some tents. It took him a few seconds to remember that Sierra and Gabe's wedding had taken place two days before.

He hadn't been invited. But why should he have been? Yeah, the men at the farm had extended friendship to him beyond the foreman/client relationship, but they'd probably been waiting to see how things developed with him and Allison. And when there was nothing, he'd been dropped.

No, it was his own fault for bolting from Finnley's birthday party like he'd been shot out a pneumatic nail gun.

Brent parked in front of the farm school. He closed his eyes. *Lord? This is all beyond me. I don't know how to do this.*

Sometimes a guy had to fling himself off a cliff and pray for the best.

A middle-aged couple exited a motor home and crossed to the straw bale house.

Sometimes a guy had to wait for the best time to jump off a cliff. Wait until the farm had resettled into its routine. He wasn't backing out. Just being selective of the best time to find Allison and apologize.

The apologizing wouldn't be that hard. It was the explaining that would kill him.

oOo

Finnley knelt on the ottoman, staring out the front window at an acute angle.

"What's there, buddy? What do you see?"

"Brent," he whispered.

Allison's heart surged into her throat. She'd known he'd be back today. She had barely slept all night and gotten up early to shower and spend some quiet time with her Bible open.

Brent. He was here.

"That's cool, buddy. Soon we'll be able to move into our house beside Maddie's. That'll be nice, won't it?"

The house that had been planned for one person and a dog. And would now contain two people… but probably not a dog. And which she wished would hold three people. Maybe, some day, more.

Finnley glanced into his bedroom, where the mural on his wall was in plain view.

"Are you going to miss the farm picture Brent painted, buddy? Maybe we can ask him to paint another in your new room."

"He promised."

Allison tilted her head. He what? "Did he tell you?"

Finnley nodded, peering back out the window. "He makes Rover."

Her nephew hadn't mentioned his imaginary dog in weeks. Allison crossed the room and sat on the chair nearest the window. "How is Rover doing since you came to Green Acres?"

The little shoulder lifted in a slight shrug.

"Do you like it here now? Playing with Maddie and riding the horse with Keanan? Living with me?"

She almost missed that wee nod. Finnley turned wistful eyes to her. "See Brent?"

Her heart clenched. "Remember you can't go in there without a hard hat."

"But he's not working."

Must've been the longest sentence he'd come up with yet. "True. Well, ask him then."

Finnley slid off the ottoman and headed for the door. He fumbled with the knob for an instant then stepped outside, pulling the door shut behind him.

Allison took his place on the ottoman, watching as he crossed the yard toward Brent's truck. Brent opened the truck door and slid out. He noticed Finnley and crouched down, arms wide.

Finnley ran into them and wrapped his arms around Brent's neck, holding tight while Brent rose and swung him in a circle.

This was what a family could look like. Her and Finnley and Brent. She'd never marry a guy who didn't love her nephew like his own son, but Brent could. Look at him grinning into the boy's face.

It would be hard to tell him about her past, but she'd do it. For Finnley's sake. And maybe, for Finnley's sake, Brent would hold off judgment on her, and accept them both into his life.

She turned away from the window and walked to the bathroom. She brushed her hair and checked her makeup. Time to follow Finnley to the unfinished school building.

Time to follow her heart.

o0o

Brent set the little boy on the ground and ruffled his hair.

Finnley looked up at him with big brown eyes that dissolved his heart. This child was worth the attempt to set things right with Allison. Not that Brent would humble himself before her only for the boy's sake. Not at all.

He loved her.

He knew it now. Having Finnley would be the icing on the cake, the cherry on top, the mural on the wall. But it wouldn't do the little man any good to woo his aunt without love.

Not a problem. Love was definitely present. If only it wasn't for Mallory. How would Allison take that?

Brent sensed as much as heard or saw Allison leave the duplex. She stood on the stoop, her lean body clad in two shades of gray with a yellow scarf around her waist, like a chain of dandelions. She stood, arms around her middle, watching him. Waiting.

"Come on, squirt. Let's go talk to your aunt." She wouldn't shut the door on him, would she? No, then she wouldn't have come outside at all. Unless Finnley had come outside without her permission, and she just wanted the boy out of Brent's clutches.

He'd take his chances. He walked toward her, his hand on the back of Finnley's head. The little man seemed willing to be guided back. Brent stopped several feet away from her. Far enough away that he couldn't hold her and kiss her without consciously moving a few steps closer. He soaked up the sight of her. "Allison."

She offered a tremulous smile. "Hi, Brent."

All the things he'd said to her six weeks ago rocketed through his mind for the millionth time. "I-I'm sorry for the way I left that day."

Her gaze slid to Finnley, who looked from one to the other. "I'm sorry, too."

His heart surged. That was a good sign, right? Not that she had anything to be sorry for. It was all him. He was the one with the nasty icy wave waiting to slosh over them all. He was the one who'd closed the doors back then, trying to forestall the wave. "I need to talk to you."

The door to Sierra's duplex next door opened and a curly-haired blond woman strolled out. Her quick gaze took in the three of them but, instead of going back inside or heading across to the big house, she closed the few steps between them.

"Hi, I'm Chelsea Riehl, Sierra's sister. You must be the guy from Timber Framing Plus?" She held out her hand.

He shook it. "Yes, Brent Callahan. Pleased to meet you." He glanced at Allison, but she was looking down. At what, he couldn't tell. Maybe at the toe of her sandal tracing the edge of the concrete step.

"I'm going over to the big house for breakfast. You coming?" Chelsea held out her hand to Finnley, but her eyes were on Allison.

"I'll be there in a few minutes. Want to go with Chelsea, Finnley?"

The little man's head shook, hair brushing against Brent's hand.

"Okay, then. I'll see you in a few. Nice to meet you, Brent."

"Likewise."

Chelsea strolled away. Brent looked back at Allison. "You okay?"

She lifted her chin and looked him in the eye. "Not sure."

Brent ran his fingers through the soft hair of his son. "Maybe... maybe this evening I could take you for a drive down along the lake?"

"I'll see if someone can sit with Finnley for a little while."

"Sounds good." It sounded way more than good. It sounded like a hopeful start to a new beginning. One where he was honest with her, laying out his whole sordid past, and seeing if she wanted anything to do with him afterward.

The result could be bliss, or it could herald several months of misery as he worked on her house and school, seeing her every day, but having a wall between them. The only way to know was to walk forward. Take the step, open his heart, and wait for the results.

"The windows will be here soon," he said instead. "You'll be amazed how quickly things take shape once those are in place. Your house will look like a home in no time."

Well, maybe not "no time." But it would sure feel like progress compared to the past couple of months.

"That's great. I can't wait."

Her words were so soft he barely heard her. The words didn't match her voice. Maybe she was as nervous to hear what he had to say as he was to say it.

Several vehicles came down Thompson Road, the other Timber Framing Plus vehicle in the forefront. Franco and Curtis, ready to unload windows. He'd rather not be caught talking to Allison, but he couldn't walk away abruptly just so the guys wouldn't razz him.

"You need to get to work, I guess." Allison glanced at him.

"Yes." He touched her arm then retracted his hand. "Later." He tried to pour a promise into the look he gave her.

The guys' truck jounced past them up the driveway. Franco waved from the passenger side, a smirk on his face.

Two cars drove in behind the truck, parking between the pole barn and the straw bale house. Four young women poured from one of the cars. From the other, a tall man exited the driver's side and rounded the vehicle to open the passenger door. A woman with short red hair climbed out.

She looked vaguely familiar. Where women were concerned, that was never a good thing. She said something to the man then her gaze slid past him and landed on Brent.

Even from here he could see her eyes widen. She grabbed at the man's arm and said something. The man turned to look, too.

"I should be going," Brent said to Allison. He had two choices. Run for his truck and leave the property, or try to catch up with Franco and Curtis.

But it was too late for either. Hand in hand, the couple strolled toward the duplex.

"Brent Callahan? Is that really you?"

He remembered the voice. Remembered the face. But the name escaped him.

"Hi." As noncommittal as he could come up with as a cold wave rolled over him chilling him from head to toe.

"Gina Dalles. Well, I was Gina O'Haran when I knew you. This is my husband, Parker."

Gina.

Not in front of Allison.

Chapter 26 ---

*T*he look on Brent's face spoke volumes. He remembered this woman... but wished he didn't.

The woman — Gina — seemed to notice Allison and Finnley for the first time.

Allison straightened, dropping her hands to her sides. She stepped closer to Finnley. That it also put her closer to Brent was incidental. "Come on, buddy. Breakfast is waiting."

Wait. This couple had been to the wedding on Saturday. The guy was Sierra's cousin or something like that. So that meant they were here for a hearty farm breakfast, too. "On second thought, Finnley, I think we'll just have toast in our house."

Whoever that woman was, Allison wanted to stay clear. She reached for her nephew's hand, and he edged closer to Brent. "Finnley. Come now."

The little guy's lip quivered. He glanced at Brent, who nudged him forward.

Allison grabbed her nephew's hand and all but dragged him back into the duplex. When she shut the door, he slumped against it, his face buried in his drawn-up knees.

She crouched in front of him. "Finnley, you must listen to me. Not Brent. I'm your auntie, and Brent is just..." Just what?

Just the construction guy? Not hardly.

Finnley sniffled.

Impatience rolled over Allison. Something was going on out there. Something she wanted to hear, and yet didn't. The kitchen window was open a few inches. Maybe she could hear from there. And if she didn't like what she heard, she could turn on the blender or something.

"I hated you for a long time, Brent."

What? Allison leaned on the counter, closer to the window.

"It was my fault as much as yours, of course. But I was the one who was pregnant."

The room swam. Allison couldn't have stopped eavesdropping if she tried.

"I'm sorry." Brent's voice. Quiet. Sincere.

"I-I had an abortion. I couldn't handle the thought of bringing a child into this world. Into *my* world."

Silence for a moment. If only Allison could see their faces. Especially Brent's.

"I'm sorry." His voice broke.

"It was through that experience I found Jesus. I've been praying for you ever since, asking God to help me find you again to tell you I forgive you. To tell you that He forgives you, too."

"Thanks, Gina. That means a lot to me. I became a Christian about four years ago. God has forgiven me so much."

Allison's head buzzed. She clutched at the faucet to keep her upright. Water poured into the sink. She fumbled with the handles to make it stop.

"I'm so glad to hear that, Brent. Parker and I have been married almost two years now. He's helped me to get over the past. He's stood by my side even when it's become apparent I'll never conceive. The abortion..." Gina choked on her words. "The abortion messed up my insides, the doctors say. I'll never have children. If I'd only known."

Soothing murmurs came from the other man.

"I-I don't know what to say." Brent's words were so quiet Allison strained to hear them. "I'm sorry. I wish I could undo those years in Denver. The drinking, th-the drugs, everything."

Those years? The *what?* How long had Brent and this Gina...?

"I know I wasn't the only one, Brent. I knew it then."

Even worse. He'd preyed on women. Allison's legs threatened to give out. Only her elbows planted firmly on the counter beside the sink supported her.

This could not be happening. That woman outside. Brent's quiet voice responding. It was all a bad dream. Right?

He'd said he wasn't good enough for her. Was this what he'd been talking about? Maybe he was right. Maybe he wasn't good enough. How far did forgiveness go, anyway?

What Allison had meant to tell Brent — but not anymore — was in a different category altogether. She'd been a victim, not a perpetrator. Brent was no better than Lori. Than John.

The expression on Brent's face as he looked at Finnley filled Allison's mind. The ways they looked alike. The fact he'd been in Denver four years ago and more. So had Lori.

No. Her legs couldn't hold her up any longer. Allison slid to the floor, wrapped her arms around her knees, and wept.

oOo

The delivery truck bearing windows rumbled down Thompson Road before Gina gave Brent a hug. Then Parker shook his hand with a look containing more respect than the derision Brent knew he deserved. Parker slipped his arm around Gina's waist as the pair made their way over to the big house.

Brent glanced at Allison's duplex behind him as the big truck's air brakes stopped the vehicle on the driveway. His gut writhed like a den of snakes. How much had she heard? He hadn't missed the sound of water running just beyond that open window.

He had to assume she'd heard everything.

The passenger window slid down and the driver leaned across. "Callahan? Where you wanting these windows?" He jerked his thumb at the farm school. "There? Your old man said there were two jobs at this address."

Brent pointed out the driveway wending up the hill. "You can't miss it."

"I ain't offloading these by myself, Callahan."

He needed to talk to Allison. "Two of my crewmembers are up at the site. They'll give you a hand."

The guy shook his head. "Could use all hands on deck. Many of them are a two-man job."

"I'll be right there." He couldn't resist a glance at Allison's door, firmly shut against him. It wasn't like she'd talk to him, anyway. It might be ten times worse if he didn't make an attempt right now, but the starting point was so horrible it didn't take a magnitude of ten to be a no-go. He had to try, though. Find out what she'd overheard.

He waved the driver up the hill. "I'll be with you in a minute." The truck pulled ahead and Brent turned to the door. *Lord? I could really use some help here. Please help Allison to understand...* To understand what? That it wasn't as bad as Gina had said? It had been every bit as bad, and worse. He hadn't known about Gina's abortion until today. He hadn't known about Mallory's son until a few months ago.

It was almost better, knowing. *God, I know You've forgiven me. I hold to that fact. If Allison is the right girl for me to commit to for the rest of our lives, please straighten this horrible mess.*

He knocked on the door. No one answered. "Allison? May I talk to you?"

"Go away." The muffled words came through the open kitchen window just a few feet to his right.

Yeah, she'd heard. She'd added enough things up. "Allison, please."

The door opened, but she wasn't there. Brent's gaze dropped to the sad little boy peering through a crack at him. "She crying."

Should he take Finnley's words as an invitation to enter? Brent crouched down to his son's eye level. "I'm sorry." He'd been saying that a lot — and meaning it. "You tell Auntie Allison that the men came to bring the windows for your new house, okay? I have to go and help them unload the truck, and then I'll come back and talk to her." Right. The boy barely strung three whispered words together. Like he was going to pass along that whole message.

He reached out and smoothed Finnley's shock of black hair. "I'll be back as soon as I can, squirt."

Finnley pushed through the crack. "Come with you."

Brent's heart seized. "No. You have to stay with Auntie Allison, okay? Give her a hug."

The boy's face fell.

"Back inside with you. I'll hurry."

Finnley's lip quivered as he nodded and allowed Brent to nudge him through the doorway. The door closed.

He looked at the open window. "Allison? I love you."

She did not reply.

Brent stumbled to his truck and drove up the hill.

oOo

"Auntie Allison?" Finnley patted her knee. "Okay?"

How many times had he seen Lori crying? How much did one little kid need to go through?

"Brent come back."

It would be better if he didn't. She couldn't get to the other side of this, no matter what he said. How fervently he apologized. How much she longed to lose herself in those deep brown eyes, feel his arms around her... Stop. She had to pull herself together for Finnley's sake.

219

She wiped her eyes with the sleeve of her gray hoodie and met Finnley's worried gaze. "Sorry, buddy." She took a deep breath, trying to gain control of her emotions. Like she could, ever again.

"You sad?"

"Yes, I'm sad." If that's how she could sum up a broken heart. She reached out to tug the boy closer, but he shifted out of reach. Right. Anger flashed through her. He leaned into Brent, but not her. Brent, the — no. She was not going to think about that man.

"Brent make better."

"Finnley, no. Brent cannot make this better. Okay? You need to stay away from him. Let him do his work and finish our house. Then he'll go away again and never come back."

Tears filled the little guy's eyes. "Never come back?"

Allison scrubbed at her face. How had this bond formed? How had she allowed it? But she hadn't. Not really. It had just happened. Did something in their genetics call each other? "It'll be okay, Finnley. You and I are a family now. I'll take care of you."

The tears dribbled down his cheeks.

Oh, man. If only she could pack the boy up and go to Portland for a month or two. Her parents' house was for sale, but she and Finnley could live in a corner of it in the meantime. Of course, she was needed to make decisions here. With the windows in over the next week or so, Brent and his guys would start the drywalling and soon be on to the finishing touches.

She was going to have to see a lot of Brent. This meant Finnley would be exposed to him, too.

His father. Was it right to keep them apart?

Wasn't it worse to encourage them? Brent had more right to Finnley than she did. What if he wanted custody? She could lose her nephew, just when she'd found him. Rescued him. How many times could she survive her heart being torn out and stomped on?

Brent was Finnley's father. Brent had been Lori's lover. As much as Allison's mind tried to avoid that fact, she had to face it. How long had he known? He'd bolted from the birthday party. What had been said to disrupt the peace?

She had no clue. It didn't matter anymore.

"Want Brent..."

That made only one of them. Allison surged to her feet. "Come on, buddy. We're going to the beach, okay? Go get your swim trunks on and get your toys."

His little jaw set.

"Finnley, do it."

He turned away as she sagged against the counter. Disappearing for the day was only a temporary solution, but she needed time to come up with something more permanent. All she knew for sure was that she needed to be gone before the window-delivery truck left and not come back until she was certain Brent was gone for the day.

She'd agreed to talk to him this evening, but there really wasn't any way he could still expect that to happen. Could he?

Chapter 27 ---

*H*er car was gone. Had been gone all day, since before the window truck had left. Probably right after Brent had gone up the hill to help unload it.

Brent knocked on her door again. Not that it would do any good. She wouldn't have loaned her car to anyone.

"Looking for Allison?" The curly-haired woman approached. Chelsea.

"Uh, yeah. Have you seen her since this morning?"

Chelsea shook her head. "No, I haven't. We were going to hang out this afternoon, as we were friends in Portland. But she hasn't been around and didn't let me know she had other plans."

If she'd stood up her presumably nonthreatening friend, she wouldn't think twice about avoiding Brent.

The sun touched the mountain on the west side of the valley. Allison wouldn't keep Finnley out much longer, would she? It was past the little man's bedtime already. Daylight lasted so long so far north at this time of year.

"She was going to ask someone to sit with Finnley this evening so we could talk."

Chelsea shot him a glance, her eyes crinkling. "Oh, is there something interested friends should know?"

Brent ran a hand through his hair and forced a laugh. "Not sure. I'd hoped so, but... well, it's complicated."

"Isn't it always? I mean, that's why Facebook even has it as one of the relationship categories."

He looked at her blankly. "Huh?"

"It's complicated." She looked at him expectantly then sighed. "Never mind."

"No, I mean this really is complicated." Best not to tell a friend of Allison's too much, though. But maybe... "How well do you know Gina?"

"Gina Dalles? She's married to my cousin Parker and they live in Boulder. I don't know her all that well." Chelsea eyed him thoughtfully. "She did come in this morning mentioning she'd run into an old friend outside. Said something about it being a small world... and an answer to prayer."

"Oh." Brent scratched his head. "Is that all she said?"

"More or less."

That was good. A relief. She hadn't aired his dirty laundry in front of all Allison's friends. Of course, she hadn't needed to, because Allison heard it firsthand. She must've.

"There must be something in the water around here." Chelsea turned away.

"The *what?*"

"The water. Green Acres. Everyone who comes here seems to fall in love." Her mouth twisted to one side. "I don't know if it's a good thing or a bad thing that I want to move here myself. It may seem like I'm coming just to meet a guy."

Brent gave his head a shake. "You're moving here to get married?"

"No, silly. I want to come because I'm an event planner, and I think this crew could use my talents. And because I like it here better than Portland."

"Then why...?"

Chelsea shook her head. "You've got it bad, don't you? When

my sister bought this farm with Jo and Claire, they didn't expect to get married. None of them. And look what happened. Ping. Ping. Ping. Like ducks in a row."

"Uh… yeah?"

"I figured it was coincidence. Not that I have anything against marriage, mind you. Zach and Noel and Gabe are great guys. It's all good. But I figured someone as hardened against men as Allison would be safe. Yet here you are, camped on her doorstep like a lost puppy. It must be the water."

Lost puppy? Was this woman for real? His guts had been removed from his body and trampled in the dirt, and she mocked him for saying it was complicated and blamed it on the water?

Wait. Chelsea had known Allison before. He shouldn't dismiss her as flighty and weird. He shifted to his other foot. "How long have you two known each other?" Childhood friends, maybe? He could hope.

"We had a passing acquaintance in college, but lost touch until her parents died last year. She hired me to plan the funeral."

His eyebrows shot up. "She what?"

Chelsea shrugged. "I plan events. She didn't know what went into a funeral. Neither did I." She grinned. "But I was less emotionally involved and had a good reason to learn. So I did."

"That's just… strange."

"People with money hire out a lot of things normal people just deal with themselves. And trust me, she has money." She pointed at the school building. "But I'm guessing you know that. The estate left her pretty well set up."

Brent hadn't stopped to wonder if the farm had taken a mortgage for the projects or not. It wasn't any of his business how the contract was paid for, so long as it was. On the other hand, he knew exactly how much the bid had been for and what had been added to it since. To think anyone might simply write checks for that was beyond his comprehension.

Maybe she thought he was only interested in her for her money. Or maybe she'd try to buy him out of Finnley's life.

No, surely she knew him better than that. Surely he knew *her* better.

Daylight faded into twilight, and still she hadn't returned. Was he supposed to simply accept she didn't want to talk to him? She couldn't avoid him forever, not while he was building her house and school. Maybe it wasn't necessary to push her the first twenty-four hours he was back.

It went right against his fix-it mentality to drive away now, but he couldn't sit on her doorstep all night.

He glanced at Chelsea. "Well, let her know I came by. I'm sure I'll see her in the next day or two."

She smirked. "I'll pass the message on."

oOo

He'd sure worked late.

Allison passed the white Timber Framing Plus pickup on her drive home from Galena Landing. She glanced at Finnley in her rearview mirror. "Did you have a good time at the beach, buddy?"

He nodded against his car seat's headrest, clutching the teddy bear she'd given him months ago.

"And you made some new friends. Avery and Christopher." Maybe *made new friends* was too strong a term. She'd seen the single dad with his two kids at church a few times. "You built sandcastles in the sand."

So much safer on the beach of an inland lake compared to the ocean, where tides or even rogue waves could wipe out the construction. Much like the rogue wave that had smashed her dreams of Brent this morning, leaving nothing but sand particles that would irritate everywhere.

No. She wasn't thinking about Brent. Ever again.

"They have a daddy," said Finnley's quiet voice from the back.

Allison's heart twisted. "Yes, they do. But no mommy."

"I have no daddy. No mommy." There was a slight pause. "Where is my mommy?"

"Oh, buddy." How did you tell a kid his mom was in prison? "She did some bad things. Some really bad things." She glanced in the mirror in time to see his nod.

Could she summon up any sympathy for her sister? Their upbringing hadn't been the best, in either case. Lori had made her own decisions. Extremely stupid ones, it turned out.

But she was still a human in need of love. God's love. The reality slammed into Allison like another rogue wave. All she'd done was judge. It was hard not to, when she saw the shell this little boy was.

"Time out?"

Allison jerked her eyes to meet Finnley's in the mirror. She summoned a chuckle. "Yes, buddy, your mommy is in time-out." Not that Finnley had experienced that punishment for himself — the kid didn't have the confidence to do anything bad — but he'd seen Maddie's penalty a time or two. "Your mommy has a really long time-out. That's why you came to live with Auntie Allison, because it was too long to wait for Mommy."

He stared thoughtfully at her in the mirror. Processing.

"So you came to Green Acres. So you can play with Maddie and Jane Eyre and Danny Boy. And..." She'd been about to say the baby chicks, but remembered in time that the birds would be butchered for the freezer later this week. "And Keanan," she added, needing to finish the sentence.

"And Brent." He sounded wistful.

Her hands froze on the steering wheel as her mind fast-forwarded through the morning's overheard revelations. Had Brent admitted to being Finnley's father openly enough for the boy to catch on? No. Finnley couldn't know.

Allison turned on the signal light and turned into the farm driveway. "Buddy, Brent is a nice man." It burned to say the words, but she couldn't deny it in front of the boy. *And a great kisser.* He'd kissed her sister, too. And more. "But he's here to build our house. Then he'll go away again and never come back."

She parked the car in front of the duplex and unbuckled Finnley. She tried to hold his hand on the short walk to the door, but he pulled away from her. Right. He'd soak up all the male attention he could, but not hers. How could she get through to him? How could he come to realize that it was Auntie Allison who loved him and kept him safe, not Noel or Gabe or Zach or Keanan? Or Brent.

Finnley ran into his room.

Allison glanced in a moment later. The little guy sat on the floor in the corner of the bedroom. She frowned. He'd put himself in time-out?

No. His little fingers traced the outline of the dog Brent had painted on his wall. Tears trickled down his cheek as he stared at the image with such longing it made Allison's heart squeeze.

Rover was back. Or was the longing for Brent?

It was past his bedtime, but she couldn't force him away from the mural. Not yet.

oOo

"He's asleep?" Chelsea poked her head around the door of Allison's duplex.

Allison nodded. "Finally." She'd heard sniffles from Finnley's room long after he should have succumbed to dreams, especially after a long day of playing in the sand and water.

Chelsea gave her a hug.

For once, Allison felt like she could return one of those. Whether it was the emotional upheaval of the day, Finnley's rejection of her, or just that she finally considered Chelsea a real friend, she didn't know. But it felt good to let someone in, if only for a moment.

She put a kettle on for tea. "Sorry for bailing out on you today. I should've texted you and invited you to the beach with Finnley and me."

"Oh, is that where you were? Yeah, I'd totally have come. I see my relatives often enough."

Her relatives? Her blank look must've shown, because Chelsea laughed.

"Everyone who came for Sierra and Gabe's wedding. Most of them cleared out today."

That meant Gina was gone. Not that it mattered. She'd left her bombshell behind.

"Then I hung out with Jo and Claire in the afternoon and helped put things back in order."

Guilt descended. Allison should have done that. Instead, she'd run like a toddler having a tantrum. She'd make it up to them tomorrow.

Chelsea tilted her head. "They wondered where you were. We all did."

Allison reached into the cupboard for two mugs. "I should have texted sooner." Or, at least, responded to the ones she'd received.

"What happened?"

"I told you. I took Finnley to the beach."

Chelsea rolled her eyes. "Uh huh. But why? No one knew that was your plan for the day."

It hadn't been. Until Gina. Allison opened a drawer full of tea. "What kind do you want?"

"Is that for real?" Chelsea pointed at a small tin with a dandelion on the lid.

"Yes. Roasted, ground, dandelion root. They say it tastes like coffee, but those of us who mainline java can tell the difference."

"Caffeine-free?" Chelsea picked up the tin and examined it. "I'll try it. I'll try anything once. Well, almost anything."

Allison finished prepping the two cups and they settled into chairs in the living room.

Chelsea eyed her over the rim of her mug. "You didn't answer my question, by the way."

Was it time to open up to a friend? Chelsea might be the safest bet. After all, she was leaving Green Acres in a day or two, and likely wouldn't be back before Brent had finished his work and was gone. "Blame Brent."

Her friend's eyes twinkled. "Do tell all."

Allison shrugged. "There's not that much to tell. He seemed like a nice enough guy. Funny. Sweet."

Chelsea held up a hand. "Just a sec. Are you really Allison Hart? Because the Allison Hart I know would never have called a man nice, sweet, or funny. She had no use for men."

"And Brent proves my point."

"Sorry?" Chelsea took a sip.

"Okay, I'll give you the short version." The long version would require too much time and would mention kissing. Not going there. "Men are not trustworthy. Even men who seem nice, funny, and sweet. Brent is no different."

Chelsea waited, her eyes fixed on Allison's.

"He used to sleep with different women. How many, I don't know. But your cousin Gina for one." She bit her lip and closed her eyes. "And my sister Lori for another."

"He's Finnley's father?" Chelsea's voice rose in a squeak.

"Shh." Allison glanced at Finnley's bedroom door. Closed. Surely her nephew was sound asleep and hadn't heard that. "Short answer. Yes."

"Whoa. I'd never have guessed. I mean, there's the whole Asian thing, but other than that. But ewww."

That about summed it up. Her gut quaked. "Yeah, I know."

"So when did you find out?"

230

Allison held Chelsea's gaze. "This morning."

"This morning?" Chelsea frowned. "But you guys looked like you were having a cozy conversation when I went by."

"We had been." And to think she'd even agreed to go out. To talk to him. That wasn't going to happen now. She did not want to hear the sordid details. Him and Lori. No way.

"I don't get it."

"Gina recognized him and came over to talk to him. She said she'd been praying for him for years and that she wanted him to know she'd forgiven him for…" Allison took a deep breath. "For getting her pregnant."

Chelsea's eyes bulged. "Pregnant? But—"

"A few years ago. She had an abortion."

"No way." Chelsea sank back in her chair. "Well, that explains a lot. And now she and Parker want kids and can't have any."

Allison nodded.

"And Finnley. Wow, that must've been a shock to you. Is that why you disappeared?"

"Yeah. I just… just couldn't face it." Not that a day at the beach had helped. It had occupied Finnley while her mind looped the morning scene endlessly, teasing out nuances. Trying to block mental images of Brent and Lori together.

"So you haven't talked to Brent since then."

"No. There's nothing to talk about."

"Sounds like there is."

"Well, you're wrong. Do you think I want to be involved with a… a womanizer like him? Do you think it's fair to *him*—" she jerked her chin in the direction of Finnley's bedroom "—to have that for a role model?"

Chelsea pulled her feet onto the chair and curled up sideways. "Have you ever heard of forgiveness? Of God's redeeming love?"

In principle. Allison's jaw clenched. "You don't understand."

"Listen, Allison. I'm no psychologist, but I've noticed something in my observations of humanity."

Allison's eyebrows rose as she stared at her friend.

"Sometimes those who find it hardest to forgive others have deeper issues." Compassion flowed from Chelsea's eyes. Not condemnation. Not judgment.

"What do you mean?" The words choked past the lump in Allison's throat. What she really meant was, how had Chelsea seen?

"I'm guessing..." Chelsea's hand came up in defense. "I'm guessing you're not very good at forgiving yourself. I could be totally off base here and, if so, I guess I've just blown what might have been a promising friendship to smithereens."

"But it wasn't my fault." Allison plucked a tissue from a nearby box, dabbed her eyes, and blew her nose.

Clearly not the response Chelsea had expected. "Huh?"

She got the words out between sobs. "I was the victim."

Chapter 28 --

*F*or two days Allison never seemed to be on the farm when Brent was. If her vehicle was parked out front, she wasn't in the duplex or out in the garden. When five o'clock rolled around, her car was gone. Soon he'd be desperate enough to pound on the big house door or ask Noel where she was.

Not yet, though. He didn't have a game plan besides prostrating himself on the ground and pleading forgiveness. He doubted that would be enough.

Even Curtis had quit razzing him. It took a lot to make the guy shut up. Apparently Brent's tension was obvious to anyone paying attention.

That didn't seem to include Allison.

The drywallers were coming Monday. They'd have Allison's house sheeted, taped, and mudded by the end of the week. Painters the week after. Floor-layers. Cupboard installers. Trim carpenters. The electrician and plumber again. Long before the end, the process would begin again down at the school, slower because of the size.

It felt like he'd soon be done at the farm. It wasn't true. Several months remained. But the clock was ticking. The calendar turning. Time was running out to gain Allison's attention. Her trust. Her forgiveness. Whatever was needed.

At the moment, that was screwing the frame for the French doors in place while Curtis and Franco lifted a large pane into place in Allison's bedroom. Everything he touched, he imagined her touching. She'd open these doors several times a day to sit on her deck, walk over for a visit with Jo, or let Finnley out to play.

A middle-aged man strolled up the hill from the straw bale house. Brent had thought all the wedding visitors were long gone, but apparently not.

The man stopped just off the deck. "So this is where all the construction noise is coming from."

"It is." But it wasn't really that loud, was it? Loud enough to disturb anyone from down the hill?

"Things have sure changed on this farm in the past few years. I used to visit Grace Humbert when she lived here, years ago."

At Brent's blank stare, the man shook his head. "I'm sorry. I'm Daniel Rubachuk. Father of the groom. Grace Humbert was Rosemary Nemesek's mother."

Brent brushed his hand against his work pants as he crossed the deck. "Pleased to meet you, Daniel. I'm Brent Callahan, foreman of this build."

"My wife and I used to live in town here. Now we're missionaries in Romania. It was our great pleasure to return for our son's wedding." He pointed at the log cabin next door. "That's Zachary's place?"

Brent nodded. "Zach and Jo, yes. And little Madelynn."

The man's eyes crinkled when he smiled. "That monkey is something else, isn't she? And another baby on the way. It's good to see Zach settled down with a family. He and Gabe have been good friends since they were gaffers the size of that little Finnley."

He appraised the house behind Brent. "And this is Allison's new place. Why, this farm is growing faster than I can keep up with. Gabe and Sierra might want a place bigger than that duplex eventually." Daniel shook his head. "I still can't believe he went and sold that health food store. And that Keanan fellow is thinking of staying on, too. The farm will be bulging at the seams."

"Keanan?" Wasn't he the guy with bushy hair and a tent? Oh, and a guitar.

"You hadn't heard?" Daniel chuckled. "Well, I guess there's no reason you would have, I guess."

Right. He was just the contractor. The day-to-day life on the farm was none of his business.

"Must be lots of work for a talented fellow like you around here. I can't believe how much Galena Landing has grown since we left here ten years ago. Or is it eleven now?"

"I've had a few requests to bid on new construction, it's true. I'm not sure if any of them will come through." A guy named Tyrell Burke was planning a mansion on his farm south of town, while the Smiths wanted to build a more modest house on an empty lot in Galena Landing.

Brent wasn't sure he wanted to stick around this town, though. It all depended on Allison. Sooner or later he'd catch her unawares and lay his soul bare before her. Meanwhile, praying was his best option. His only option.

oOo

Allison had found a rhythm. She helped out with work around the farm in the morning, staying well clear of anywhere Brent might see her, and took Finnley to the beach in the afternoon. Mason Waterman and his five-year-old twins were frequently there, too, so Finnley was finally starting to make friends with children his own age.

Mason Waterman was completely safe. He didn't seem inclined to smoldering gazes or spine-tingling touches or multi-layered conversation. How could she make anything out of, "It's my turn to get ice cream for the kids"? She couldn't.

235

Mason and Christopher flew a kite along the beach, the fragile plastic kite dancing in the breeze as Mason expertly dipped it then allowed it to regain height with just the right tension on the string.

Being a kite looked like fun, except for the tether. No cares, just cavorting with God's wind. But maybe the tether was necessary.

It was impossible to miss noticing that she was letting her guard down around men, and it didn't seem to be a good habit. Look where that got her with Brent — an ache that would not go away. And Keanan — no, she wasn't going there, either. The guy thought too much and, when he spoke, it was some kind of poetry. Besides, who knew where a man with that much wanderlust was going to wander off to next, and when?

Mason handed over the kite string to his son. For a moment the kite remained high on the breeze then plummeted into the lake. Mason tousled Christopher's hair and reeled it in, the kite skipping on the waves as it came.

"Anything exciting online?" Mason dropped onto the sand beside her, the kite at his side.

Christopher joined Finnley and Avery as they packed sand into turret-shaped buckets for another sandcastle attempt.

Allison thumbed her iPad off, snapped the keyboard cover over it, and tucked it in her bag. She adjusted the angle of the beach umbrella a little more. "Just writing a class for the farm school for next year." She didn't have to mention she'd gotten a whole five sentences written. Her mind had done too many spins to concentrate.

"That's a cool thing you guys are doing there. My parents can't say enough good things about you all."

His parents? "You grew up around here, then?"

He nodded. "My folks have a farm across the valley. I was a couple of years behind Zach and Gabe in school."

"Oh." She forced a laugh. "Silly me. I thought you were probably here on vacation."

"I wasn't sure at first." His eyes followed the children at play. "But sometimes, when life kicks you in the teeth, you retreat to what was once familiar. Safe. You know?"

Best to choose her reply carefully. "My familiar wasn't safe."

She felt the glance he tossed her but kept focused on the kids.

"I'm sorry," he said simply.

"It's just how it was. You were telling me about your plans."

"Guess I'm a bit like the prodigal son. Spent a while wallowing in the pig pen before remembering I had perfectly good parents who would welcome the kids and me back into their lives." He angled a glance her way. "I'm sure you know how challenging it is to be the only parent."

"Finnley is my nephew. I've only had him a few months." That didn't mean Mason's assumption was wrong. It simply meant she didn't have all the same experiences.

"You know what they say about small towns when you're looking for a job. It's not what you know. It's who you know."

"Oh? You found something?"

He nodded. "Starting soon as the farm extension agent. Harry Rigger is retiring."

"Good for you." She meant it, too. But it changed things. The guy was moving here permanently. He might be angling for a wife and a mother for the twins. That was definitely not going to be her.

This was the problem with having guys for friends. There was always another level, or the potential for it.

She glanced at her watch and feigned surprise. "Oh, I need to get going. Finnley! Time to pack up."

His little jaw set.

She'd liked it better when he didn't have his own opinions. Hadn't she? Oh man, she hadn't meant to admit that, even to herself. That was the controlling Allison speaking. The one who liked life in neat little organized rows, alphabetized and color-coded for maximum efficiency. The one who didn't like surprises.

"Come on, buddy," she called, softening her voice. "We have time to get a hamburger if you like."

He grabbed a stick from the sand, jabbed it into the half-formed castle then kicked over the remaining turret.

"Hey!" Christopher yelled. "Daddy, Finnley broke the castle."

Allison surged to her feet. "Finnley!"

He glowered at her, jaw set.

"It's okay, Christopher. I'll help you build it again." Mason rose to stand beside Allison and quirked her a grin. "Kids, eh?"

Like she was supposed to accept this behavior as normal. It wasn't. Not for Finnley. She collapsed the beach umbrella and picked up her bag. "Say you're sorry to Christopher."

He glanced at his friend, who stood with hands planted on his little hips. Finnley's lips moved. They might have said sorry.

"Say it so he can hear you, Finnley."

Another scowl in Allison's direction before he focused on his toe, scuffing sand. "Sorry."

"It's okay, Finnley." Christopher threw his arms around Finnley. "My daddy is going to help me make a new one. It will be even bigger, huh, Daddy?"

Finnley shrugged out of Christopher's embrace and plodded toward Allison. She handed him his sandals, and he sat to put them on.

"See you tomorrow?" asked Mason. "Same time, same beach?"

"Probably not." She tossed a laugh, hoping it sounded more natural to him than it did her. "Tomorrow's a full farm work day." She cupped her hand on Finnley's head to nudge him toward the car, but he sidestepped her touch. "See you."

"Daddy, do you have a bigger bucket?" came Christopher's voice from behind them.

"Why did you kick over the castle?" She looked down at the

shock of black hair. The brown shoulders she could barely see lifted and dropped. "Buddy, you have to play nice. You have to treat other kids like you want them to treat you. Would you like it if Christopher ruined your hard work?"

No response.

She buckled him into his car seat and his brown eyes met hers. "Christopher has daddy."

"Yes, he does."

"Where John?"

He'd looked to that despicable man as a father figure? She brushed the hair out of Finnley's eyes. He needed a haircut. "He did bad things, buddy. He's in time-out like your mommy."

Finnley nodded. "Where Brent?"

So few words, but every one of them packed a punch. "He's working on our house, so you and I will have a nice place to live. Remember? It's right next door to Maddie's house."

"Brent live there too?"

If only. "No, buddy." Wait, had she really wished he would? Allison shut the back door, climbed into the driver's seat, and drove out of the parking lot, past the Landing Pad.

"Brent live there?"

Hadn't she just answered that? But this was excessively talkative for Finnley.

"He lives in another city, far away." Okay, Coeur d'Alene wasn't that far, but certainly far enough on Finnley's scale.

"Truck there."

Allison glanced sharply at the hotel. One Timber Framing Plus pickup angled in near the building. "That's not Brent's truck, buddy. That's the one Curtis and Franco drive."

"Oh. Brent live there?"

She sighed. "He kind of lives there when he's not at his other house." Time for a subject change. "Do you want a burger?"

"Brent come?"

"No, buddy. Just you and me. We're a family now, just the two of us." She glanced in the mirror as she shifted the car into gear. "I love you, Finnley. I'm so glad you came to live with me."

His dark eyes still gleamed with unshed tears. He stared at the Landing Pad as they drove past, likely focused on the lone Timber Framing Plus truck.

Brent was probably still sitting on her doorstep. The jerk.

Chapter 29 --

*A*llison watched Noel sharpen knives for fill-the-chicken-freezer day. Zach turned on the feather-plucking machine so the rubber fingers spun on the drum. Claire turned the heat down under the large canner they'd use for scalding the birds.

Covered in a rubber apron, Allison cringed. Jo stood ready to show Keanan and her the fine art of gutting chickens. The best she could hope was that the laid-out assembly line and everyone else's experience would get her to the end of the day.

She knew this was part of farm life. Local eating and optimum health made vegetarianism out of the question. Not that she'd ever been all that tempted to skip meat, but then she'd never raised fluffy yellow chicks to fill a freezer before. Never taken part in the process. It didn't look like Keanan had, either.

They'd set up near the tire swing, sandbox, and toddler-sized slide that functioned as a mini-playground for Maddie and Finnley. The idea was to keep the kids nearby but not underfoot. At the moment, Finnley sat on top of the slide platform, watching the adults, while Maddie tried to climb into the tire swing.

"Ready?" called Zach. He pulled a chicken from a large sack in the back of the pickup. The guys had spent the better part of an hour rounding up the birds earlier.

"Water's hot." Claire glanced down the table where cutting boards and gleaming knives awaited. "We're ready."

Allison squeezed her eyes shut, unable to bring herself to watch as Zach lifted the first bird to the chopping block. A resounding thwack cut through the air, followed by the sound of fluttering feathers as the bird's nervous system petered out.

She stole a glance over to see Claire sink the headless bird into the vat of hot water. The stench of hot wet feathers filled the air. Allison glanced at Jo. How would that smell to a pregnant woman?

Jo met Allison's gaze with a grimace, her nose twitching.

Allison raised her eyebrows.

"I'll be okay," Jo whispered, the last word cut off as Noel flipped the plucking machine on and accepted the bird from Claire. He held the bird inside the machine. Wet reddish brown feathers poured out onto a tarp below.

Meanwhile another thwack resounded, and Claire reached toward Zach for the next bird. Noel handed the nearly naked one to Jo, who stripped the residue of feathers, pulling out a few black pinfeathers.

That bird was headed straight for Allison. Why couldn't she do Jo's job instead of removing guts with Keanan? Right, feathers were probably bad enough on a pregnant stomach.

"Ready?" Jo asked Allison.

"No" wasn't the right answer. Allison nodded, gut queasy, as she pulled on a pair of surgical gloves.

"Okay, see? Here's the bottom of the rib cage. You cut here, but only deep enough to pierce the skin. You want the innards to come out in one ball, not lacerated." She glanced at Allison. "You think it smells bad now, just wait until one of us slices an intestine."

Great. And Noel had made sure the knives were sharp, too. It was only a matter of time before one of those slit too deep.

Keanan leaned over Allison's shoulder as Jo demonstrated the rest of the cut then worked her hand between the ribs and the guts. A few seconds later, she dragged the mass out and dumped it into the bucket beside her.

Allison needed a deep breath, but was afraid of what she'd inhale. She managed to get enough air without gagging.

Jo peered into the cavity. "Now you just need to scrape out the bits that are still stuck to the ribs. Like this. And cut off the feet." She showed how to wiggle the feet to find the joint. "And then a rinse…" She turned on the hose and squirted water into the void. "Now into the cooler. We'll cut most of them up for parts before freezing, but we can do that inside later. For now, they need to get cold."

Keanan touched Allison's shoulder. "You up for this?"

She nodded, a quick jerky nod. She lived on this farm. She and Finnley took meals with everyone else. She'd do her part.

By now two more birds sat waiting. Keanan set one on Allison's board and arranged the other in front of himself. Jo leaned across to watch and guide.

Allison reached for her knife. Buying fried chicken at the drive-through had never sounded so good.

oOo

Brent's heart lurched. She was there, with the others. Not that it helped. The Green Acres gang obviously had an assembly line going on as chickens squawked before they were forever silenced. This wasn't a good time to invade her space or push her.

Finnley turned on the little slide to watch Brent drive past.

Brent lifted his hand to wave but dropped it before he'd finished the motion. Though he ached for the child, he couldn't flaunt Allison's wishes. She was Finnley's guardian, not him. And if he wanted to win her approval — and he certainly did — it was best not to get on her bad side. Again. Or more?

243

Who knew his past would haunt him for years to come? He'd thought — hoped — that receiving God's forgiveness would wipe his slate clean. Yeah, so God promised to put his sin as far as the east is from the west, but it was different with people. Funny to think humans had a longer memory than God did.

He parked the truck by the gorgeous structure he was building for Allison and Finnley. He tried to be thankful every day for the opportunity to construct this house for them while wishing he could also help create a home.

To see Allison puttering in the little kitchen or glancing up from the computer nook he was building her with a look of love in her eyes. To see Finnley running down those log stairs and leaping into his arms.

Should he push for custody? DNA tests would prove his paternity.

He could talk to Patrick about opening a satellite office in Galena Landing. He could nail down the building projects that dangled as possibilities. But then he'd need to put Finnley in daycare. The kid sure didn't need that, not when his life had been so disrupted already.

Of course, with full custody, he wouldn't need to stay in Galena Landing. He could cut Allison right out of Finnley's picture. That certainly wasn't the way to her heart. He'd do that only if there was no other way to keep in touch with his son.

Would she agree to joint custody? Then he'd have to keep seeing Allison, but he wouldn't win any points from her. He snorted as he slammed the truck door shut and crossed the yard. He had no points to lose, as far as he could tell. The judge would be the one to decide whether to allow either of them access.

Could he stand trading Finnley off at the beginning and end of every weekend and looking Allison in the eye? Their relationship would never recover. And besides, he couldn't do that to her. He just couldn't.

The guys had set up scaffolding across the front of the house.

Curtis sat in the Bobcat, raising a pallet of fiber cement siding to the scaffold while Franco directed him. Now that the windows were in, they could finish the exterior.

Brent gave the guys a thumbs-up and headed into the house through the French doors. Would anyone even use the front door across the room? He winced. Didn't look like that was going to be his problem.

For now, he was back to creating the best shelter he could for the two people he loved most in this world.

oOo

After Brent's truck rumbled by, Allison kept a closer eye on Finnley for a few minutes. The boy had definitely noticed. He looked glummer than usual when he turned back from staring up the driveway, chin resting on both fists as he scowled at Allison.

"You guys haven't talked yet?" asked Jo.

Allison shot her a sidelong look. Was nothing private around here? Oh, right, the famous full-disclosure thing that had gotten Sierra into so much trouble with the group last fall when she'd kept information from everyone. But that had been info the group needed. Allison's love life — or lack of it — was no one's business but her own.

"What happened?" Jo went on. "Seemed like you might be onto a good thing with our resident contractor for a while."

Did Allison mistake Keanan's sudden interest in the conversation, or was it her imagination that he shifted slightly closer to her, his head tilted just a little?

"Nope." Allison elbowed Keanan. "Pass another chicken, please."

Jo chuckled. "You may think you're the only one who's ever felt confused in love, but you're wrong."

Allison's back stiffened. A bird plopped onto her cutting board. She stabbed it just below the ribs. An odor more putrid than usual exploded from the bird. Allison bit back a bad word. Great. She'd split the intestines.

Jo waved her hand in front of her face. "You'll have to rinse that one extra well."

Allison glared at her. If Jo weren't pregnant, Allison would blame her for the error in judgment and make her gut this chicken. She turned aside and took a deep breath. She could pretend Jo was at fault, but no one's hand but hers had held this knife. Better get it over with.

She held her breath as much as possible as she hurried the bird through the process then held it under the garden hose until the stench dissipated. "Is it really clean enough?" She held it up to Jo.

Her friend looked a little green as she peered inside. "Yep, it's good. Give your gloves a good wash, then rinse this guy again and drop him in the cooler."

"Okay." She sprayed water on each hand in turn. "I promise to pay better attention to what I'm doing in the future."

Keanan chuckled. "I bet you will. So will we all."

When Allison resumed her station, Jo said, "What happened there kind of answered my question. You and Brent Callahan have some unfinished business, and it's eating at you."

Allison wiped her cutting board clean.

"Brent's been looking for you every day this week. Sometimes several times a day."

Allison reached for a chicken.

"He seems really concerned about something."

Her knife would go in just so. Not too deep this time.

"He's got all the signs of a man in love."

Perfect. Only the skin slit. Now to slip the blade under the skin and make the next cut.

"What signs are those?" asked Keanan.

Thank you, Keanan. You all just talk about love without me. It's better that way.

"Oh, you know," Jo said. "He's always watching for her, always brightening when someone mentions her name. He's working long hours, but comes down to the yard oftener than he used to. Drives a nail or two into the farm school building, stares at the duplex, then goes back up the hill."

"I get that he's watching for her." Keanan reached for the water hose. "But he's building her house. Maybe he just has a question to run by her."

"Wouldn't he leave a message for her, then? A note on her door? Or—" Jo put in an effort to snap her gloved fingers "—send her a text, maybe? He's got your number, doesn't he, Allison?"

In more ways than one. She nodded sharply but didn't look up.

"Is he sending you texts?"

Seriously. It was time Jo stopped poking at this. There'd been a flood of texts on Monday. Tuesday through Thursday had seen dozens more. She no longer clicked through to see his words. The first few had all been the same. Reading them over and over again was like picking at a wound. Why make the pain repeat? Maybe time would numb it.

"A sign of unrequited love, Keanan, is what Allison is doing right now. Moping. Refusing to talk about it. Being sullen."

She'd show Jo sullen. She'd show her refusal. If only they weren't tied to the chicken line for hours to come. They'd done, what, a dozen of the hundred scheduled?

"Which is exactly how Brent is acting, too," Jo went on. "And then there's the whole thing where they glance at each other when they think the other isn't looking."

She had not done that. She'd stayed right off the farm as much as she possibly could.

"That's rough," Keanan said. "This whole love business. You'd recommend they just talk to each other?"

Jo leaned on the table. "Have you ever met a problem between two people that was solved without talking things through?"

"Good point."

However, there was kissing. Six weeks ago it seemed, for a little while, as though kissing might solve the problem without the need for words. Hadn't brought lasting results, though.

"The thing is, Keanan," Jo went on. "It's not just affecting Allison and Brent. It's affecting all of us."

Thanks, Jo. How about talking directly to Allison instead of pretending to have a discussion with Keanan? And what possessed the guy to go along with this charade?

"It's even affecting F—" Jo gasped. "Allison, where did he go?"

Allison's head jerked upright and she stared at the children's playground not ten feet away. Empty.

Chapter 30 --

*N*ow that the windows were in and the early July heat wave had hit, the house needed air conditioning. Brent opened all the windows on the main floor wide. When could he get the heating contractor over to hook up the air exchange system? He climbed the stairs and opened the clerestory windows in the loft and Finnley's bedroom. A slight breeze tickled his face as he ran his fingers over the smooth window frame Franco had installed just yesterday.

A slight movement at the edge of the trees caught his eye. Finnley.

How could a man's heart leap and sink at the same time? He wanted nothing more than to spend time with the boy. Okay, that was a lie. He wanted Allison more, but she and Finnley were a package. They came together... or stayed away together, if Allison had anything to say about it. He'd bet anything she didn't know the boy had followed Brent up to the house, though she'd notice any minute.

Brent skidded down the stairs and hurried out through the French doors. "Finnley? Does Auntie Allison know you're here?"

The little man crossed his arms over his chest and gave Brent a disapproving glare so similar to one of Allison's that Brent's throat caught.

"Listen, squirt. You have to obey Auntie Allison. You can't come up here without her."

"Hard hat?"

Brent squatted in front of the boy. "It's not because of the hard hat. It's because it's her job to take care of you. To keep you safe."

Part of him balked. It should be him. He was the boy's father. Obviously something in Finnley pulled him in Brent's direction. Like deep inside he knew there was a deeper connection than the contractor-client thing.

The fact remained that Allison was his legal guardian.

Finnley's dark eyes filled with tears. "Want you."

Brent raked his fingers through his hair. How had this happened? This was wrong, wrong, wrong. "Thanks. I appreciate that." His arms twitched with the effort of resisting the impulse to gather the child tight.

"Finnley?" Allison's voice called from down the hill.

The boy didn't blink.

"Better go back, squirt. She's looking for you. Worried about you. She loves you."

Finnley's jaw set as he shifted.

Brent'd seen the same posture in the mirror a time or two. He nudged Finnley's shoulder. "Go find your aunt."

"No want to," whispered Finnley.

"I know. But sometimes we have to do what's right, even if we don't want to." One of life's hardest lessons. Brent's heart ached that a four-year-old needed to learn it.

"Finnley?" Allison's voice was closer now. Louder.

Brent jerked his chin toward the path. "Better go, squirt."

A tear trickled down the little brown face.

Brent couldn't stand it anymore. He scooped Finnley up in his arms and nearly stumbled when thin arms tightened around his neck, all but cutting off his next breath. He started for the path.

"Finnley? Where are you?"

"He's right here. We're coming." Brent walked toward Allison's voice. If nothing else, Finnley had precipitated their meeting. She'd have to talk to him now, wouldn't she?

One glimpse of her face a moment later dashed that thought. Her lips were drawn into a tight line and her eyes flashed fire. "Finnley Daniel Hart. You may not run off without asking me."

Brent felt like he'd never get a full breath again as the little man buried his face in Brent's throat. He tried to unwind the boy's arms, but it was impossible. An octopus couldn't have held on any tighter, even with double the appendages. And besides, Brent kind of liked the trust his son had in him. A trust that Brent would keep him safe from his aunt. Yeah, no good could come from this one.

"Put him down, Brent Callahan."

Desperation tinged his words. "Can't you see I'm trying?"

Allison stepped closer and pulled one of Finnley's arms loose. "Come on, buddy. Brent has work to do. You need to come back with me."

The boy's head movement was so slight Brent doubted Allison could see it. Brent only felt Finnley's chin twisting against his collarbone. He met Allison's exasperated gaze. Something lay behind it though. Something like panic, maybe. Anger. Sorrow. Regret.

All that was gone in an instant when she broke contact.

It occurred to Brent that he didn't need to hold Finnley to keep him from falling. The kid was doing all the work. That left Brent with two sort-of free arms. He turned sideways, got an arm around Allison's waist, and pulled her close.

For half a second he thought his ruse might be successful before she twisted out of his grasp.

"Don't."

"Allison, I — we need to talk." He held both hands out away from his body so she could tell this embrace wasn't his idea. The boy clung like a leach.

Her eyes went everywhere but to his face. "I don't think so. There really isn't anything to discuss." Her arms crossed in front of her, just beyond his easy reach.

Saying anything in front of Finnley was dangerous. He knew that, but nothing else had worked. "Allison, I love you. I know what you heard the other day. I'm sure you don't doubt whether it's true or not, but I'll admit it. It's true." Brent wrapped his arms around the child who clung to him. "About him." He'd stop before making it so clear Finnley could understand the meaning. The time for that would come later, but not now.

Allison's jaw clenched as she stared at the ground. But hey, she was here. She was listening. That was progress.

"I lived a wild life. I didn't figure I was hurting anyone. I know now that I was wrong, but it took a while to get that through my head. I've confessed my sin to God, and He has forgiven me. I know it."

Still no response.

"That doesn't undo the consequences. I have mixed feelings about that, I'll be honest. I never imagined the powerful feelings from… this." Brent ran his hand down his son's warm back. He took a step closer to Allison.

She didn't back up.

"But it's definitely not the only reason I want to be part of your life. I loved you before I ever knew about… this." He continued to caress Finnley's back.

Allison took a deep breath. He was close enough to hear the shudder in it. He took another step, but this time she sidled away. "Finnley, please get down and come with me." Her voice shook. "I need you to obey right now."

This time Finnley let Brent disengage his grip. Brent crouched as he set the boy down. "Go with Auntie Allison, squirt." He nudged Finnley toward Allison then glanced up at her. "This isn't over," he said quietly.

"You're right. It's not." But the glimmer in her eyes still shone more anger than love.

He had a feeling the kind of "over" she had in mind was not going to be the kind he'd like.

o0o

"You stay here and play with Maddie. No more running off." Allison pointed Finnley toward the tire swing. No missing the resistance in his shoulders to both her touch and her words.

What was his fascination with Brent? She clenched her jaw so hard her teeth ground. The stress of all this was not good for any of them.

She returned to her spot at the table and tied her apron back on, angling her body to keep a better eye on Finnley.

He dropped to the ground with his back to her, obstinacy in every line of his body. Well, two could play that game. Half his genetics were her sister's. Allison was at least as stubborn.

On the other hand, half his DNA was Brent's. Somebody else who was stubborn as sin and twice as black. How was she going to win this one?

"I'm thinking of going to Portland for a few weeks," she told Jo barely above a whisper. A glance at Finnley revealed no sign he'd overheard. "I need to get *him* away from *him*." Her chin jerked from her nephew to her house.

"Have you ever considered talking things through?"

Had Jo ever considered minding her own business? "Do you have any idea what he's done?"

"Uh…" Jo glanced up the chicken line and leaned over the table. "No. Why don't you fill me in?"

It would be a relief to dump it on someone else. Then maybe they'd stop assuming it was something that could be merely talked away. As if talking could undo what Brent had done. What her sister had done. What her father had done.

"This is hardly the place."

"That bad?"

Allison raised her eyebrows and looked Jo in the eye. "You have no idea."

"We're half done with the chickens," Keanan said conversationally, as though reminding them of his presence.

Not that Allison had forgotten. Too many people stood within earshot, and that included her nephew. A sharp glance in his direction revealed Maddie tackling him. He shoved her aside, and she fell. A loud wail rose.

"Finnley Daniel! I saw that. No pushing. Say you're sorry to Maddie."

He slumped, his back still to her.

"Maddie grabbed him first," said Jo. "She instigated it."

"That doesn't give him the right to push a smaller child."

Jo shook her head. "Maddie, tell Finnley sorry."

The toddler peered into his face. "Sowwy."

He twisted, turning his back to her.

What on earth was Allison going to do with this child? She'd been losing her grip on her nephew ever since Brent had laid eyes on him. When had Brent figured out the relationship? All he wanted from her was access to his son. It wasn't her he loved, no matter what he said. He was using her.

She was done being used. Done having a specific purpose and then discarded. She'd done what her dad wanted and it had never been enough. Shame burned her face as she remembered what it was like to have that held over her every day. Never good enough. Never loved for herself. Always being used.

No more. At least she'd eventually pulled free of her father and tried to rebuild herself. And with his death last year, she'd thought the bonds were shattered. It didn't feel like it. They'd be part of her forever, pulling her down, pulling Finnley down.

How had she thought she'd be a better parent than Lori? She had just as much baggage as her sister. Different baggage, but it was still there, like their father lived beyond his grave.

"Allison?"

She became aware of Jo's gentle voice, of the tears blurring her own vision.

Keanan pulled her into his arms. She stiffened and pushed away. He probably didn't mean anything by it, but this wasn't the time to find out.

"I'm fine." It didn't sound like her voice, all scratchy and loud and defiant, but it was.

"Allison, what time does Finnley go to bed? Because I'm coming over tonight. You need someone to share the burden."

"B-but Maddie…"

"She goes to bed at eight. Her daddy will be home for her." She raised her voice. "Right, Zach?"

Zach gave a thumbs-up to Jo and a worried glance to Allison. Oh, man. It was bad enough letting another woman into her private space. What if Jo told Zach? She couldn't stand him knowing. Or Noel, or Gabe, or Keanan. Was this what the farm team's full disclosure meant to everyone?

All her dirty laundry, hung out for everyone to inspect. To be horrified over. To shake their heads at what she'd done, what she'd allowed to happen. She'd been weak. She wasn't anymore, and she didn't want to remember.

But she couldn't keep the memories back. Not with all this stuff with Finnley and Lori and Brent crowding in. She'd been trying to manage on her own all her life.

She met Jo's concerned gaze. "He goes to bed at nine."

Jo nodded and reached for the next chicken. "I'll be there."

Chapter 31

*B*rent eyed Curtis as the truck turned southward for another weekend in Coeur d'Alene. After another week where he'd been unable to make headway with Allison. "What's on your mind, man?"

It wasn't like Curtis to relinquish control of the other truck to Franco and request a ride with Brent instead. Could he hack the younger guy's chatter all the way to the city? Or worse, his snipes against Allison?

Curtis flexed his shoulders and glanced sideways at Brent. "Got a problem."

"Oh?"

"You know I've been seeing Nya."

Not precisely news. "The waitress at The Sizzling Skillet."

Curtis nodded. "She's, uh, pregnant."

Brent gripped the wheel and breathed a prayer for the right words. "Yours?"

"Yeah. That's what she says." Curtis took a deep breath. "Probably true."

"What are you going to do?" The girl couldn't be over twenty.

"She said she's getting an abortion. She can't tell her parents."

The words stabbed Brent deep in the gut. Gina hadn't even been able to tell him. Had her parents known? Probably not, at the time. He managed to keep his voice level. "Is that what you want?"

Curtis grimaced. "I don't know what I want. To erase everything, I guess."

"Abortion doesn't erase things. Just sayin'."

"Seems like it would."

"It doesn't. They try to tell you it will, but it doesn't." *Please, God, give me words.* "A woman is haunted all her life knowing she killed her baby."

"Embryo, dude. Not a baby."

"Oh, come on, Curtis. You're a grownup." Though that might be debatable. "You know where babies come from. Fertilized eggs turn into embryos that turn into babies. And there's only one way eggs get fertilized."

"Yeah. I guess."

"Abortion isn't the only option, you know. You could—"

"I'm not marrying her. That's so old-fashioned."

"With that attitude, you're right."

Curtis's jaw jutted out. "What do you mean?"

"Two wrongs don't make a right. You're not doing the baby or Nya any favors getting married if you're not committed to raising a family together. To staying together no matter what."

"Whew."

Silence reigned as they drove south. "Look, I know where you're coming from on this."

Curtis chuckled. "Yeah, right."

"Really."

"Oh, Mr. Perfect is only an illusion?"

Brent's knuckles turned white on the steering wheel. "I'm not sure how you ever got that impression. I'm so not perfect." But hadn't he been doing his best to hide everything in his past that wasn't? Still, flaunting it was stupid, to say nothing of humiliating.

Here went humiliation.

"I was pretty messed up in college. I barely attended enough class to get by. My life was full of alcohol and girls."

Curtis swung in the passenger seat to face him. "No way."

"I just found out the other day that I got one of my girlfriends pregnant and she had an abortion. She hated me but didn't tell me. But then she found God—"

"Don't even start on the religious stuff."

"It's part of the story."

Curtis crossed his arms. "Whatever."

"Gina found God and forgave me for what I'd done to her. After a while she met a great guy and they got married. Now she can't get pregnant. The abortion messed up her insides." Brent shot a glance at Curtis. "Do you want something like that on your conscience? Because it's not that great a reality to live with."

"You said *one* of your girlfriends. How many did you have?"

Yeah, he'd hoped Curtis would miss that. "Quite a few."

"You? I'd never have guessed."

"I've changed my ways, Curtis, but not before a lot of things happened I regret. Gina's pregnancy and abortion was only one of them. I lived a very selfish life and it took some major stuff before God whacked me upside the head to get my attention."

"I said no religious talk."

"Look, you came to me for advice, and you're stuck in this truck with me for another couple of hours while I give it. We've got a few things to cover here, like the realities of being a single parent, about the option of adoption, and about the fact that God cares what happens to you, Nya, and the baby. Feel free to ask questions, but we're going in."

Maybe God had allowed him to run wild to the end of his rope so he could talk to guys like Curtis from a position of understanding.

o0o

"You were just a child trying to please your father." Jo said over a cup of tea.

Allison's long hair shielded her from Jo's gaze. "I should've known better."

"Listen to me. You're not the only child in this world who's been violated by a parent. It was not your fault."

"But—"

"Allison."

She didn't want to meet Jo's gaze, but she did want to be free of this weight. She'd already told Jo more than she'd ever divulged to another human being other than her mother. Fat lot of good that had done.

Stop making things up, Allison, and pretending they're real.

Yeah, stop being like Mom, who'd pretended her own ideals were reality. And if Mom wouldn't believe her, who else would have? Only Lori, and she'd been trapped in the same nightmare until she ran away, leaving Allison to be the sole recipient.

"You've never talked about this with anyone, have you." Jo wasn't asking a question.

Allison shook her head. Even Chelsea had gotten the skimmed-over version the other day.

"Have you thought of getting some counseling? Talking to someone who can help you break the bonds of the past? Because they're like a forcefield on your shoulders, and you need rid of it, girl."

"You don't understand," Allison whispered. "It can't be gotten rid of. It happened. I can't undo that." God only knew how hard she'd tried. Begged for relief.

Jo surged to her feet and paced the small living room. "Have you met Pastor Ron's wife, Wanda?"

Allison blinked. "Um, I think so?"

"She's a trained counselor. She can help. May I call her for you?"

"No." The word shot out of Allison's lips. "I'm sorry, Jo. I shouldn't have told you all this. Promise me you won't tell anyone else. I couldn't hold my head up."

Jo knelt in front of Allison and grasped both her hands. "It's not your burden to carry."

"Whose is it then?" Allison yanked her hands away and stood, putting the chair between them. "It's me it happened to."

"Jesus."

The name hung in the air between them, almost visible. Allison stared at Jo.

"Allison, you're a Christian. You've accepted Jesus' sacrifice on your behalf. But you have to claim it and live it. I don't know how to help you with that, but Wanda does."

Part of her yearned for it. But she'd opened up to Jo, and Jo didn't have answers, only the name of someone else she should talk to. What if Wanda didn't have the answer, either, and referred her to someone else?

"You don't understand. I've prayed."

Man, she hated seeing sympathy in Jo's eyes. "I'm sure you have, sweetie. But this freedom is worth pursuing."

Allison shook her head. "Did anything like this ever happen to you when you were a kid?"

"No. My stepfather didn't give me the time of day. I guess I can be thankful."

"Yeah."

"But he still nearly ruined me for marriage. He and my mother didn't model anything I wanted."

"Men are idiots. They take and take and take."

"Women are idiots, too."

Allison narrowed her gaze at Jo.

"Look, we don't have to be victims. Men and women — we're all human. We're all tainted by sin. It's got nothing to do with gender. We've all had different upbringings. Some were raised in solid homes where their parents loved and respected each other. Like Zach. You've seen Rosemary and Steve. Can you imagine either of them a victim? Can you imagine them unhappy in their marriage, even with Steve's disability?"

Allison shook her head. But if she'd had a decent upbringing, she'd be good to go, too.

"Claire, Noel, me… we had messed-up lives as kids. Not the same as you, but there's more than one brand of dysfunctional." Jo leaned closer. "Jesus can heal them all."

What had Brent's childhood been like? What caused him to live a wild life in college?

If she forced herself to admit it, his lifestyle wasn't that unusual. Lots of young people that age partied. Drank. Did drugs. Slept around. Why did she hate it so much in him?

Because of Lori. Because she couldn't think of kissing Brent without thinking about him kissing her sister. Living with her. Having sex with her.

"Tell me why you can't relax and get to know Brent. He seems like a great guy. He loves the Lord."

It was like Jo read her mind.

"Is it only because of your childhood? Or is there something more with him?"

Jo had no idea. A sob caught in Allison's throat and she fought it down, turning away to hide the tears that threatened to overflow.

"Allison? Tell me about Brent."

"Didn't Gina tell everyone?" The bitterness in her voice surprised even Allison.

"Gina?" Jo sounded perplexed. "Gina who?"

That name should never have erupted from Allison's mouth. She knew Jo well enough to know everything would come out now. Allison glanced toward Finnley's bedroom door — closed — and took a deep breath.

"Gina and Parker were here for Sierra's wedding."

"Oh, right. I remember meeting them. They stayed over and came out to the farm for breakfast on Monday with a bunch of other people."

Allison squeezed her eyes shut and nodded.

"Sh-she used to be Brent's… girlfriend. She got p-pregnant and had an abortion."

"Oh, no."

"He didn't know anything about it until Monday." She peered at Jo from behind lowered lashes, waiting for the reaction.

Jo's eyebrows pulled together. "She and Parker came in the house talking about how good God is. That doesn't sound—"

"She said she'd been praying for him. That she forgave him."

"Well, that's awesome then." Jo looked at her again. "Isn't it?"

Allison bit her lip.

"So there's more. Keep going."

"Gina…" Allison swallowed hard. "She said she knew she wasn't the only one. They talked about Denver. About when this happened."

"And…?" prompted Jo when Allison paused.

"My sister was there then."

"Uh huuuh?"

Did Allison have to spell everything out? She raised her jaw and faced Jo. "Brent is Finnley's father."

Jo sank into the nearest chair. "No."

"Oh, yes."

"Did he tell you that? Or did you…" Jo fluttered her hands.

"Make it up due to them looking alike? He told me. After the thing with Gina."

"Oh, man."

Allison couldn't look at Jo while thoughts and emotions ran across her friend's face. "Can I make you another cup of tea?"

"Sure. Please."

Her hands trembled as she added water to the kettle and turned the element on.

"That must've been a blow. All of it."

"You have no idea."

Jo laughed without humor. "I can imagine. But this isn't the Brent we know today."

Allison pivoted. "What do you mean? Same guy."

"But he's changed his ways. He's a Christian now."

"It's still him inside. Don't you get it? He used women. He slept with my sister."

"Sweetie, when we come to God and ask Him to forgive us, does He do it?"

Trick question, but there was only one right answer. Allison forced it out between clenched teeth. "Yes."

"We are not the same people after accepting God's gift. How can we be? The Bible calls us new creations. Says the old is gone and everything is new."

If only that undid Brent and Lori. Finnley.

The kettle boiled and Allison fixed the tea. She brought a cup to Jo and curled up in the other chair. "I wish I hadn't said anything."

To Jo's credit, she did not roll her eyes. "Why?"

"Because..." Allison studied the tea in her cup. "Because now you know too much about me."

"You think it gives me power over you? That I'd use it against you?"

Allison swallowed hard and tried to still the trembling teacup.

"Oh, sweetie. Never. God is big enough to deal with the pain in your past. He's big enough to give Brent forgiveness and a new hope for the future, too." Jo leaned forward in Allison's peripheral. "He's big enough to forgive your sister for what she's done."

Forgive Lori? "But... Finnley..."

"I know," Jo said simply.

"And Brent." Even harder.

Jo nodded. "God is bigger. More compassionate."

It didn't take much to be more compassionate than she'd been. She could almost forgive Lori. After all, she understood the circumstances that started it all. But Brent… she'd almost trusted him.

"Everyone has weeds in their lives, Allison. You have a crop of uncommonly stubborn burrs. The big burr got plucked when you came to faith in Jesus, but some of the little hooks stayed stuck inside you. It's time to let Jesus remove those, too."

"But how?" The whispered words hung in the air before Allison realized they'd left her mouth.

"I'll pray with you. For you. But would you consent to talking to Wanda? She'll know the right way to guide you to freedom."

Freedom. It sounded so impulsive. Like twirling in the sand. Like dancing to unheard music. Like a kite flying with no tether.

Could she handle freedom? It might mean giving up control. Everything could blow up in her face.

But what could be worse than reality? It might be worth the chance to let God do some weeding in her life. It might be painful, but life already was.

I love you, my child. Let me take over.

If she couldn't trust God, there really was no hope.

She met Jo's gaze and nodded. "Okay. I'll talk to her."

Valerie Comer

Chapter 32 --

*I*t wasn't like Finnley to sleep so late in the morning, even on a Saturday with few plans. Hopefully he hadn't stayed up listening to Allison and Jo talk in the other room. They'd really tried to keep their voices down so he wouldn't overhear.

What if he had, though? Allison eyed his closed bedroom door.

Was it fair to keep the knowledge of who his father was from him? But he was barely four. It couldn't matter to him yet. And besides, Brent should be the one to tell him if anyone did.

Allison pulled her class planner out and spread the material on the kitchen table. Almost as dangerous, because thinking about the farm school made her think of the builder. Brent.

She'd give Finnley a bit longer. She'd push Brent out of her mind and get some work done.

An hour later, her stomach rumbled. Mid-morning? She glanced again at Finnley's bedroom door. She'd better wake him. It boded ill for the rest of the day and the next night if he slept this long.

"Buddy?" She tapped on his bedroom door before opening it slightly. "Time to wake up." She crossed to the blackout blind, adjusted it to allow some light into the room, then turned to his bed.

It was empty.

Allison froze.

She couldn't have missed hearing him go to the bathroom, could she? "Finnley? Where are you?"

Not in the bathroom. She hurried back to his bedroom, heart pounding. Sleeping in the closet? But he wasn't in there, either. He was so quiet and disappeared so often. Where could he be?

Allison tried to swallow the panic that rose in her throat, but it kept welling higher, faster, harder until she thought she might pass out.

How could she lose a four-year-old?

Her gaze swung to the front door. He could reach that knob. He'd done it before. She focused on the shoe shelf by the door. His shoes were missing.

She ran back into his bedroom and flipped on the overhead light. His mussed bed sat in the corner with no pajamas lying on them. But his Superman backpack was missing.

Allison sank onto the edge of Finnley's bed.

He'd run away. And every single time he'd done it before, she'd found him with Brent. So he was probably up at the house. When had he slid out without her noticing? She needed a bolt high up, out of his reach. But it was too late, at least for this time. *Please, God, let there be a next time.*

She shoved her feet into her sandals and ran up the path to the half-finished house. Yes, he could manage the knob at the duplex, but the doors up here were heavier. No sign of entry. But it was still the most logical place. She opened the French door and stepped inside, closing it behind her, imagining Finnley doing the same thing.

"Finnley? Come to Auntie Allison."

Silence.

She took a deep breath and climbed the stairs to the loft. "Buddy?" She hurried into Finnley's room, still clad in vapor-barrier covered insulation, the closet but a row of studs to divide

268

it from his bedroom.

Definitely not here, or anywhere in the loft. She hurtled down the steps and checked the entire house, which only took a few minutes. With no furniture and unfinished walls, hiding places were few. Brent kept the worksite tidied right up.

Allison pressed both hands against the wall, squeezed her eyes shut, and tried to banish the ringing in her head. The desire to scream nearly overwhelmed her. No. She had to think clearly. Think. Where could Finnley be?

Time to go next door and see if he'd showed up to play with Maddie, maybe. But Jo would have let her know. Her phone was charged, right? She patted her pocket. She'd left it on the table at home. Well, she didn't need it to walk next door.

Allison crossed the small yard in a few heartbeats and jogged up the steps to the log house deck. Jane Eyre stretched her way out of the box, and two kittens tumbled out. No Danny Boy. But that wasn't unusual. Finnley's favorite kitten had been known to curl up down by their place. He'd even snuck inside a time or two.

Zach opened the door to Allison's knock. "Hi! What's up?" He looked past her, obviously expecting to see her nephew.

"Have you seen Finnley? I can't find him anywhere." She hated that her voice rose with every word.

Zach frowned. "No, I haven't seen him. Come in a minute." He turned from the door, leaving it open. "Jo! Have you seen Finnley? Allison can't find him."

Please please please.

Pajama-clad Maddie perched on Jo's hip, little legs straddling the bulge of her sibling.

Jo shook her head, her worried gaze meeting Allison's. "No, I haven't seen him since yesterday afternoon. He was already in bed when I came over last night."

"When did he go missing, Allison?" Zach asked.

Valerie Comer

"I don't know. I tucked him in bed, and I didn't check on him. I mean, I never do. Why would I? He's asleep."

Jo nodded as she handed Maddie off to Zach. "So you haven't seen him this morning?"

Numbly, Allison shook her head. "I went to look a few minutes ago, thinking this was rather late for him to be sleeping in. But he wasn't there. His shoes and backpack are missing."

Jo and Zach exchanged a glance.

"You've checked the house, I gather?" Zach's chin jutted next door.

Allison nodded. "Not a sign of him. That's as far as I've gotten."

"I'll go roust out Noel and Claire," Zach said. "And Keanan. We'll find him in no time."

"I'll come, too," said Jo.

Zach shook his head. "We need someone to stay put in the big house, and that's you and Maddie. A command center."

"But—"

Zach leaned over and kissed her. "No buts, love. It's you."

Jo gritted her teeth and accepted Maddie back from him. "Okay, fine. But hurry. It may be July, but he could still have gotten really cold last night." She looked at Allison. "Do you think he wandered up the mountain?"

Allison spread her hands. "I don't think so? But I don't know. He's never seemed really interested in it."

"What is he really interested in?" Zach guided Allison back out the door.

"Brent." The word came out with bitterness.

"Let's check Keanan first. He likes him, too."

Allison pulled away from Zach's hand at the bottom of the steps. "You talk to Keanan. I'll go find Claire."

"I'll be there in a minute!" called Jo as she shut the door.

Zach nodded. "I'll meet you back at the big house. If no one has seen him, we'll make a plan from there."

Allison ran down the trail. First she'd grab her phone, then she'd find Claire. Surely Finnley wouldn't have gone too far. She could imagine him perched on a tall stool at the peninsula while Noel whipped up breakfast for him.

Only someone would have let her know.

oOo

"Your mind seems elsewhere, Brent." Patrick glanced his way before lining up his next swing.

Brent was an indifferent golfer at the best of times, but he couldn't shake the feeling he should have stayed in Galena Landing this weekend. For the five thousandth time he reminded himself that the ball was in Allison's court. He'd made it clear how he felt about both her and Finnley. Hanging around on his days off wouldn't accomplish anything.

"She pretty?"

Very. Brent grimaced. "Nice try, Patrick."

"Well, you do keep a man guessing." Patrick drove the ball. "Still have Allison Hart on your mind?"

And on his heart. Brent watched as the ball flew toward the distant green. The way he'd been golfing today, it was going to take at least four swings to get his ball where Patrick's had gone in one.

"Guess that answers my question."

Brent angled a look at his uncle. "What does?"

"Your silence. A few months ago you couldn't stop talking about how much she annoyed you. Last time, you dropped a bombshell. Now you don't want to talk about her at all."

"She's not talking to me." Brent lined up his golf club and eyed the distance.

Patrick shook his head. "And the boy?"

Brent pulled back and swung the club, connecting with the ball. It soared toward the green, but a bit far to the right.

271

Shouldn't be too hard to get it back on course.

"Tell me what's happening." Patrick climbed onto the golf cart.

Brent rejoined him. "There's nothing to tell."

"What about the little boy, your son? Have you talked to her about him?"

Brent's phone rang, and his heart jolted. *Allison*. He hadn't heard that ring tone nearly as often as he'd hoped when he'd added it to his contact list. He pulled the phone from his pocket with trembling hands and thumbed it on. "Hello?"

He held his breath. Which Allison would be at the other end? An Allison ready to yell at him some more? An Allison who had discovered something wrong with the house? Dare he hope for an Allison who'd decided she loved him back?

"Brent? It's Finnley. He's gone missing." Her voice broke. "Do you have any ideas where he might have gone? Anywhere he talked about to you?"

Brent stumbled off the golf cart, barely noticing it was still running. "Missing?" He pulled in a deep, shuddering breath. "Since when? Tell me what happened."

"I-I tucked him in bed last night, same as usual. And I thought he was just sleeping in this morning but when I finally checked, he wasn't there. Then I noticed his shoes and backpack were gone, too."

"You've checked the new house."

"Yes. Zach and Keanan and Noel and Claire and I have combed the entire farm. We've searched every building and the horse corral. We've gone next door to see if Rosemary had seen him, but she hasn't."

Numerous possibilities whizzed through his head, only to be discarded. He could only grab onto one thought. "I'm coming. I'll be there as quickly as I can."

"But—"

"Allison." His voice choked up as he walked further from the

272

golf cart. "Allison, I love you. I love Finnley. I can't stay here doing nothing when you guys need me. Okay? I'm coming."

"Okay. But I just wanted to know if you have any ideas."

He had ideas all right. They included kissing her. They included gathering Finnley up in both their arms in a group hug. They did *not* include not finding his son.

His son.

Brent glanced back at the golf cart, where Patrick sat with a smirk on his face. "Allison, I'll give you a call again as soon as I'm on the road. I have Bluetooth in the truck, so we can talk without me causing an accident. I'll let you know if I think of something."

She hesitated. "Okay."

"I love you."

The line went dead, but that was okay. She'd heard his words. She'd called him when she needed help, and she'd accepted his offer. He jogged back to the cart.

Patrick's eyebrows rose above twinkling eyes. "Anything you want to tell me?"

"You get the short version. Finnley has gone missing, and I'm leaving for Galena Landing right now. Sorry about the golf game."

Valerie Comer

Chapter 33 ---

Noel and Keanan had taken Domino up the hillside behind the
building site. Zach and Claire were going over both farms one
more time, looking for places a little boy in dark green
pajamas might be hiding.

Allison borrowed Keanan's bike with its little trailer and rode
down Thompson Road, calling Finnley's name. If she found him,
she'd have a way to carry him home. If no one did, they'd meet
back at the farm at noon and call the police to activate a search
team. Would that be a mark against her for maintaining custody?

How could he have disappeared right out of the duplex while
she was sleeping?

What if something more sinister had happened? Maybe
someone from Lori or John's past had grabbed Finnley as some
kind of dark punishment. No, she couldn't think that. He'd just
wandered off. He wasn't a pawn in some ominous game, just a
little boy who'd gotten something into his head and let himself
out the door.

But what?

"Brent live there?" he'd asked when he saw the Timber
Framing Plus truck at The Landing Pad.

He'd gone in search of Brent. She was certain, but it would take too long to cycle into town. She tapped Zach's icon in her phone. "Check at The Landing Pad. He may have tried to find Brent there."

"Where are you?" Zach asked.

"Just past Elmer's."

"Finnley couldn't possibly have walked as far as Galena Landing, but I'll get Claire to drive in and see. Noel and Keanan are still up the mountain. I'll hop on my bike and join you as quickly as I can."

She thumbed the call off and her phone rang again.

Brent. "How are you holding up?" He didn't even bother to ask if she'd found Finnley. He had to know she'd call and tell him if she had.

She took a deep breath and willed the panic from her voice. "I don't know."

"I'm just south of Galena Landing. I'll be there really soon. Where will I find you?"

"On the road. We think he may have tried to walk to town. He saw one of your trucks at the hotel one day and asked if you lived there."

"Oh, no. That's much too far. Does he even know the way?"

"Depends on how closely he's paid attention, I guess. We've driven it often enough."

"I'll stop by The Landing Pad and see."

"Claire's on her way there." Literally. The farm's old VW hatchback roared out of the driveway toward Allison. She scooted the bike a bit farther off the road and waved as Claire shot by.

"I'll see you in a few minutes." Then, as he'd done the other five times he'd called this morning, he began to pray into his headset, asking God to take care of Finnley and to give Allison and the others wisdom to find him. And peace.

She really needed that peace he asked for.

His "I love you" lingered in her mind after the call

disconnected. She stared blankly into the nearby field. Did the future hold anything for her and Brent? Not if she couldn't find his child.

A self-propelled swather churned toward her down Elmer's field, cutting the tall grass for hay. What if Finnley was hiding in there? Would the driver see him in time to stop?

She scrambled off the bike and ran into the field toward the contraption, waving both arms. The gears shifted and the machine slowed. A creak of brakes, then the blades stopped turning.

Elmer peered down at her through the cab's open window. "What's wrong?"

"My little nephew has gone missing, and I'm worried he might be hiding in your field. He's only about so high." Allison measured off hip height. Below the top of the grass. "I'm not sure if you'd even be able to see him if he's in here."

Elmer glared at her for a second, shaking his head. Then he took a long look around the field. "Doubt he's in here. I'd be able to see if someone pushed through. Makes a kind of trail." He pulled a lever and the blades began to whirr again.

"Please wait!" Allison shouted.

"Perfect weather to get the hay off," he called back. "It's supposed to rain by next weekend. Got no time to lose."

"But a little boy—" She jumped in front of the machine and stood, arms akimbo.

Elmer gave an irritated wave. "Get out of my way, missy!"

She shook her head. He wouldn't dare run her over on purpose. That would be murder, plain and simple, the way those blades cut.

He waved both arms in a shooing motion, his face pulled into an angry glower.

"What's going on here?" yelled Zach.

Allison glanced over her shoulder at the man making his way through the waist-high grass toward them. She nearly wept in relief. Zach could make this man stop.

Elmer pulled the lever and the blades stopped churning. "I might ask the same thing of you folks. Get off my property and let me cut my hay."

Zach glanced at Allison then looked back at Elmer. "We're looking for a little boy who could be hidden in the tall grass."

She didn't feel so crazy standing in Elmer's way with Zach jumping to the same conclusion she had.

"Look, you can't tromp all over my field, flattening my crop, on the off chance your runaway is here. You'll ruin my cows' winter feed supply."

Zach raised his chin. "You'd rather run over a little kid with that machine and kill him?"

Allison quaked.

"Of course not." Elmer shook his head. "But what're the odds he's here? Practically zero. I got work to do."

"Look. Give us two hours. I'll get Jo to fix you lunch and bring it over along with some of that raspberry vinegar she makes. Go inside, out of the hot sun—"

"Tractor's got air conditioning—"

"—and give us some time to find the child. Please."

The man shook his head, glaring at them both.

Where was Noel, anyway? He was the only one who knew Elmer well. Maybe he could talk sense into the man.

Of course, Finnley could be somewhere on the farm between this one and Steve and Rosemary's. He could be across the road. He could be halfway to Galena Landing. There was no real reason to think he was on Elmer's property.

"Two hours?" Elmer shut off the tractor.

The silence was near deafening.

"That's all I give you. I gotta get this whole field cut today or I'll never get the hay off before it rains."

"Thanks, Elmer." Zach pulled out his phone. "I'll call Jo and ask her to bring some lunch down for you."

Elmer waved his hand dismissively. "No need. You can't bribe me that way. I'm doing this out of the goodness of my heart."

The *what?* Allison managed to keep her face expressionless. Two hours wasn't long, but hopefully it would be long enough. If rescue crews had to be called, doubtless they *would* tromp all over this field and ruin Elmer's hay.

Who ever let her pretend to be a responsible adult? She was no better than Lori or John. No, she hadn't starved or beaten Finnley, but she also hadn't made him feel loved and secure.

If she'd done it right, he'd be safe and sound right now. Wouldn't he?

oOo

Brent hit the brakes as he rounded the final corner before Green Acres Farm. Two bicycles, one with a kiddy trailer he recognized as Keanan's sat along the roadside. Jealousy surged through him.

Loving and protecting Finnley and Allison was his responsibility, not Keanan's, but he'd done a poor job. He'd let her push him aside. His pride had made it easy to acquiesce. Instead of allowing himself to be vulnerable and showing his love, he'd hidden his past, telling himself it was for the best.

It had *not* been for the best. A guy didn't get to have experience — good or bad — without becoming responsible to help others. Like Curtis, who at least now planned to talk to Nya and see where the situation took them.

Brent leaped from the truck as his gaze snagged Allison and Zach walking toward him through the tall grass. He allowed the immensity of the field of tall grass to soak in. How would they ever find Finnley in that?

Claire pulled in right behind his truck.

He couldn't let her get to Allison before he did. Brent burst into a run and caught Allison in his arms. Her hands slid around his neck as he picked her up in a tight squeeze. With everyone watching he didn't dare — nah, he didn't care what they thought. Her lips were right there, waiting for his to brush across them.

One kiss wasn't enough. Brent clutched her in his arms and nuzzled into her neck for a brief moment. Allison melted against him and he stifled a groan. Zach. Claire.

Finnley. His son.

He set Allison back down but kept one arm firmly around her as he turned toward the others. "What's the plan?"

He didn't miss the wink Zach gave Claire. Whatever.

Zach's face quickly sobered as he outlined where all they'd searched in the few hours since Allison had noticed Finnley had disappeared. "Anywhere we missed?" he finished up.

Brent sorted through the information. They'd covered the house and farm school. The entire farm, for that matter. Allison's thought that Finnley had tried to find him rang true.

If only he hadn't encouraged the boy's adoration. No. He wasn't going there. It was counter-productive. The past was past. The future would be different.

He surveyed the field. "No one could get in here without leaving a trail, could they?"

Claire shook her head. "No. If we had a plane or helicopter, I'm sure we could see clearly. There's been just enough wind in the past few days to blow down the edges of the field a little so an entry point wouldn't be obvious."

Brent pivoted toward her. "Who do we know with a plane?"

"Uh..." Claire looked at Allison.

"Search and rescue," Zach put in. "Time to call them, I think. We've done what we can without help."

Allison cut off a sob, and Brent pulled her closer. "I agree. Do you have a number for them? Will 9-1-1 get to the right place?"

"I think so." Zach made the call. After he'd spoken to the dispatcher, he turned the phone off. "It will probably take an hour before they're mobilized."

"I'll see if Noel and Keanan are off the mountain yet." Claire tapped her cell. After listening a moment, she shook her head. "Goes straight to voice mail."

"They're searching up there?" Brent asked.

Claire nodded. "No one knows that mountainside better than Noel." She smirked at Zach. "Even the guy who grew up running wild on it."

"Could be," said Zach. "I trust him to know how to scour it." He looked around the hayfield. "Okay, if search can get an overview here in an hour, that's all we can ask for. Elmer is giving us two hours before he resumes cutting hay. Says he can't wait any longer than that."

Anger boiled up in Brent. And fear. "But—"

Zach held up a hand. "Yeah, I know. But it will be fine. Really. Look, why don't you take Allison back to the farm? Claire and I can keep looking in this area until help arrives." He started toward the road, Claire behind him.

Allison pushed her way out of Brent's arms. "No. I'm staying. He's my responsibility."

"I'm staying, too. He's my…" Brent hesitated, holding Allison's gaze. "Finnley is my son."

Zach turned slowly, but Claire whipped around. "*What?*" Her gaze dashed between Brent's and Allison's.

He reached for Allison's hand and — thank God — caught it. Her slight squeeze gave him the strength to speak out. "I lived a rather promiscuous life for a while in college. Allison's sister Mallory was only one of the girlfriends I had in those years. I made every kind of mistake. I've asked God to forgive me, and He has, but the consequences still exist."

"Whoa. I never guessed." Questions still flared on Claire's face. "When we find Finnley, I need to hear more." She pinned

Allison with her gaze. "But for now, we've got a little boy to locate." She followed Zach to the road.

Brent stood rooted in the field.

Allison stepped in front of him and he locked his hands behind her back. "I'm sorry if I shouldn't have said all that in front of your friends."

"I'm glad you did. I'm done hiding things. There are things you need to know about me, too."

He met her gaze from a few inches away. "Like what?" Did she have a secret child hidden away? An abortion in her past? That would explain her reaction to Gina's revelation. Maybe they should have this conversation later. After they'd found Finnley.

"My father... he abused me. Sexually. Many times while I was growing up." Allison's eyes focused on her hands fussing with the collar on his shirt.

Brent slid his hands up her back and into her long hair. He swept the strands away from her face and cupped it with both hands. "Allison?"

Her eyes darted to meet his then shifted back to his collar.

"Allison. I'm so sorry to hear that." He pressed a gentle kiss on her lips.

"I was never good enough," she whispered. "He used me and never loved me. He was my dad. He should have done better."

"He should have." Brent kissed her again.

"I decided all men used women, so I'd never get close enough to be caught again. Never be a victim again."

That explained a lot. He tipped her chin, but her eyes refused to meet his. "Allison, look at me, please. I want to make you a promise."

She swallowed hard. "It's too soon."

"Not for this one. Please? Trust me?"

Her brown eyes shone with tears as she met his gaze. Vulnerable in a way he'd never guessed she could be. "Allison, I love you. I will never ever use that to get my own way. I won't push you. I won't force you." How could he make her believe him? He couldn't. Only time would prove his words. "Listen to me, darling. I give you my heart. Not because of Finnley. You had it before I ever met him."

Her jaw trembled beneath his palms.

Gentle. He had to let her lead. He knew it with certainty down to the soles of his feet. "Allison, you have my heart. It will always belong to you. There's no one else for me in this entire world. I don't want an answer today. I'm not even going to ask you the big question today. In fact, I'm not going to ask it, ever."

Her startled eyes met his and her lips parted.

He brushed his against them gently. "I want to marry you, Allison. I want to make a home with you and Finnley and the little ones God will bless us with. But I won't push you. I won't beg you. It's up to you, sweetheart. When you're ready, tell me. I'll be waiting for you."

She swallowed hard. "What if I'm never ready?"

Brent rested his forehead against hers. "I'll be praying every single day that you will be. My heart is in your hands. And we are both in God's." He kissed her once more then released her until only their eyes held them together.

Chapter 34 ---

*A*n hour later, a helicopter had criss-crossed Elmer's field from every angle.

Allison watched, hand tucked firmly in Brent's, as Zach took the call from the pilot. Zach rubbed his temple with his free hand and thanked the man.

"He sees no sign of a path into the field." Zach's gaze met hers briefly. "He'll check the next tall field down the road."

"Any point in joining the group on the mountain?" asked Brent.

Twenty experienced searchers searched alongside Noel and Keanan.

"I wish I knew." Zach rubbed his forehead.

Allison had badly misjudged Zach and Noel. She'd never dreamed these men would give so selflessly for her. For her nephew. To say nothing of Brent. After all she'd put him through, he held her hand and stood by her side.

She didn't deserve him. Didn't deserve all this care.

No. Jo had told her to stop the negative self-talk. Reminded her that Jesus' sacrifice covered it all.

She took a deep breath and looked from Brent to Claire. "How hard did either of you watch for him from the vehicle windows between here and Galena Landing?"

"I was driving pretty fast," Brent admitted. "I needed to be here with you."

Claire shook her head. "I went fast, too, but I was watching. Too bad he didn't wear the orange Tigger pajamas last night. Those green ones are practically camouflage. He definitely wasn't walking down the road, but I can't guarantee he wasn't peeking out of the ditch or something."

Brent tugged Allison toward his truck. "That's what we'll do, then. We'll drive slowly and each watch out our window. We'll call his name."

Zach looked at Claire. "We can quarter the field across the road. There aren't as many hiding places as in this hayfield."

Claire stared at the barbed wire fence. "Does he know how to get through one of those?"

Allison grimaced. "Keanan taught him. He knows the difference between the barbed wire ones and the electric ones, too."

Zach poked his chin toward the fence. "Percy's isn't electric. No power hook-up. And he rotated his cows out a few weeks ago. He usually takes a late summer cut of hay off this field."

Allison climbed into the passenger side of Brent's work truck. As soon as he started the engine, she slid the window down. He backed into Elmer's driveway to turn around then drove slowly toward town. She kept her eyes roving the ditch, the fence line, the little copses of trees near the road.

"Finnley!" she called out, alternating with Brent calling out the driver's window.

She caught a glimpse of a patch of odd green. "Stop!" she yelled, opening the door and sliding out before Brent had time to follow through. She stumbled and surged through the ditch, thankfully empty of water in early July. Her heart sank almost immediately. The little bush by the fence did not provide enough cover, and the green she'd seen had simply been a discarded pop bottle. She tossed it in the back of Brent's truck and got back in.

Brent reached across the console and rested his hand on her knee. "We'll find him, darling."

Allison blinked back tears. Tried to blink back memories of snatches of newscasts where children went missing. Sure, some were found safe and sound, but others had been abducted. Molested. Killed. Others were never found at all. And then there were wild animals. Bears coming off the mountain. Coyotes. Maybe even wolves or cougars. At least it wasn't snake country.

Finnley was such a little boy with scrawny little boy muscles. What could he fight off? Nothing bigger than Danny Boy.

Brent pulled her against him as much as the console would allow. "Father God, we are still here. Still asking You to protect Finnley. Still asking You to help us find this small child. Please give the searchers wisdom and sharp eyes. Lord, I pray especially for Allison." His voice trembled. "And for me. Please give us peace. We claim the peace of Jesus in our hearts. In His name we ask these things. Amen."

"Amen," she whispered, trying to smile. How had she thought all men were alike? All out only for their own selfish interests? No. She'd been so wrong.

Brent released the brake and the truck rolled forward.

Allison stared out the side window, looking for a little boy who needed to know he had a daddy who loved him and prayed for him.

oOo

How far could a four-year-old walk? A mile? Possibly more? At the two-mile mark from Green Acres, Brent turned the truck around.

A glance at Allison showed her mouth open in protest. She clamped it shut.

"There's no way he could have walked farther than this." Brent kept his voice light. "He's a kid, not Superman, no matter what his backpack says."

"I know. It's just..."

Brent squeezed her hand. "I know. We'll do the same thing driving back, but we'll be on opposite sides."

"And then what?" Her voice rose. Panic wasn't far below the surface.

Brent rubbed his thumb over the back of her hand. "And then we look some more."

Where, he had no idea. The professional search team was focused on the mountainside. The leader said it was the most likely place. Brent knew it was also the most dangerous, and the most important to cover before dark. They still had a few hours.

"Finnley, where are you?" he called out the truck window. "I love you, squirt!" He eased the truck forward a few yards while Allison called out the other side.

Twice he scrambled out of the truck, sure he'd seen something unusual, but it was never Finnley. "We'll find him," he said to Allison, but he could feel the panic clawing its way up his throat. It was all he could do to keep it together for her.

They rounded the last corner and coasted to a stop behind the VW. Far from the road, Zach bent back a bush, while Claire nearly disappeared into a hollow Brent hadn't even known was there.

He frowned. "I thought this land was flat."

Allison followed his gaze. "Mostly flat."

He put the truck in reverse and peeled backward around the curve then hit the brakes. "Come on." Brent shoved open the door.

She didn't wait for him but hopped out and came around the front of the truck to meet him. "What are you thinking?"

Brent scanned the terrain. "We're what, half a mile from the farm? Maybe a little more?"

She nodded.

288

"Far enough he'd be tired by now." Brent took Allison's hand and started down the embankment. "I think that dip Claire was in is an old creek bed." He skidded down, holding Allison's hand. "Aha. Just what I thought. There's enough water here during spring run-off to justify a culvert under the road."

Allison crouched down beside him as they peered in.

"Finnley?" called Brent. "Come here, little man."

He'd said the words so many times he'd almost given up hope for a reply. Had he really heard something this time?

"Finnley? Where are you?" His voice echoed in the metal tube.

"Hey, buddy, are you in here?" called Allison.

A faint scratching sound came from within and a tiny voice said, "Brent?"

"Yes!" It was all Brent could do not to leap to his feet with his fist thrust to the sky. "Can you come out now, squirt? I'm right here with Auntie Allison."

A hunched silhouette moved toward them.

Brent, still squatting, tugged Allison closer. She fell against him, knocking him over and, in a second, he was sprawled on the rocky ground with her practically on top, kissing him fervently.

A guy could get used to this. He kissed her back, holding her tight, but only for a moment before setting her aside and turning back to the large metal culvert.

A little boy in dark green pajamas crawled out, wearing a squirming Superman backpack and numerous bright red scratches. He hurled himself in Brent's arms, nearly knocking him over again.

"Brent! You came!"

Brent held the warm little body tight. He seemed okay. No broken bones, no lasting damage. "I'm so glad we found you, squirt. Auntie Allison was so worried about you." He closed his eyes. "And so was I."

Finnley sniffled against his neck. "She say you my daddy. Are you my daddy?"

Brent became aware of Allison's hands on his shoulders and her legs pressed against his back. He tilted his head back to meet her eyes. Would she be jealous of Finnley's attachment?

She blinked back tears but managed a smile with a shake of her head.

Could this really become his family?

Finnley squeezed Brent's cheeks between his little hands and peered into his eyes. "Are you?"

For a second, Brent struggled to remember the question. Ah, right, the daddy question. "Yes, squirt, I'm your daddy."

Allison massaged his shoulders.

"Where you live? Why you not here?"

Brent managed to clamber to his feet with Finnley in one arm. He pulled Allison tight with the other, and her arms wrapped around both of them.

"I love you, buddy," she said. "I'm glad you're safe."

"Rover keep me safe."

Allison frowned.

Brent rested his forehead against Finnley's. "You mean Jesus. Jesus kept you safe."

The little guy nodded. "Jesus."

"I should let everyone know we found him." Allison pulled out of the hug and tugged her phone out of her hip pocket as she climbed back to the road. She stood beside the truck, twisting long strands of hair behind her ear as she talked.

"Come on, squirt. Let's get you home. You hungry?"

"Yes. Danny Boy too."

"Danny Boy?" That would certainly explain the scratches on Finnley's hands and face.

Finnley nodded. "I keep him safe."

The wiggling backpack. Well, they wouldn't unzip that until they got back to the farm. The kitten was sure to bolt for freedom at the first chance he got, and Brent didn't want to waste time looking for him when he wanted to revel in the little boy's tight grip and Allison's love. Not that she'd said the words yet, but she would.

oOo

Allison held Finnley in her lap in the truck for the half-mile home as he clutched his backpack in front of him. "Why did you run off, little buddy?"

"You said he my daddy." Finnley squirmed so he could look at her with reproachful eyes. "I want daddy."

That much was pretty obvious. She'd spent months taking care of this child, her sister's boy. She'd fed him and clothed him and cared for him. And yes, loved him. Still he'd turned to Brent time and again.

Brent wanted to marry her. Not just because of Finnley, he said, but because he loved her.

Did she love him the same way? Or was this just the simplest solution? The easiest way for Finnley to have his daddy and for Brent to get what he wanted and for her to have... what? Security? Love?

She didn't want to choose Brent for Finnley's sake. Just the thought of it made her push away.

Brent turned into the driveway. Searchers already filed off the mountain to see the little boy that had been lost but was now found. Claire was right behind them in her beat-up car, and Zach was not far behind that on his bike. Someone would have to go back for Keanan's.

Jo rushed out of the straw bale house with Maddie straddling the baby bump.

Everyone had pulled together for her. For Finnley. They belonged here at Green Acres.

Brent grasped her hand across the console. "It's okay, Allison. No need to make big decisions in a time of stress and relief."

How could he always know what she was thinking? She met his gaze and, like a magnet, it drew her in until their lips touched.

"I love you," he whispered.

"Yes," said Finnley.

Claire yanked the truck door open and lifted Finnley from Allison's arms. "Hey, little guy. Good to see you safe and sound. What have you got there?" She pulled the zipper tab and a little orange paw emerged.

A second later Danny Boy erupted from the backpack and streaked across the farm, free at last.

"Where Danny Boy go?"

Allison slid out and gathered Finnley in her arms. This time, he didn't resist. "Off to find his mama and his breakfast. Let's get some food into your tummy, too, okay?"

Chapter 35 --

*A*llison drove the few blocks from Galena Gospel Church to
Lakeside Park on a late August afternoon. Even from the
parking lot she could see Brent's tanned back next to Mason
Waterman's gray muscle shirt.

Christopher ran down the sandy beach with Finnley at his
heels and a kite in tow. After a whole summer of trying, he'd
recently learned to keep it in the air most of the time. That kid
had stick-to-it-iveness.

So did she. After weeks of meeting with Pastor Ron's wife,
Wanda, Allison felt the freedom to fly. She kicked off her sandals,
grabbed them up, and ran across the sand, her yellow sundress
flowing around her knees.

Some sixth sense alerted Brent before she reached him. He
turned to watch her, a wide grin on his face. How could she ever
have allowed the weeds of doubt to crowd out the beauty of this
man? Yes, God had done some weeding in his life, too. They'd
made major errors in judgment. Both of them. They were human.
Yet God cherished them anyway. Cherished her. His long-lost
daughter.

"Look, Auntie Allison!" Finnley called, as Christopher handed
the kite spool off to him. "I can fly a kite, too!"

She stopped only a few feet from Brent to watch her little guy
bite hard on his lip and frown in concentration as the kite dipped
around him. In just a minute or two, it fell against the sand.

"Yay, Finnley!" she yelled. "You did a great job."

"Yes, you did," said Christopher. "If you keep prakkising, you'll be as good at it as me." He darted to the fallen kite and threw it in the air as Finnley began to run. Once again the kite rose.

Brent stood beside her and slipped his arm around her. "How did your session go?" His eyes watched Finnley, but his hand caressing her waist told her his attention was on her.

"Good." Allison couldn't help herself. She did a little jig on the sand. "I'm ready to write my sister a letter. Wanda helped me see that I need to forgive Lori for what she did to Finnley. For what she did with you. She needs to know Jesus loves her, too."

"Let's walk," suggested Brent, tugging her along with him.

She slid her arm around his waist and strolled beside him in the direction the little boys had run.

"I've got a question for you."

Allison's heart nearly stopped. Was it time? But no, he'd said he wouldn't ask her that one. It was up to her. She swallowed hard. "Oh, what's that?"

"Do you mind if I write her, too? I want her to know I forgive her, as well, and ask if she'll forgive me. I want her to know this little boy means all the world to me." He tightened his arm and nuzzled her hair. "I want her to know this little boy's auntie is more precious than gold. Most of all, like you said, she needs to hear that Jesus treasures her."

Allison's eyes brimmed over and she buried her face against Brent's strong warm chest. He cradled her against him, rubbing his hands up and down her back.

"I don't know what I've done to deserve you," she whispered between sniffles.

He kissed her forehead. "I don't deserve you, either. I'm thankful love and forgiveness aren't things we only get if we deserve them. I love you because of you. Who you are." He tilted her face up so their eyes met. "I don't mean because of your relationship to Finnley. I mean because of the amazing woman

God created in you."

"I don't think I can live up to that."

He kissed her lips gently. "Stay close to Jesus, and all the rest will be taken care of."

She tangled her hands in his black hair and held his head in place so she could kiss him properly. "I love you, Brent," she whispered against his lips then reclaimed them with hers.

It was time. She was ready.

oOo

Brent ran his hands down the wooden beams inside Allison's new house and looked around the space. Hickory cabinetry created a small L-shaped kitchen with an eating island. The built-in desk he'd handcrafted just for her sat tucked beneath the stairs. Down the hallway lay a bathroom with a jetted tub. A bedroom beyond opened to a small patio nestled into a private hollow against the mountainside.

The half-log staircase rose to the upper story where a mural nearly identical to the one in the duplex awaited, and a railing fashioned of tree branches would keep Finnley safe as he played in the loft.

It'd been hard work keeping Allison and Finnley out for the past two weeks while he'd worked overtime on the finishing touches. He'd spent time every evening with Allison, going for a twilight walk before tucking Finnley into bed.

She'd made a quick trip to Portland a few weeks before to select the furniture she wanted to bring here. The truck should arrive Monday evening.

Tomorrow.

Was Allison ready for the next step? Sometimes it seemed the moment was in front of him. At other times, he wasn't sure. But he was committed to her and to Finnley, regardless. He'd moved into an apartment in town. Signed a contract with Tyrell Burke to start on his timber frame house this fall so they could do the finishing over the winter. Two other possible projects loomed.

Was he ready?

Oh, yeah. No doubt about it. He'd been more than ready for weeks. Ever since the day Finnley had been lost and found. The day he'd promised not to push Allison. He'd made it clear enough, hadn't he? That it was all up to her now?

He'd done his part. He brushed an invisible speck off the tiled island. Her house was ready for her. He was ready.

Brent pulled his phone from his pocket and tapped a message in: *Meet me at the house?*

She texted back in seconds. *It's finished? Be right there!*

How had a fingerprint gotten on the French door? He wiped it away with the hem of his shirt.

What did "be right there" mean, anyway? He knew exactly how long it took to walk the trail from the duplex to the house. He'd done it hundreds of times. He'd thought she'd be more eager. That she'd come running.

He checked his phone again, but she hadn't sent another message to say what detained her. The timestamp said ten minutes ago. Was that all? It felt like eternity.

Brent paced to the other window, but it didn't provide a clearer view of the path. He returned to the French doors.

Was that a speck of yellow between the trees? He caught his breath. She wore the yellow sundress she'd bought just a few weeks ago, practically the only real color he'd ever seen on her. Her hair was piled in a knot on her head.

Finnley clung to her hand wearing long black pants and a sunshine yellow button-up shirt. His hair was damp and perfectly combed.

Brent closed his eyes and took a deep breath. "Thank You, God." Then he opened the door, stepped out onto the deck, and swept a bow. It only seemed fitting. "Welcome. Please enter."

Finnley's eyes were round as logs as he climbed the three

steps, still holding Allison's hand.

But Brent couldn't keep his eyes off the gorgeous woman in front of him for more than a second. "Are you ready?"

Her brown eyes shone as she nodded, a little smile pushing up her cheeks. "Oh, I'm ready." Her voice was low with promise.

Did she mean what he hoped she meant? Patience. Time would tell.

He followed her and Finnley into the house and closed the French door behind them. Finnley let out a whoop, let go of Allison's hand, and raced for the stairs.

Allison chuckled. "I guess we'll see the loft first." She kicked her sandals off and followed Finnley.

"You maded me a farm!" Finnley yelled from his room. "You maded me Danny Boy!"

Brent grinned as he climbed the stairs.

"And Rover. Look, Auntie Allison."

"I see, buddy. That's a very nice farm."

Brent came up behind Allison as she leaned on the doorjamb of Finnley's bedroom. He slid both arms around her.

She leaned back into him as he rested his chin on her shoulder. She looked amazing. Smelled amazing. He nuzzled her neck. Tasted amazing.

Allison turned in Brent's arms. "It's gorgeous. You outdid yourself."

He kissed her nose. "Thank you. Are you ready to see downstairs now?"

"There Domino." Finnley traced the details on his mural.

She grinned at the boy then kissed Brent back. "Sure."

He held her hand as they descended the steps, her other gliding over the smooth surface of the banister log.

"I can't believe the details." She glanced up at him. "Does Timber Framing Plus put this much effort into the finishing touches of all the houses they build?"

Brent chuckled. "Not quite."

297

Her gaze paused on the kitchen backsplash. "You're sneaky, you know that?"

"Who, me?" He leaned forward, resting his elbows on the island as she rounded it.

"Didn't I expressly choose the gray glass tiles?"

If he hadn't heard the lilt in her voice, he might've been worried. "You did."

"Then why do there seem to be dandelions painted on some of them?" She leaned closer, touching the yellow flowers.

"They're only weeds when they're growing where they're not wanted," he said softly. "And I do think they're wanted right there."

She glanced at him, her expression unreadable. "You might be right."

He followed her to the bathroom, where he'd toed the party line for all the finishing work but hadn't been able to resist bright yellow towels. Just a few, for a house-warming gift.

She grinned, shook her head, and entered her bedroom.

Brent leaned against the doorframe and watched her, the woman he loved, as her gaze caught on the one other place he'd been a rebel. Sure, three of the walls were in the mid-gray tone with crisp white trim she'd chosen, but on the bits of the fourth that showed around the closet doors and window, he'd taken leave to paint a sun low on the horizon, a hint of orange to link the yellow with the gray.

Allison planted her hands on her slim hips. "A setting sun, Brent? Really?" Her voice, her expression, both neutral.

He couldn't tell what she really thought. "It's a rising sun, not a setting one." He swallowed hard. "To represent a new day. A new beginning."

She tilted her head to one side.

He shouldn't have done it. She probably hated it. "I can paint over it in half an hour if you want me to." Could he paint himself out of her life as easily? No. Not with Finnley.

"Hmm. It might grow on me. We'll see." She brushed past him, down the little hallway and to the foot of the stairs. "Buddy? Would you come down here, please?"

"Coming." Footsteps ran across the floorboards and down the stairs. Finnley grinned from ear to ear as he bounced to a stop beside Allison and looked up at her. "Is it time?"

She nodded.

Finnley dug around in his pocket and pulled out with a small box.

Brent caught his breath as the little man came and stood in front of him. When Finnley tilted his head way back to look at him, Brent dropped to his knees.

Finnley glanced up at Allison.

Brent carefully did not follow his gaze but kept his eyes focused on his son. *His son.*

"Brent, we want to know if you will be our daddy and live at our new house." He looked up at Allison. "Did I say that right?"

She nudged him. "Give Brent his present."

"Oh. I 'most forgot. Here." He thrust the little box at Brent.

Brent blinked back moisture as he opened the box. He unfolded the piece of paper he found inside, a paper edged with dandelions. In the middle, it said, "Will you marry me? I love you. Allison."

He scrambled to his feet, grabbed Allison around the waist, and gave her a twirl. Her bare feet scarcely missed Finnley. "Are you sure?"

She laughed. "I'm one-hundred percent absolutely certain."

He tightened his arms around her, folding her as completely into his hug as was possible, kissing her eyebrows, her nose, her cheeks, her lips. Oh, her lips.

"I haven't heard an answer," she teased, pulling back and looking deep into his eyes.

He tugged out the pins that held her hair in place and let the locks cascade down her back. "I say yes. I'm thrilled to marry you." He kissed her again.

A little hand tugged at his pant leg. "Brent?"

How could he nearly have forgotten his own son? But he didn't want to let go of Allison. He scooped Finnley up in one arm, and Allison completed the circle by hugging them both.

"Yes, squirt?"

Finnley frowned and crossed his arms. "You didn't say if you will be our daddy."

"I'm already your daddy, squirt. But yes, I'll marry your Auntie Allison and live in your house with you for always."

Finnley clenched Brent's jaw between both his little hands. "Really truly?"

"Yes, little man. Really truly. Now I have a present for her, too. Should I give it to her right now?"

Finnley leaned in, filling Brent's vision. "Can I?"

"Sure you can. But I have to put you down first, okay? I need to get it out of my pocket."

The little face contemplated that for a moment before nodding. "Okay."

Brent slid his son to the floor and handed over a little velvet box.

Finnley rotated it a few times. "It looks just like the other one."

"Trust me, squirt. It's not quite the same."

The little man shrugged and handed it to Allison. "Okay. Here you go, Auntie Allison. A present from Brent." Then he jumped up and down. "What's in it? Can I see?"

Allison tipped back the lid of the jeweler's case. Her eyes grew wide and she pressed one hand against her chest. "Oh, Brent. It's beautiful! How... when?"

"Weeks ago. I bought it not long after Finnley... you know. I wanted to be ready when you were."

"Didn't you ever doubt me?"

He shook his head, holding her gaze. "Not for a minute." He reached for her left hand. "Allison, will you do me the honor of becoming my wife and the mother of our children?" He ruffled Finnley's hair, but his eyes didn't leave hers. "This little squirt, but also any others the good Lord sees fit to send our way?"

Her eyes shone with love for him. "I will."

He plucked the diamond ring from its velvet nest and slid it on her finger.

"Are you my daddy now?" asked Finnley.

Brent patted his head. "Now and for always, squirt. Now go up to your room and see if you can find Jane Eyre on your wall. She's hiding there."

Allison grinned. "Then Brent and I can talk about how quickly we can make all this happen."

The sooner the better, in his mind. But they could talk about it after they kissed some more.

The End

Recipe for Dandelion Pesto ----------

For the mildest flavored dandelion greens, cover the emerging plants and use the leaves before they turn dark green. The darker the leaves, the more bitter the flavor.

Dandelion Pesto

Makes about 1 cup, or 2 servings

1/2 cup pine nuts
2 garlic gloves
2 cups loosely-packed dandelion greens
2 teaspoons lemon juice
1/2 cup olive oil
Salt and black pepper, to taste
1/3 cup freshly grated parmesan

Lightly toast the pine nuts in a dry cast-iron skillet over medium low heat. Remove from heat. Place pine nuts in food processor and add the garlic and dandelion greens. Add the lemon juice and olive oil. Pulse until smooth. Add salt and pepper to taste.

Serve over cooked spaghetti squash or fettuccine.
Sprinkle with a generous amount of parmesan.

Dear Reader -------------------------

Do you share my passion for locally grown real food? No, I'm not as fanatical or fixated as our friends from Green Acres, but farming, gardening, and food processing comprise a large part of my non-writing life.

Whether you're new to the concept or a long-time advocate, I invite you to my website and blog at www.valeriecomer.com to explore God's thoughts on the junction of food and faith.

Please sign up for my monthly newsletter while you're there! My gift to all subscribers is *Peppermint Kisses: A (short) Farm Fresh Romance* that follows Wild Mint Tea in chronology. Joining my list is the best way to keep tabs on my food/farm life as well as contests, cover reveals, deals, and news about upcoming books. I welcome you!

Enjoy this Book? --------------------

Please leave a review at any online retailer or reader site. Letting other readers know what you think about *Dandelions for Dinner: A Farm Fresh Romance* helps them make a decision and means a lot to me. Thank you!

If you haven't read *Raspberries and Vinegar*, the first book in the series, with the story of Jo and Zach's romance, *Wild Mint Tea*, the second book, containing Claire and Noel's story, or *Sweetened with Honey*, Sierra and Gabe's story, I hope you will.

Keep reading for the first chapter of Chelsea's story, *Plum Upside Down: A Farm Fresh Romance 5*. It will be available from most online retailers in e-book and print in the summer of 2015.

Plum Upside Down

A Farm Fresh Romance

Book 5

Valerie Comer

Chapter 1 --

*C*helsea Riehl heard the voices before she rounded the corner on her way to the big house.

"No, no. Go in peace." That was Keanan's voice. The guy hadn't been at Green Acres Farm much longer than she had, and he was more than a little strange. "She will be delighted to see the Andes once again."

Who was *she*, and why was she going to South America? Chelsea frowned, turning toward the voices. Keanan towered over a guy she didn't know standing next to a beat-up truck. Both men had hair past their shoulders, only Keanan's was tied back with a strand of leather. The other guy had dreads.

Seriously? Hadn't she left that behind in Portland?

The shorter guy pumped Keanan's hand. "I will take good care of it. I can't thank you enough."

"Shoot me an email from time to time. Photos. I will live vicariously through you."

Which still didn't explain who *she* was.

The guy tossed a nylon bag into the back of the truck.

"My prayers go with you, my friend. May God Himself bless you." Keanan clamped a large hand on the other man's shoulder and began to pray.

Chelsea was so out of there. Not that she didn't believe in God or prayer. She absolutely did. But, in the week she'd known him, Keanan Welsh repelled her as much as he fascinated her. He might be sort of good-looking underneath that mass of hair. He might be a really nice guy as her sister said. He didn't even smell bad like she'd thought he might. But what made a guy like him tick?

His upbringing was obviously vastly different from hers. She'd been raised safe and secure in an upper-middle-class Portland home, with two parents who loved each other and their three kids. Who took them to church on Sunday and a private Christian school five other days. She couldn't even imagine the hippie commune he must've lived on. He probably had a wardrobe of tie-dye — not that she'd seen any yet — and a best friend named Starshine Harmony.

She slipped into the relative coolness of the straw bale house that served as Green Acres' headquarters. This whole communal farm thing was right up her alley. Each member was equally committed to Jesus and to sustainable living. They worked together for the needs of the group and enjoyed the benefits together. Chelsea had been trying to get onboard for three years, almost since the beginning. Now she was finally here, but so was that irritating Keanan Welsh.

Her sister, Sierra, glanced over at her across the peninsula separating the kitchen from the dining area. "Whew, glad you're here. The guys just dropped off four more boxes of Italian plums. They're trying to get them all picked before the starlings beat them to it."

The raucous black birds had descended like a plague of grasshoppers yesterday. Apparently that meant the plums were ripe, and it was now a race to the finish line to see if the community could get their fair share before the scavengers pecked a hole in each one.

Chelsea rolled her shoulders as she crossed the space and into the kitchen. "Well, I'm ready to start." The words trailed off as the reality of the fruit invasion slammed her brain like a landslide. "Whoa."

Her sister grinned, brandishing a knife. "There are more boxes coming, but also more help. You get a choice. Washing or pitting."

"I thought everything was organic. Why do we have to wash them?" Chelsea took a large bite from a purple plum. Just green and crisp enough on the inside to balance the juicy sweetness of it. Warm still from the September sun.

"It's true we haven't sprayed the trees. Plums are amazingly resilient to disease and pests."

"Other than starlings."

"They know ripe fruit when they smell it." Sierra split a plum, dropped the pit in a bucket, and placed both halves cut-side-up on a dehydrator tray. "But anyway, there's still the possibility of exhaust from the vehicles creating a film on them. And wildlife in the trees. It's better to be safe than sorry."

"I'll start with washing, I guess." Chelsea eyed the deep sink full of dark purple golf balls.

"We can trade off. We'll have more hands soon. It will go quickly, I promise."

Promises wouldn't make it happen. But still, it had to take a lot to feed ten adults and several kids a varied, healthy, and mostly homegrown diet. She'd bet it had been a lot easier the first year or so when it had been only her sister and her two girlfriends.

Chelsea sighed and walked over to the sink. "Just rub them and put them in the other sink?"

"Yep. There's a basket there to fill."

Catchy praise music breezed in via the house's wireless sound system. Chelsea caught herself humming along as she turned the faucet to little more than a dribble.

"Considering you moved in next door, I hardly see you," Sierra commented from the island behind her. Plink, plink went fruit onto the trays. "Are you settling in okay?"

"Yeah, I'm fine. The duplex has lots of room for one person.

Well, you know."

Sierra chuckled. "Yes, I felt the same way when I moved into the other half. Hard to believe it was a year ago already. For the record, the unit is still plenty big enough for *two* people."

Chelsea wouldn't tease her newlywed sister about how they'd fit when babies came along. Not when pregnancy seemed like a long shot due to Sierra's endometriosis.

"You can splash some paint in there, you know," Sierra went on. "Allison's tastes run rather austere."

Allison Hart had lived in Chelsea's unit for the past several months, but now her adorable timber-frame house had been completed on the hillside, and she and her young nephew had moved up there. That'd opened a space for Chelsea.

Too bad for Keanan. He'd lived in his tent since spring. Not that anything seemed to faze the guy, and he'd welcomed her as warmly as had everyone else. No talk about how he'd been here first or anything like that. Last spring the guy had just ridden his bicycle onto the property, pitched his tent, and stayed.

Unfathomable.

Chelsea forced her mind back to the conversation. What had they been talking about? Right. "The gray walls provide a terrific backdrop, though." That would get a reaction.

"Gray?" sputtered Sierra. "A great backdrop for what? Talk about a depressing color. I'm not even sure it's an improvement over white or beige."

Yep, Chelsea still knew her big sister's buttons. There was strange comfort in that. "For art, silly, though I wouldn't mind having at least one wall of my bedroom pink. And then there's the spare room. I know the mural was painted for Allison's nephew, but it's a little much for me." She hesitated. "I hate to hurt anyone's feelings the first week I'm here. I can live with it."

"It's your home now." Sierra plunked a basket beside the sink and began filling it with washed fruit. "Besides, Brent did a new mural for Finnley in their new house. I see no reason why you can't cover it. In fact, I'll give you a hand, but it might have to wait until the garden is off."

"Now why does that sound so ominous?" muttered Chelsea.

"Ominous? Girl, if you have the energy to paint after a fourteen-hour day of canning tomatoes or cutting and wrapping meat, you're way ahead of the rest of us. Today is nothing compared to what's coming."

And she was bored after ten minutes of washing plums. Why again had she signed up for this?

o0o

Keanan Welsh pushed open the door to the straw bale house. This building welcomed him as few ever had, following the ideas of a book on pattern language he'd studied in college. Everything from the deep windowsills to the sunlight flowing in from various angles to the nook by the fireplace had been designed to ease the human spirit at a subconscious level. Even knowing how it was done didn't diminish his pleasure in the result.

The two sisters worked in the kitchen, chatting about fashion. Keanan steeled himself and crossed the dining room to enter the space. "May I be of assistance?"

He knew there was need. The fruit-pickers had said the kitchen was backlogged. Several team members were at their day jobs, and that couldn't be helped. They put more cash into the system, but fewer work hours. It somehow balanced. He was here for the work end.

Sierra glanced up, her face wreathed in a grin. "Sure. Grab a knife. We have all three dehydrators to load in the sunroom."

He lifted a paring knife. "It's a welcome change to be facing plums instead of peaches like last week."

Sierra's sister shot him a strange look from over at the sink. Her curly hair was held off her face with a pink flowered scarf. "So what do we do with all these?" she asked.

Good question. There had been few plums in the diet since he's arrived at Green Acres in May. He angled a glance at Sierra from across the island as he pitted.

"We have them for breakfast in smoothies or stewed fruit. We eat the dry ones plain as snacks. We layer the frozen ones into desserts like cakes and crumbles. We go through a lot of plum sauce on meat." Sierra set a loaded tray aside and began filling another. "Noel will make a batch of mead with some of them."

"I didn't know there was so much one could do with plums." Keanan nodded. "Nor did I realize the meat sauce was of a plum origin."

"Well, we also make our own tomato-based barbecue sauce. I'm sure you've had both variations."

"What happens to any remaining plums? Do we process each and every one?" He had visions of the boxes Noel and Gabe were filling outside. A truckload of plums seemed excessive, even for this community.

"The chickens and pigs will gorge on any we don't use."

"Ah, I wondered if there were folks in Galena Landing who might use the excess."

Sierra eyed him. "Possibly. But a lot of them have a tree or two in the backyard. I doubt anyone hankering plums can't access any."

"With your permission, I might take a box into town with my bike and trailer, and ask around? The intention is not to deny the livestock their treat, but to aid humans who need it."

"Um, we can ask what the group thinks." Sierra frowned at her knife. "Want to slide these trays into the dehydrator?"

"Certainly." He balanced several trays on top of each other and rounded the stone fireplace wall to the sunroom doors. A moment later, mission completed, he headed back to the kitchen.

"...weird," said Chelsea.

"Shh," replied Sierra.

Keanan's mind did a grand leap. They'd been talking about him, and the farm's newcomer didn't approve of him. Well, he didn't precisely approve of her, either, with her penchant for makeup and fashion. Even now she wore a pastel top to match that scarf, below-the-knee beige pants, and sandals with heels. Oh, and a chunky necklace. For working in the kitchen.

He glanced her way as he walked past.

Her head was bent over the sink — curls all but hiding her face — only serving to draw his attention to the glittering gems on the arms of her pink glasses. Surely those could not be real diamonds? But with Chelsea Riehl, he couldn't be certain.

"Who was that guy outside?" she asked.

Good, a change of subject. "Logan Dermott. I met him just the other day, but he's been in the valley picking fruit much of the summer."

"Oh? Where's he from?"

Keanan frowned and sliced open another plum. "I'm not sure."

He heard or sensed Chelsea turning from the sink, but he didn't look at her. "Then what did you give him?"

"Oh, that?" He chuckled. "My tent. He's going on a trip to Argentina, talking with mission groups about helping the indigenous people regain food security."

"You *gave* your tent to some guy you don't even know? Seriously?"

This was strange how? Keanan met Chelsea's gaze. Not only were her frames pink, she apparently looked at life through rose tints as well. "Why not? He needs it. I don't."

"But—" She shook her head hard, and those curls flew out sideways like so many corkscrews.

"I do not understand why this presents a problem." To say nothing of none of her business. His tent, his decision. End of story.

"Where are you going to sleep?"

"Don't be alarmed. I won't force myself into the spare bedroom in your duplex."

Her eyes grew large. "You better believe you won't."

This was a woman who could push his buttons. He must brace himself. Keanan took a deep breath and let it out slowly. Then again. "My grain bins will be arriving on the weekend, and I'll be staying next door in Zach's parents' spare room until my home is insulated and ready for me to move into."

Chelsea took a step closer. "I think I'm not hearing you correctly. You plan to live in a *grain bin*?"

Sierra snickered, but Keanan had no trouble ignoring that. "I do, in fact. It will be quite snug. It will have solar panels for electricity. Even a bathroom so I needn't cross the yard to shower or brush my teeth."

"You're serious."

"Uh... yes?"

"A grain bin. Wait, you said plural."

"Correct. One is fitted inside the other so straw can be tamped between them for insulation."

Chelsea looked at her sister then back at him. "Okay, joke's over. What are your real plans?"

"To live in a grain bin." Keanan's patience ebbed. "Which, truly, is no business of yours. You needn't look at it. You needn't visit. It will be tucked away on the hillside where my tent was, and you can ignore its very existence. You can ignore *my* very existence. It is all the same to me."

Her eyes grew wide behind those ridiculous glasses, and her painted lips pursed. She whirled back to the sink, her curls flying out sideways.

Perhaps it wasn't all the same to him. But it might as well be.

Author Biography

Valerie Comer lives where food meets faith in her real life, her fiction, and on her blog and website. She and her husband of over 30 years farm, garden, and keep bees on a small farm in Western Canada, where they grow and preserve much of their own food.

Valerie has always been interested in real food from scratch, but her conviction has increased dramatically since God blessed her with three delightful granddaughters. In this world of rampant disease and pollution, she is compelled to do what she can to make these little girls' lives the best she can. She helps supply healthy food—local food, organic food, seasonal food—to grow strong bodies and minds.

Her experience has planted seeds for many stories rooted in the local-food movement. *Raspberries and Vinegar, Wild Mint Tea, Sweetened with Honey,* and *Dandelions for Dinner* will be followed by two more books in the Farm Fresh Romance series, including *Plum Upside Down* (summer 2015) and a final tale set on Green Acres Farm.

To find out more, visit her website at www.valeriecomer.com, where you can read her blog, explore her many links, and sign up for her email newsletter to download the free short story: *Peppermint Kisses: A (short) Farm Fresh Romance 2.5.* You can also use this QR code to access the newsletter sign-up.

Made in the USA
Coppell, TX
08 April 2021